KILLER IN THE CLOISTER

CAMILLE MINICHINO

CHAPTER 1

It wasn't easy being conservative in 1965, even for a nun.

But I was as determined and sure of myself as only a twenty-eight-year-old could be.

My Superiors thought there was some risk, sending me away to graduate school right after my final vows, but I was firm in my faith and confident in my vocation as a Sister of Mary Immaculate. Hadn't I made a mature decision to give my life to the service of God? I would do His will as revealed to me by my Superiors.

I had no intention of opening my mind to the passing fads Mother Julia had warned us against, like priest-social workers and peace signs made of colored felt glued to burlap banners. Without saying so explicitly, Mother Julia's lessons left us with the unmistakable impression that the underlying cause of the unrest in the United States stemmed from the assassination, two years earlier, of John Fitzgerald Kennedy, the first Roman Catholic president.

I sat in my dormitory room in the middle of the Bronx, a four-hour bus ride from my Motherhouse convent in Potterstown, New York, and took a copy of St. Alban's University catalog from the deep pocket of my Sunday habit. Mother Julia had circled the required curriculum for my first semester—courses in Thomistic theology, modern philosophy, research methods, and a seminar in comparative religions. I twisted my nose at the last one, as if I smelled a bad batch of incense. I didn't see why I should be studying other belief systems when there was enough to learn in my own two-thousand-year-old tradition, thank you.

My small mahogany desk was ready with new spiral notebooks, sharpened pencils, and a framed image of St. Francis of Assisi, my patron saint.

I'd chosen my religious name not in his honor, however, but for my great aunt, Francesca Sforzo—part of the small fraction of my heritage that wasn't Irish.

I celebrated my feast day every year on October 4, and prayed daily to Saint Francis to lead my brother Timothy back to the faith—perhaps not to Holy Orders, as our parents wished, but at least to a law-abiding life.

"Sister Francesca, are you settled in?"

I recognized the voice on the other side of my door as that of Mother Ignatius, the old Albanite Sister in charge of St. Lucy's Hall, the Sisters' dormitory. She'd been on hand earlier to greet each student. I opened my door and looked down on her thin five-foot frame, a good six inches below my eye level.

"I want to remind you that we'll say Vespers at four," she said, her voice wavering, as if it had been in use for too many decades. "And then some of the Sisters have asked for a little get-together afterwards so you can all meet each other."

Mother Ignatius, wrapped in yards of black serge, seemed as uncomfortable as I was at the idea of a "get-together."

I checked that the long hallway was clear, then leaned down and whispered, as if we were standing in the sanctuary of St. Lucy's chapel. "Whatever you say, Mother. But may I ask—will this be a regular practice?"

Observing the rule of no frivolous touching, Mother Ignatius gave a slight nod to indicate that we should move into my room. Once over the threshold, with the door still open, again according to custom, she let out a heavy sigh. I offered her my straight-backed wooden chair and sat on the edge of my bed facing her, the small room now filled almost to capacity. A third person would have had to perch on the tiny sink by the window. It hadn't taken long for my first challenge to surface, I'd noticed, in the form of the small rectangular mirror above the sink.

SMIs were forbidden to look at their reflections. I shifted my gaze to a spot between the mirror and the window.

"I'm glad you asked about the get-together, Sister." Mother Ignatius leaned into me and squeezed her eyes into a gesture that was close to a wink. Her half smile revealed long, overlapping teeth. "Your Mother Julia and I had a long talk about you when she called to make arrangements for your stay here. She said I could count on you. She said that although you're very young, you have the values of the old."

"I didn't mean to question you, Mother Ignatius. I—"

"No, no, Sister. You weren't wrong to speak up. I don't mind telling you I'm not at ease with these changes, either. The Sisters want wine and cheese at this gathering. It disturbs me greatly. Even though you're all from different orders, this is still a convent." Mother Ignatius made a prayerful gesture with her tiny hands, as if to emphasize the core of her existence. "It's a slippery slope. Who knows what's next? These new Sisters make me feel that I'm the only thing standing in the way of the life they want."

I threw my shoulders back and lifted my eyes to heaven, unable to contain my opinion of spontaneous social intercourse among religious.

"It's not as if we're in a sorority house. You're our Superior, Mother Ignatius."

I seemed to have spat out my words, and was immediately sorry, but Mother Ignatius didn't seem to notice my intense response.

"I wish it were so, Sister Francesca," she said. "There's just so much authority I can maintain. Your home congregations are paying room and board for you to live here at St. Lucy's."

I rubbed my fingers along my jaw. All my muscles were tight—a sensation that came often lately as I wrestled with my feelings about the wave of modernization taking over the church. The Second Vatican Council, convened in 1962, and still in session in 1965, was sweeping through the Church like a coup to bring democracy to the hierarchical structure ordained by God himself. I agreed with Mother Julia:

Consensus and collegiality are fine for President Johnson and his administration, Sisters, but it is not what Our Lord had in mind when he anointed Peter the first Pope.

Solemn high Latin masses had become harder and harder to find, especially in university chapels. Guitars and secular banners replaced the pipe organ and priestly vestments in Roman Catholic churches everywhere. Each day brought a burning issue to the fore, and convent life—up to now a bulwark of permanence—had turned into an arena of debate, as frantic as secular election campaigns.

But until my arrival at St. Lucy's, I'd had to deal with the issues only in the abstract, with Mother Julia always on hand to interpret. I wondered if I was prepared to face the consequences alone in my daily life. I pushed my hands far up into my sleeves, grasping my elbows, as if to hold onto my resolve to stay with the rules I'd promised to live by on the day of my final vows.

Mother Ignatius seemed also to have disappeared into a different century. She sighed and shook her head inside her stiff black bonnet, which stayed pointing straight ahead.

"It certainly was easier in the old days," she said.

I felt a twinge of regret. "I'm sorry I missed them."

CHAPTER 2

B ehind St. Lucy's was a yard, large by Bronx standards, a long
stretch of green lawn dotted with maples and elms. From my
window, I could see wide rows of flowers brightening the
landscape with September colors—oranges, deep yellow, purple, and
red.

I remembered reading in the brochure that St. Lucy's property,
which was about a mile from St. Alban's main campus, was owned by
the Albanites, the same order of priests who ran the University. At one
edge of the lot, I could see the beginnings of a new development, and I
guessed it wouldn't be long before we saw the lovely convent lawn
absorbed by a housing project and a row of shops.

A stone pathway led to a shrine of Our Lady of Sorrows at the far
end of the yard. I took my spiritual reading and light summer shawl—
heavy wraps weren't permitted until October first, no matter what the
weather—to one of the benches farthest from the house.

I breathed in the dry, crisp fall air. For about a half hour I visited
the thirteenth, the greatest of centuries, enjoying the flawless logic in
The Summa Theologica of Saint Thomas Aquinas.

Human nature needs the help of God as First Mover, to do or will any
good whatsoever, as was ...

The bell for chapel.

I closed the book immediately and walked toward the house. As I
entered through the back door, I resolved to go straight to my room

after Vespers if I detected the smell of wine from the gathering in the parlor.

———————————

Apparently, Mother Ignatius had prevailed, at least as far as keeping an alcohol-free environment, so I stopped in at the social hour that followed prayers. I was greeted by a Sister in a modified habit. Teresa — she hadn't included her title on her name sticker — looked like a schoolgirl, with a calf-length dress and hose in dark blue, a white Peter Pan collar, and a silver cross pinned over her heart.

"You're Francesca," she said, with a broad smile. Wisps of dark, curly hair slipped from under the pretend veil hugging the back of her head. "I think we're neighbors. I'm in Room 26."

Neighbors live in suburbs, I wanted to tell her. They're married with two children and have afternoon chats in coffee shops.

"Good evening, Sister," I said. I managed a smile while I emphasized her title.

I moved past her and found Mother Ignatius.

"A glass of punch, Sister Francesca?" She held up a ladle of pink liquid that smelled to me like at least a partial victory, but her face had a worried look, her forehead even more wrinkled than her advanced age allowed.

"Is something wrong, Mother Ignatius?"

"You're a St. Lucy's resident now, Sister," she said, her voice low and shaky. "So you should be aware of this." She pulled a piece of yellow lined paper from the folds of her skirt and gave it a slight wave under my chin, which was about as high as she could reach with comfort. "This is a list of demands I received."

I drew in my breath. I'd heard of sit-ins that were popular on college campuses and lists of demands by unruly students. Mother Julia had summarized the news for us, informing us of students' cries for more participation in classes and better food in the cafeterias. I didn't expect to experience the phenomenon in a convent.

"I'm sorry to hear that, Mother. How can anyone have a demand so soon? We've just arrived. Classes haven't even started yet."

"The list was drawn up by the Sisters returning for their second or third year. Sister Teresa, Sister Veronique especially. You'll meet them all." Mother Ignatius swept her short arm to encompass the parlor. "They warned me when they left last June that they expected changes this year."

"What kinds of changes?" We already have mirrors in our rooms and social hours, I mused.

"For one thing, they want keys to this building to come and go as they please."

I clenched and unclenched my fists as Mother Ignatius talked, as if I were keeping count of unpleasant notions.

"How does Sister Felix feel about this?" I asked her.

"I'm afraid my assistant agrees with most of the new rules, or I should say, lack of rules. Even our chaplain, Father Malbert, is of the same mind." Mother Ignatius tilted her elaborate headdress in the direction of the fireplace, where a sandy-haired man—I put his age at about mid-thirties—in khakis and an Irish knit crew neck sweater was the center of attention for a group of Sisters.

"That's our chaplain?"

She nodded toward the man. "That's our chaplain."

I looked across the room at Father Malbert and saw no outward sign that he was Our Lord's representative on earth. No collar, no cross, not even a decent pair of black pants. Just brown tassel loafers and a hail-fellow loud voice as he entertained his audience. I turned back to Mother Ignatius.

"May I see the list of demands, Mother?"

"Not here, Sister." Mother Ignatius had tucked the yellow paper out of sight as if it were a top-secret document for a modern-day Inquisition.

As I straightened up from talking to Mother Ignatius, I nearly bumped into a large white-haired man in casual slacks and a maroon sweater who had moved in right behind me. The gardener? Another priest? It was hard to tell these days.

"Good evening, Mother Ignatius," he said, giving both of us a broad smile.

He looked at my white bib, where a name sticker might have been if I'd chosen to use one.

"Sister ...?" he asked.

"Sister Francesca."

"Sister Francesca," he said, taking my hand although I hadn't offered it. "You're a Sister of Mary Immaculate. I recognize the SMI habit. I'm Jake Driscoll. Had your order in school, K through six. Before you were born, I suppose." He laughed as if he'd told a clever joke.

"Good evening, Mr. Driscoll."

I couldn't say why, but the name seemed familiar to me. Probably because every third family in the Irish neighborhood where I grew up was Driscoll, I thought.

I noticed Mother Ignatius tightening her arms across her chest, as if to keep her body and soul together. Or to prepare for battle.

"If you'll excuse us, Sister Francesca, Mother Ignatius and I have some unfinished business."

"On the contrary, Mr. Driscoll," Mother Ignatius told him, "our business has been finished for quite some time."

Jake Driscoll managed to place his body in front of mine, cutting me out of the conversation and blocking my view of Mother Ignatius, so I couldn't tell whether or not she wanted me to stay. I chose the conservative route and edged past them.

Looking for a Sister who might be a kindred soul, I found one without a name tag, sitting on a straight chair by the window. She balanced a small plate of cheese and crackers on her lap and seemed to focus on eating, one of the few Sisters not in the group paying homage to Father Malbert. I approached her, having decided to consider the gathering one of those occasions Mother Julia had referred to, requiring conversation.

"I'm Sister Francesca," I said to the Sister who was snacking. "I'm in theology."

She covered her mouth as she finished chewing, then smiled up at me.

"Sister Ann William. Pharmacy?" she said, her voice ending in a question mark. "I'm from Texas. I guess that's clear?"

I shrugged my shoulders. "I've never been west of the Hudson River or south of Washington, D. C."

She laughed. "And I've never been this far north."

"I didn't know St. Alban's offered a pharmacy curriculum?" I seemed to have caught her accent already.

"Oh, yes. The School of Pharmacy is pretty big. Lots of our Sisters have degrees from here. Sisters of Holy Charity? We run small hospitals and convalescent homes all over Texas and the Midwest." Sister Ann William brushed crumbs from her habit—a royal blue with white trim—and from the chair next to her in a gesture of welcome.

I sat down and turned my body so I could see Mother Ignatius and Jake Driscoll. I wasn't happy about my behavior. Giving only half my attention to the person I was with, and eavesdropping—if reading body language could be called that—on other people at the same time.

Simultaneously I heard from Sister Ann William that she'd located a Latin mass on campus, and I saw that Mother Ignatius and Jake Driscoll, who towered over her, were at odds. They stood across from each other, arms folded, their faces wrinkled with frown lines visible even at room's length.

After a few minutes of surprisingly pleasant small talk with Sister Ann William, I made plans to walk to campus with her the next day. I excused myself and walked toward the hallway and the stairway to the dormitory rooms, anxious to escape a sing-along that had started up.

I was nearly out of the parlor when I heard Mother Ignatius's voice.

"Sister Francesca."

I turned to find her in an agitated state, rubbing her hands together and shivering, as if a cold wind had blown through the room.

"Sister Francesca, some pressing matters have come up, and I need to talk to someone. And I sense Mother Julia was right. In spite of your youth, you seem to be wise in the ways that count. Will you meet me in the small parlor after Compline?"

"Of course, Mother. Is something wrong?"

Mother Ignatius seemed out of breath, although as far as I could tell she hadn't been rushing. "Frankly, yes, Sister. I'm afraid of … well, I don't wish to speak of it here."

"If I can help in any way …"

She nodded and licked her lips. I sensed her mouth went dry when she was stressed, as mine did. "About eight-thirty this evening? I need to take some action and perhaps you can help me order my thoughts. I get confused at times."

I nodded, although I considered myself utterly inadequate to the task Mother Ignatius seemed to be giving me. I'd just met her. She was easily fifty years my senior. Why wouldn't she turn to an older Sister or to our chaplain for guidance?

I glanced at the jolly group at the end of the parlor. A group of Sisters in various stages of habit sang something about all God's children while a young man I guessed was a seminarian strummed a guitar. Our chaplain sat on the couch between two Sisters, with one arm around each, mouthing the words to the song with a vaudevillian flair.

"I can see why you might get confused, Mother," I said.

———————————

At eight-thirty, I went to the parlor for my meeting with Mother Ignatius. The fruity smell of punch lingered in the air throughout the main floor, reminding me of my first departure from SMI custom. I sat by a window, alternately reading Saint Thomas and watching the lights come on along Marian Avenue, which St. Lucy's Hall shared with multi-story apartment buildings and an occasional small shop or grocery.

This time, as I looked out over the lawn, I saw the developer's large sign in a new light. As hard as it was to read the letters by the dim glow of the street lamps, I made out the name of the construction company — J. DRISCOLL & SONS.

No wonder the name had sounded familiar. The world of real estate and property management was as foreign to me as the multitude of Protestant religions, but I had no trouble believing it offered a wealth of possibilities for the conflict I'd witnessed earlier between Jake Driscoll and Mother Ignatius.

When the Westminster clock chimed ten o'clock, I realized more than an hour had passed. I decided Mother Ignatius had been sidetracked or was too tired for a serious discussion. But on the way to my room, the memory of her worried look and fearful demeanor nagged at me.

I said a prayer for her well-being, just in case.

By the end of my meditation period the next morning, I was ready to rid myself of the annoyance I'd felt at my new community of Sisters, most of whom I hadn't met. For all I knew, many of them shared my outlook. I reminded myself that uncharitable thoughts were never in vogue, and I'd already found an ally in Sister Ann William. I thought of how often in the world a small minority makes a fuss that, in the end, amounts to nothing. As St. Paul said, *All things come to those who wait.*

At mass, I prayed for humility and guidance and focused on the excitement of the school year ahead—studying theology full time. My mood was also helped by delicious aromas of coffee, fresh cinnamon rolls, and bacon reaching my pew from the kitchen at the back of the house.

After Father Malbert's final blessing, I fell into line for the refectory. I found a napkin ring with my name on it and stood at the long wooden table with the other Sisters. There were thirty-nine of us, I'd been told. We waited in silence for Mother Ignatius to arrive and begin grace.

After several minutes, Mother Ignatius' assistant, Sister Felix, appeared at the head of the table. She folded her hands in front of her and took a long breath.

"Sisters," she said in a solemn voice, "I have very sad news. Last night, Mother Ignatius died in her sleep."

CHAPTER 3

I sipped plain black tea from a mug that seemed almost too heavy to lift, certain I wouldn't be able to manage solid food. Although I'd known her for only a day, I'd felt a bond with Mother Ignatius, and I mourned the sudden loss of a Superior.

Fortunately for my upset stomach, breakfast at St. Lucy's was family style, and I could allow large platters of eggs and bacon and a basket of rolls to float past me. At my Motherhouse, we had no choices at mealtime. Postulants, the newest members of the community, laid a plate of food at each place and we were expected to eat every crumb, whatever our relative metabolic needs or the conditions of our digestive systems.

Maybe some flexibility in custom is good, I thought, but changed my mind when I realized that another departure involved talking at meals—permitted in St. Lucy's refectory, to my dismay.

Several Sisters still had name stickers, to facilitate conversation or because they were unaware they were wearing the remnants of last evening's party, I guessed. I looked for Sister Ann William and found her on the opposite side of the table, too far down the row to speak with. I caught her eye and raised my eyebrows until they hit against the starched white linen band across my forehead. She tilted her head in my direction, her otherwise perky features drawn into a sad smile.

Up and down the table, a limited rainbow of black, brown, blue, and white habits, talk was of little else besides Mother Ignatius. Wasn't it a blessing that she died in her sleep? How old was she? Seventy-five was the average of the ages bandied about. Had she been ill? Not that anyone knew. Did she have any family? None, was the consensus.

I wondered where the information came from and what prompted the free-flowing conversation about a deceased member of the community. If it had been an SMI Superior who died, we wouldn't have been allowed to ask such questions.

I cocked my head when I heard a remark outside of the usual queries and expressions of sympathy. The speaker was Sister Teresa, the official greeter at the get-together the evening before.

"I guess that's it for the contract," I heard her say in a loud voice. She threw her head back as if she'd just won a verdict from the College of Cardinals. I noticed her plate was piled high with scrambled eggs and rolls. Sister Teresa was as skinny as I was, but she wore the dress of her blue habit tight across her chest, calling attention to herself in a way that was decidedly unbecoming a Bride of Christ.

I leaned past the Sister between us—another gesture that was frowned upon at my Motherhouse. I marveled at how quickly I was adjusting to an environment that was almost secular in its practices.

"What contract?" I asked.

"There's an agreement between St. Alban's U. and the Sisters of St. Lucy's Hall. It was created about twenty years ago—in the Middle Ages," Sister Teresa said, drawing a laugh from several nuns around her. "It requires the signature of the Mother Superior of this house for any legal transactions, even though, technically, St. Alban's owns the property."

"They did business a little differently in those days," I heard from a heavyset Sister with thick glasses whose name sticker identified her as Sister Veronique. From the coarse white fabric of her habit, I guessed she was a Dominican. Her wide girth gave her the appearance of a cartoon monk. "One person could dictate for a whole group back then," she said, as if she were referring to centuries past. "There wasn't the accountability we expect these days."

"We have Vatican II to thank," another Sister said.

Thanks, or regrets? I asked myself.

In the next few minutes, many of the old-timers—Sisters who had been at St. Lucy's for four or five years finishing a doctorate—offered information and opinions regarding the antagonism over the contract. What I pieced together sounded like a battle with Mother Ignatius on one side and powerful, influential men like Jake Driscoll and Father Malbert on the other.

I was struck by the accuracy of my pessimistic prediction as I'd strolled through the yard the afternoon before. J. Driscoll & Sons did want the property adjoining St. Lucy's, and for more than a year Mother Ignatius had refused to sign it over to them. I was impressed she'd been able to hold out for so long, given her advanced age and diminutive size, not to mention her secondary position as a female in the Church.

It made sense to me that Driscoll would lobby for the space to expand his development project. But I couldn't imagine why anyone connected to St. Alban's U. or St. Lucy's would feel any differently from Mother Ignatius. The beautiful lawn and stone pathways were perfect for study and meditation, and for visiting days.

I looked at Sister Felix, seated at the head of the table, and wondered what was going through her mind, whether she looked forward to taking over, if that were the case. Her angular face, surrounded by a soft black veil, was animated as she talked to the Sisters to her immediate right and left. Her plate, too, overflowed with food I noticed, unable to curb my tendency to measure the level of a person's emotional involvement by her ability to eat.

"Why would the new Superior at St. Lucy's be any more likely to sign away our yard than Mother Ignatius would?" I asked.

"The contract dies with Mother Ignatius," Sister Veronique said. Her fingers traced the edges of a large wooden crucifix that hung from her neck on a black cord.

"Sister Veronique always has the scoop for us," Sister Teresa said. "Her department chairman—Father O'Neill in History—is *the* important person on campus. Head of the Faculty Senate." Sister Teresa sounded like a proud parent, although both women seemed about the same age, probably as close to thirty years old as I was.

Sister Veronique continued, as if on cue from the director of a Christmas pageant. Even at a distance of several place settings, I could see that her pale blue eyes were magnified by her heavy lenses. "St. Alban's drew up a new contract, effective with the next Superior, that gives the Sisters no power over St. Lucy's property. They'll just manage the daily operation of the house."

"Of course, St. Alban's stands to make a lot of money on the sale of the property, and right now that means more to them than land," Sister Teresa added. "David—uh—Father Malbert says the money would go to scholarships for the poor youngsters in Harlem."

"Sister Teresa knows 'David-uh-Father Malbert' really well," Sister Veronique said, with a high voice and a teasing smile.

Sister Teresa blushed, and other Sisters giggled in a way that said they knew something I didn't. I hoped my guess was very wrong.

"It's not that anyone wants to lose the yard," Sister Veronique said. "But there were lots of little clauses to that contract that affect us. Things about the quality of our lives. We couldn't even have keys since Mother Ignatius didn't think it was a good idea."

"Or television after nine in the evening," the Sister on my left added.

"Or extra telephones on each floor."

"Or guests for dinner."

"Or access to the kitchen between meals."

One by one, the veteran Sisters addressed those of us who had just arrived, as if they'd been given the mission to train us in everything that was wrong with life at St. Lucy's. I wanted to ask how many of them had such so-called privileges in their home communities, or if they'd entered their orders expecting no change in how they'd lived as secular women.

I held my tongue, and finally heard what seemed a more appropriate response to losing a Superior.

"I think it's very sad," a Sister named Miriam said. "Mother Ignatius was nice."

Sisters around her uttered sounds of sympathy and agreement, but to me the tribute seemed like an afterthought. I had the feeling I'd been listening to the list of demands Mother Ignatius had clutched in her hands on the yellow paper.

I wondered what it meant that Mother Ignatius' death was so convenient for so many people?

CHAPTER 4

Sister Ann William and I had made plans to walk to campus together after breakfast, for registration and an afternoon rosary. The removable white collar on her royal blue habit dress looked fresh and clean, as was the round white bib I wore. Like two grade school girls, about the same size and height, in new fall clothes, we carried our bag lunches and our umbrellas down 198th Street and across Webster Avenue toward the Gothic towers of St. Alban's University.

A light rain fell, giving the Bronx the dark gray look it was famous for, even at ten in the morning.

I wished I had a hand free to check on the cash I was carrying. The set of two large blue denim pockets attached to a cord under my habit seemed extra heavy, but I knew it was all in my mind. Besides the required equipment of a handkerchief, a small cloth relic of our SMI foundress, a pen and pencil set, and a prayer book, I had money in my pocket for the first time since I'd entered the convent. I'd stuffed three ten-dollar bills for my textbooks into the small leather purse Mother Julia had given me. I said a quick prayer to St. Anthony of Padua, the patron of lost and potentially lost things, to keep the money safe.

If I'd been walking with a Sister of my own order, say, on the way to teach Sunday School, we would have been silent the whole way, except for a "Praised be Jesus Christ" and a "Praised forever. Amen" as we started out.

"Do you have a rule of silence?" I asked Sister Ann William.

"We did until a few months ago. At the summer congress our delegates voted to dispense with it except during Lent."

"What do you think prompted these changes? I know they're from the Vatican Council, but why now?"

Sister Ann William shrugged her shoulders. "My Superior, Mother Clarisse, says it's happening all over the country. The world, even. Changing values. More rebellion, she says."

"We have to believe our Church knows what it's doing. No Pope or College of Cardinals institutes changes that would weaken Holy Mother Church."

I said this mostly to reassure myself.

"I'm getting used to the changes," Sister Ann William said. "There's a good chance we'll have a modified veil by the end of the year. I suppose I should start letting my hair grow out."

Without thinking, I shifted the brown lunch bag to the hand that was already holding my enormous black umbrella and pushed my bonnet down on my head, as if to secure it in the face of a windstorm. I tried to imagine myself maintaining religious decorum while my red hair spilled out around a short, skimpy veil pinned to my curls, reappearing unruly as ever after six years of being shaved off.

"I hope we never change our habit," I told Sister Ann William. "It's based on the outfit of our foundress, Blessed Mary Anaclete. She was a peasant woman working in the fields outside Paris more than a hundred years ago." As we walked, I pointed out the pieces—a long black dress, a half apron tied under a white bib, a white linen band around my head, and a bonnet covered with a veil that came to my waist in back.

I thought of the prayer we said while pinning on our habits each morning.

As Mother Mary Anaclete donned a bonnet and veil to shield her from the sun, so we don ours to shield us from sin and the ways of the world.

"Our community doesn't go back that far," Sister Ann William said. "It's only about fifty years old. The Sisters of Holy Charity mission is hospital work, and I think the blue is supposed to be soothing."

"Do you think you'll like studying pharmacy?"

"Oh, my, yes," she said, stretching the three letters of *yes* into two syllables. "I was a chemistry major in college. I entered a hospital order because my two aunties are in it, not because I wanted to do nursing. But God's will, you know, and I would have, of course."

"Of course."

"Are you looking forward to theology?" she asked.

"Very much. I know studying the writings of Saint Thomas Aquinas will be my favorite class."

"For me it's going to be plant pathology. Pharmacy and premed students take this class together. You'd be amazed at how often parents call their pharmacist or rush into an emergency room with children who've swallowed detergent or a gardening chemical. Or they've eaten a plant."

"Sounds interesting," I said, without enthusiasm. I had no happy memories of the science classes in my past.

Sister Ann William smiled, as if she were enjoying a private joke. "Some of the prettiest flowers can be deadly in the right doses. In high school we used to call this the Poison Class."

I perked up my ears. "Now, that really is interesting."

Sister Ann William and I split up to go to our respective registration desks in St. Alban's imposing administration building, constructed in the flat gray-stone Gothic style I'd seen on so many Catholic university campuses.

I had to admit this sight—men and women in flowing robes, teaching in a majestic setting dedicated to God—was one of the inspiring images that drew me to religious life. From my high school days, I easily pictured myself in a nun's habit, living a life of prayerful scholarship. No worldly cares. Paying the mortgage, raising children, worrying about car maintenance or Easter outfits—all concerns of the laity—wouldn't interfere with my spiritual goals.

The rain had stopped by the time Sister Ann William and I met again for lunch in an aging student union building. A more modern version was under construction behind the old one, the reason for a bright orange crane perilously close to the administration building tower. I looked at the signage for J. Driscoll & Sons but saw a different name. EDSON & SONS. I wondered if anyone's daughters ever went into construction.

On the way to the cafeteria, we passed several bulletin boards with business cards, flyers, roommate searches, jobs available, and jobs wanted. I was glad I didn't need any such help. I'd done my share of babysitting, house sitting, and gardening chores and felt lucky now to be able to concentrate on my studies. I found it amazing how freeing a vow of poverty could be. No money, but no money problems, either.

Sister Ann William and I carried our umbrellas next to the bright maroon and gold bags that held our new textbooks and joined the cafeteria line. The room was noisy, the hot food smells unappetizing. I was happy to be carrying a St. Lucy's lunch bag, needing only a drink. Aidan Connors, a tall, broad young man whom I'd just met in my department office, was three people ahead of us in the cashier's line. He offered us his place, and we accepted.

It had taken me a while to get used to the deference most people afforded anyone in a religious habit. Now I hardly noticed when a woman old enough to be my grandmother held a door for me. When my Sisters and I showed up to teach Sunday School in a parish church, weak old men offered to carry our briefcases and throngs of parishioners parted like the waters of the Red Sea.

Sister Ann William and I took seats at the back of the cafeteria. As we arranged identical St. Lucy's sandwiches, apples, and chocolate cookies on green plastic trays, Aidan Connors approached our table.

"May I join you?" he asked, sitting down at the same time. "I guess we'll be seeing a lot of each other this semester." He introduced himself to Sister Ann William just before pouring ketchup on a large pile of French fries.

What is this? I asked myself. Less than forty-eight hours away from my Motherhouse I'm sitting in a college cafeteria with a Sister of a different order and a lay man.

I almost forgot to say grace before picking up my sandwich.

———

The Mary Chapel, the smallest of three on campus, was assigned to those who still preferred the traditional rituals of the church. A pamphlet by the baptismal font at the entrance announced the schedule of services: rosary at one o'clock on weekday afternoons, Latin mass at eight on weekday mornings, and at ten on Sundays. Unlike most churches, which had added free-standing altars in the sanctuary to allow the priest to face his congregation, the only altar in the Mary Chapel was the ornate marble table built into its rear wall.

Sister Ann William and I were among a dozen people, Aidan Connors included, who were led in the rosary by a bent old priest. His black St. Alban's cassock, a full-length robe with tiny buttons from top to bottom, was no different from that of a parish priest, except that he wore an over-sized wooden rosary around his waist, much like the one I attached to my apron cord every morning.

As I fingered my rosary, I looked up at the stained-glass windows depicting the joys and sorrows of Our Lady, sending multi-colored sunlight in streaks across the dark walnut pews. Aidan Connors knelt next to me. He held a small rosary, its shiny blue glass beads seeming all the more miniature and delicate in his large hands.

"From First Communion," he whispered. "They did pink for girls and blue for boys that year."

I smiled at him, hoping I hadn't stared at his hands so long that he thought he needed to explain.

As I prayed, *Thy will be done,* I thought about my naiveté in assuming that once I'd chosen to answer God's call to religious life, I'd be forever free of worries and decisions. But both had followed me into the cloister.

Although I put great faith in Saint Paul's assurance that for those who love God, all things work toward good, I still worried about my family, especially my brother, Timothy. I wondered if he'd try to contact me, which he usually did when he was in trouble. This time, however, I was nearly three hundred miles away.

And in the last two days I'd had to make decisions at every turn. To study or meditate? Or attend a punch party. At our Motherhouse, I'd consult the enormous bulletin board in our main hall and learn exactly where God wanted me to be at any moment. On scullery duty, at my desk, at my place in chapel, walking around the yard for meditation. I knew I must wear my wool serge cloak outdoors from October 1 to April 1, not a day sooner and not a day later, regardless of the weather. In this blind obedience was God's will for me.

Now, in my two-day-old life as a graduate student in the Bronx, even an activity as basic as daily mass presented me with a dilemma — whether to attend a Latin service at the Mary Chapel on campus, or the more convenient English liturgy offered at St. Lucy's by Father Malbert, our Chaplain in khakis. My upbringing in an Irish Catholic family hadn't prepared me for a priest I might not be able to respect.

To top it off, I had a nagging feeling about Mother Ignatius's death, that it was not completely natural or peaceful, as Sister Felix had intimated. I pictured her dying from the stress of modern life in the Church and thought vaguely that I might have prevented it. Perhaps if I'd sought her out when she didn't appear for our scheduled meeting, though I couldn't for the life of me imagine what difference that would have made.

CHAPTER 5

W hen Sister Ann William and I returned to St. Lucy's, we entered through the foyer at the front of the house where there was a wooden structure, painted green and divided into slots for our mail. I looked for my name and saw that I already had two pieces of mail, one a postcard from my sister Kathleen who was on her honeymoon in Bermuda.

Kathleen had addressed me in care of the Theology Department at St. Alban's University. The card had been directly forwarded to me at St. Lucy's, never passing before the watchful eye of Mother Julia in Potterstown. Another first—uncensored correspondence from the outside world. I briefly considered sending the card, unread, to Mother Julia, but decided she would have instructed me to do so if that's what she expected.

A shiver went through my body as I unfolded the second piece of mail, a sheet of white paper folded in thirds, without an envelope—a note from Mother Ignatius. I realized it must have been there since the night before. Sister Ann William and I had left in the morning by the back door, never passing the mail station.

I looked at the note as if it had come to me from the dead, which, in a way, it had. Like most of us beginning a letter, Mother Ignatius had drawn a small cross at the top of the paper, with the date and time below it: Sunday evening, 8:00 PM.

"Are you all right, Sister?"

I'd forgotten Sister Ann William had been standing next to me. Her face had a look of concern that told me I was as pale as I felt. I folded the note and put it in my pocket to read later in my room and assured her I was fine.

I hurried up to the third floor, sat on my bed and opened the note again. Mother Ignatius's handwriting was even and oversized, the few sentences filling the page. I read slowly, as if by doing so I could bring her back and prolong her life.

Sister Francesca, I've been called to another meeting. When I finish, I'll look for you in the parlor, then check your room. If I see your light on, I'll knock; otherwise, I'll see you tomorrow. God bless you, M. Ignatius, A. S.

The designation of her order, A. S., for Albanite Sister, was larger than her name, as if she were proudest of that part of her identity. I recalled the thrill I'd felt right after first vows when I was able to sign my name, Sister Francesca, S. M. I.

I stared at the unadorned wall of my room as if the timetable for the past twenty hours were written in broad strokes across the white paint. I'd left chapel at seven forty-five on Sunday evening, after Compline, so I was in my room at eight when Mother Ignatius put the note in my box, perhaps too tired or in too much of a hurry to climb the two flights of stairs to tell me in person. I'd gone back downstairs to the parlor at eight thirty and waited there until after ten.

My light had been on until at least twelve while I'd finished organizing my belongings and read through some undergraduate texts I'd brought along. If Mother Ignatius did check my room for a light, as she'd said, that would mean her meeting didn't end until after midnight. We were told of her death at seven o'clock in the morning.

In between, she died in her sleep.

A string of questions went through my mind. What had Mother Ignatius wanted to tell me? What had she been afraid of? Something or someone connected to her impromptu meeting? Mother Ignatius hadn't known about the meeting at five o'clock that evening when she made plans to see me. How can a spontaneous meeting go on for more than four hours?

And most important, Mother Ignatius had felt energetic and well enough to attend two meetings, and she died soon after. Could someone actually die of stress?

I needed some answers. Before I could talk myself out of it, I was downstairs knocking on St. Lucy's office door.

"Sister Felix, may I speak to you for a moment?"

"Certainly, Sister ... Francesca, isn't it? What can I do for you?"

Sister Felix's voice was high and crackly, in keeping with her pointed witch-like features. She was probably not much more than fifty, but her manner was confident and full of authority. She sat tall and straight behind her name plate at the large mahogany desk that dominated the small room. Behind her was a poster-sized photograph of a stern-looking Pope Paul VI.

The sight was enough to make me abandon my mission. In the midst of my struggle to invent another reason for my appearance at Sister Felix's door, I heard a sneeze from somewhere in the hallway behind me. I thought of my sister Patty. When she had an allergy attack, Patty needed several pillows on her bed, at times sleeping in an almost upright position.

"Sister Felix, may I have an extra pillow?" I asked.

She gave me a quizzical look. For a moment I thought she'd seen through my pretense, but Sister Felix stood and walked to a closet which, to my surprise was stuffed with extra bedding. She pulled a pillow from the shelf and handed it to me without a word.

Perhaps it was the thick down pressed against my body, serving as armor, that renewed my courage.

"Do you know who Mother Ignatius had a meeting with last night?" My voice was shaky, a far cry from that of the brave St. Joan of Arc.

Sister Felix folded her arms across her chest and brought her eyebrows together under her high white wimple.

"She had no meeting that I'm aware of, Sister. Why do you ask?"

I took a step back and reached for the rosary hanging at my waist, under the pillow.

"She was supposed to meet me, and I got a note from her, and I waited until midnight."

I realized I had the sequence of events jumbled, as if I were creating a time anagram for Sister Felix to solve.

"Mother Ignatius was not feeling well. She went to her room right after Compline and died sometime in the early morning hours."

Sister Felix had come from behind her desk to tell me this. For every step she took toward me, I took one back. Our conversation ended with both of us in the hallway, Sister Felix leaning so close to me that I almost sneezed from the dust in her heavy habit.

"Thank you, Sister Felix."

I turned and hurried back upstairs, as confused as if I'd fallen asleep and awakened in a Protestant church.

Strange as it seemed, my first thought as I entered my room was to look in the mirror. I needed to see if I recognized myself. I had approached the acting Superior of my residence and asked unnecessary questions. This is what comes of frivolous talking, I decided. I'd talked more in two days than during a whole Christmas season at the Motherhouse. My tongue was out of control.

I felt my face flush as I thought of Mother Julia and how she would view my behavior. But even as I reprimanded myself for my audacity and my serious departure from my avowed station as lowest, last, and least of God's children, I evaluated Sister Felix's response to my questions. Hard as it was to pronounce the word, even silently, I couldn't escape the conclusion that Sister Felix had told me a lie—that Mother Ignatius had no meeting last night. Unless Mother Ignatius had lied to Sister Felix. Or to me. None of the options pleased me.

In any case, I had no right to know anything.

I shook my head as if to clear it of gratuitous thoughts and wonderings and reached into my pocket for Mother Ignatius's note. I started to tear it up, but stopped midway, read it once more, then put it at the back of my desk drawer.

Taking matters into my own hands, I assumed the role of Mother Julia and imposed a severe penance on myself—I'd wear my arm chain for the rest of the week.

I opened the drawer of the small armoire next to my desk and pulled a ten-inch metal chain from a leather pouch next to a neat pile of handkerchiefs. I held the barbed chain tight in my hand until the tiny spikes hurt enough to bring tears to my eyes. Folding back my wide sleeve, I fastened the chain around my upper arm, then lay down on my bed, the spikes digging into my arm, until I heard the bell for dinner.

CHAPTER 6

I was surprised to find another clean napkin in my wooden ring on the table. It was my third meal in St. Lucy's refectory, and so far there'd been a fresh white cloth at my place for each sitting. At our Motherhouse we changed napkins only on Sunday mornings, adding the soiled ones to the enormous piles of wash for our shifts in the laundry room the next day.

The most unexpected practices I'd met when I entered the SMI novitiate had to do with hygiene. My mother, Helen Sforzo Wickes, who was half Irish, half Italian, God rest her, had always told us *cleanliness is next to Godliness*, but that adage held no sway among religious orders.

"The world gives too much attention to personal appearance," Mother Julia told us at a lesson early in our training. "Think how much time people waste taking care of clothing and making themselves clean and attractive on the outside. They use soaps and perfumes. They color their faces and adorn their bodies. But what we concentrate on, my dear Sisters, is how pure and pleasing we are on the inside, how our immortal souls appear to Our Lord and Savior. Our spiritual beauty is achieved through prayer and penance and following God's will."

Each Sister had only two habits, one for daily wear and one for Sundays. Our chemises and nightgowns, both white cotton, were washed once a week, as were our thick black stockings. With nearly two hundred Sisters in the novitiate at any given time, there was still always enough laundry to keep the huge machines going all day on Mondays.

Our underwear consisted of a one-size-fits-all chemise. I remembered looking at the list of clothing and supplies we were told to bring when we entered—our dowry, it was called. I scoured the list for *underpants*, *brassieres*, or any similar item of lingerie. Finally—like most Postulants, I realized later—I'd broken down and asked my sponsor, Sister Pauline.

"What about, uh, underwear, Sister?"

Sister Pauline had coughed and swallowed elaborately.

"The list is complete, Susan Marie. Just follow it exactly," was all she'd said.

We wore long, thin-boned corsets over our chemises, and these were washed on what seemed like an irregular schedule. Every now and then we'd see a sign at the end of the dormitory hall: CORSET WASH ON WEDNESDAY, and we'd dump them into a huge basket until we'd created a sculpture of stiff flesh-colored fabric and tangled lacings.

At the end of each year, we turned in our everyday habits, close to threadbare, to be used for patches and smaller parts. The Sunday outfit was cleaned and ratcheted down to everyday wear, and we got a new Sunday habit from Sister Seamstress, as we called her.

"Did you hear that Jake Driscoll and the Albanites have already signed a new contract?"

I'd been concentrating so intensely on laundry as a metaphor for holiness that I'd missed grace before dinner, apparently mouthing it automatically and sitting down when everyone else did.

The latest news on the St. Lucy's contract came from Sister Teresa, her department chairman having come through again with a scoop.

Her chubby neighbor at the table, Sister Veronique, also in the History Department, picked up the story, like a co-anchor on television news shows that I remembered from my college days, except they were always men.

"Mr. Driscoll was ready with his lawyers this morning. He's a man of action."

"Is everyone *happy* we're losing our yard?" I asked.

"It's not that we don't like the nice lawn," Sister Veronique said, filling her plate with mashed potatoes. "But Mr. Driscoll has done a lot for this neighborhood already. He's torn down dilapidated buildings and put in housing for people with low incomes. He's cleaned up vacant lots and made playgrounds."

"Yes, thanks to him, it's much safer to walk around here," Sister Teresa said.

"Besides, we do have the entire Botanical Gardens across the street from the University," added Sister Miriam, near me at the table.

"Father Malbert says Jake's being very generous, leaving a large area intact where the shrine to Our Lady is, although that will technically be part of his property." This official-sounding bit of propaganda came from Sister Teresa.

"He's a good Catholic and likes working with the priests," Sister Veronique said.

"I wonder if he made one last try to persuade Mother Ignatius last night," I said, before I could screen my words. Without realizing it, I'd turned my head toward Sister Felix in time to see her reaction to what amounted to an accusation of murder, or at least intimidation, and her complicity in the deed.

Her forkful of roast beef was poised mid-air, her eyes like the blades of a sharp knife. The look on her face set my teeth on edge, and I drew in my breath as if to retract my comment.

"What do you mean?" Sister Teresa asked, almost in unison with at least two others.

What indeed? I asked myself. Before anyone could speak again, Sister Felix clanked her knife against her glass of water, the standard way Mothers Superior got attention at the table.

"Sisters, I'll ask you not to speculate on the final hours of Mother Ignatius, except to pray for her. Mass tomorrow morning will be in her memory. Later in the week, there'll be a formal memorial service. I'll keep you informed as I know more."

"Will you be staying on here as our Mother Superior, Sister Felix?"

I couldn't tell who had asked the question, but I noticed a slight smile come across Sister Felix's face.

"I'll let you know as soon as our Motherhouse makes an announcement, Sisters."

I remembered with gratitude that Sisters at St. Lucy's could leave the table when they'd finished eating, not waiting to say grace together after meals. I stood up, made the sign of the cross, and left the refectory, my roast beef dinner untouched.

Back in my room, I turned to my books, deciding the best course of action was to forget Mother Ignatius, except to pray for her soul as Sister Felix had recommended. My extracurricular activities were doing no one any good, especially me.

My new textbooks were piled on my desk, taking up at least half the surface. I looked at the spines and read the titles, from the top down.

I'd bought a required text by the renegade French Jesuit, Pierre Teilhard de Chardin, plus Harvey Cox's *The Secular City*, which appeared to be more like a sociology book. Another author was the German theologian Hans Kung, whose name I'd heard in conjunction with a controversy with the Pope. From what Mother Julia told us, Kung questioned a central doctrine of Catholicism—the divine nature of Christ.

Three other paperbacks were by non-Catholic philosophers and theologians. Except for an anthology of the writings of Saint Thomas Aquinas, and a church history text, I could hardly tell from the collection that I was enrolled in a Catholic university.

I longed to bury myself in the traditions that had sustained me, but it seemed unlikely that I'd be able to hide from the twentieth century.

I'd removed my bonnet and untied my bib when I heard a gentle knock on my door. I added this event to the growing list entitled *Never Before In My Life As A Nun*. My SMI community kept the Great Silence, the rule that no one speak a word on the dormitory floor after dark, unless it was a life-threatening emergency. We assumed this was a precaution against latent homosexuality, although the term was never used by Mother Julia at our formal lessons.

"It's wise always to avoid temptation, Sisters," was all she'd ever said about the practice of Great Silence.

"Sister Francesca?"

I heard Sister Ann William's soft voice and lilting accent. I pinned myself back together and opened the door to find her holding a plate of food covered with waxed paper.

She held it out to me. "I thought you might get hungry when you were feeling better?"

"Thank you so much, Sister," I said, taking the warm platter from her. "I'm better, and I am hungry."

"The Sisters told me this would not have been possible with Mother Ignatius in charge. She wouldn't allow food on this floor."

Although Sister Ann William's whispery drawl turned these statements into questions, the terrible implication remained. Possibly because of a horrified look on my face, she covered her mouth and drew in her breath.

"Not that I'm glad she's dead," she said. "And not that I believe in all the reforms of Sister Teresa."

"Ironic isn't it?" I asked.

"You mean that a nun named Teresa would once again be instigating a reform?"

I nodded. "Yes, but in the opposite direction wouldn't you say?" I knew she'd also been thinking of St. Teresa of Avila, who'd brought her sixteenth century Carmelite nuns from the relaxed, worldly environment they'd slipped into, back to poverty, hardship, and solitude. "This Teresa seems to want to blur the distinctions between us and women of the world," I said, lowering my voice to keep our conversation private.

While we were still standing at my door, several Sisters had come up the stairs and gone into rooms, some in twos and threes, chatting with a gaiety I hadn't heard since glee club trips I'd taken in college before I entered the convent. I considered inviting Sister Ann William into my room, but decided I'd broken enough rules for one day.

"Thanks again, Sister," I said, cradling my dinner tray. "Shall I meet you after breakfast for our walk to campus?"

"That would be lovely. Good night, Sister Francesca."

A few minutes later, as I finished up my lukewarm potatoes, I sent up a silent prayer of gratitude that I'd met someone as thoughtful as Sister Ann William. She'd even remembered to include silverware with her room service. The term particular attachment—we called it PA for short—came to my mind. I mentally replayed the lessons I'd heard about the dangers of forming friendships as religious.

"Human friends are for people of the world, Sisters. They are the greatest distraction from doing the will of Our Lord," Mother Julia had often said. "How are we to know God's will if we're following our own likes and dislikes? Our own preferences have no place in religious life. It will be our life's work to rid ourselves of ourselves, Sisters."

Mother Julia drilled into us the wisdom of the three-person rule we followed. We'd walk in threes, and we'd talk in threes, to reduce the likelihood of forming one-on-one bonds. For SMIs, as for most religious orders, *recreation* was a formal term—the only time of day when talking was permitted. During inclement weather, recreation might include a game of cards or a board game. At other times we were allowed to take our mending to the room and sew as we talked. For the most part, recreation periods were immediately after meals, after we'd finished our scullery chore, and seldom lasted more than thirty or forty minutes.

We were admonished to enter a recreation area with our heads down and our eyes lowered as far as it was possible without tripping. We didn't survey the room first for Sisters we might like to be with, and we never planned to meet someone.

"When we have reached some measure of spiritual perfection, Sisters," Mother Julia told us, "we will find ourselves praying to be at the card table with the Sister who most annoys us."

I hoped I hadn't acted outside the bounds of detached collegiality toward Sister Ann William. It's not that I'm making friends with her, I told myself. I'm just being charitable, as Our Lord also commands.

———————

At about nine o'clock, while I was sitting at my desk writing a note to Mother Julia, I heard the house bells ring in the sequence of my room number—two rings, a pause, then five rings. It meant I had either a phone call or a visitor in the parlor, neither of which I was expecting.

I pinned on my bonnet and walked half way down the corridor to the intercom connecting the dormitory floors to the main office.

"This is Sister Francesca," I said into the speaker grille, my voice sounding extra loud as it echoed down the hallway. From the other end, I heard the unmistakable high-pitched tones of Sister Felix.

"Sister, you have a visitor."

"A visitor?"

"Yes, Sister." Sister Felix sounded annoyed. "Please come to the small parlor."

"Yes, thank you, Sister," I said, although I had the feeling that my acting Superior had already walked away from the phone.

I tugged at my veil, checked that I had all the pieces of my habit on, and headed down the stairs, my mind empty of guesses about my visitor.

The first person I saw when I reached the first floor was Jake Driscoll. He was in a dark suit, leaving Sister Felix's office, his arms full of long rolls of paper, as if he'd come from a real estate meeting.

"Evening, Sister," he said, giving me a wide smile as he touched a scroll to his forehead in a gesture of salute. "Your young man is in there." He used the thin tube to point to the parlor next to the front door and across from the mailboxes.

I nodded without saying a word to him. I found myself blaming him for Mother Ignatius's death, for no reason I could pinpoint, other than he was alive and happy and she wasn't.

I entered the parlor and saw the young man Jake Driscoll referred to—handsome in spite of his disheveled appearance, unshaven, wearing an old sweatshirt minus its neck ribbing, and jeans torn at both knees. His sad face tugged at my heart.

"Hi, Sis," he said.

CHAPTER 7

I searched my brother's scruffy face and long, untended hair for his trademark impish grin, and grew melancholy for a moment when I couldn't find it. When I went to embrace him, he stepped back and turned away from me.

"I'm kinda dirty," he said.

In profile, nineteen-year-old Timothy Wickes appeared as stooped over as an old Cardinal of the Vatican. Unlike the clerical hierarchy, however, Timothy wore greasy denims with American flag patches spaced at random around his hips.

"I don't care if you're messy. I—"

"I know. You changed my diapers."

Timothy turned and I put my arms around him. I felt his body relax. We gave each other our standard playful poke in the shoulders before breaking apart and I was grateful for any sign that he was still my little brother.

When it was clean, Timothy's hair was dark brown with hints of red, not carrot-like. His was the only normal-color mane among the Wickes children. Probably he had my mother's Italian side to thank for that. He was tall and thin like most of the family, except for Kathleen. Katie's wide hips and our younger sister Gabriella's name were two other constant reminders of our mother's Italian heritage.

"Did you—?"

"Yes, I reported to my parole officer."

"We were worried about you."

Timothy frowned. "I wasn't that late checking in. He said I needed professional help. So I came to see you. You're a professional, right?" Timothy grinned, and I was grateful for whatever reason he'd found to recover his sense of humor.

"Does he—?"

"He knows I'm here."

"Since you're finishing all my sentences this evening, try this one. Does Dad … ?" I trailed off.

"Funny," he said, giving me another grin. "I called Dad. He said, 'Timothy, young man, we have a few things to talk about.'"

Timothy did a near-perfect imitation of our father's throaty voice, seasoned by alcohol and cigarettes, although he'd finally given up both after a heart attack a few years ago. It had been a mild one, but enough to frighten him into healthier habits.

I sat down on a low cushioned sofa that matched three other chairs in a dark, rosy brocade with wood trim. For a moment my mind drifted to the last time I'd been in the small parlor, waiting in vain for Mother Ignatius.

Timothy looked around at the spotless furniture in the dust-free room and threw up his hands as if to indicate he'd found no available seating.

"It's all right to sit down," I said.

"I'm kinda dirty."

"You said that. There must be more important things for us to talk about, Timothy."

"You sound like Dad. And you're the only two people who still call me Timothy."

"I didn't say 'Timothy, young man.'"

We both laughed at my attempt to imitate our father, not as good as my brother's had been.

As he sat in front of me, having finally plunked himself down on a footstool, I had a hard time thinking of Timothy as a criminal. But he'd sold drugs, even if it was only marijuana, and even if it wasn't more than once or twice. For all I knew this is how every big-time drug dealer in the country got his start.

For the next half hour, Timothy and I talked about the crises of his life. Timothy was only nine when our mother died, leaving him with four older sisters to fill the role. When he ended up in jail for selling marijuana to his college classmates, we all blamed ourselves.

"Four mothers are worse than none," he'd said, more than once.

Our conversation today was as circular as the so-called dialogues I'd heard between Christians and Jews, or Catholics and Methodists, for that matter. No common starting point.

"I don't want to go back to college. But if I don't, I'll be drafted."

"Your suspension ends in January. You can go back then, and no one will bother you for at least three or four years."

"But my classes are meaningless. Bourgeois professors teaching the children of the bourgeoisie. Promoting the glorification of the military industrial complex."

This was not my little brother speaking. I dismissed the idea that Timothy had become one of the raving liberals Mother Julia had read to us about. More likely his professors at Potterstown Community College were filling his head with sloppy thinking and words he didn't even know the meaning of.

"What do you want to do with your life, Timothy?"

"Maybe I'll be a priest." Another grin. "Oops. Too late."

"Timothy!"

He scratched his head. "Sorry. I don't know. Hang out with Melody."

"I thought her name was Maureen?"

"She changed it. She says she feels more like a Melody."

I had a hard time stifling a laugh. I wondered about a young woman who'd abandon a name that was a form of Mary, in favor of one that was a common noun used by the doo-wop disc jockeys I'd heard in college.

"You want to hang around with, uh, Melody, but still have Dad pay your expenses?"

"Oh, like you have a job? Dad paid *your* expenses all the way through college, and you haven't exactly paid him back."

Timothy had stood up to deliver this remark. The small parlor seemed to collapse to minute dimensions as my insides shrank from the stinging comment. I thought I'd gotten over the guilt I suffered when I left my family, even though—except for Timothy—they looked upon my vocation as an honor for the Wickes clan.

I remembered the conversation I'd had with my father about my vocation as if it were six days ago and not six years.

"I could wait another year so I can help out," I'd said. "I'll get a job, live at home, and enter later."

"God is calling you now, Susan Marie," my father'd said. "And I'm so proud He wants one of mine. Your mother prayed for this every day of her life."

I'd tried to explain to my father that a vocation wasn't like a call from a radio quiz show where you had to have the right answer in less than a minute. Nor was it a trumpet sound from an archangel telling you to show up immediately for a habit fitting.

For me, God's call was a more ordinary summons. I believed in everything the Catholic Church had taught me, and I wanted to spend my life doing work that I could be sure was God's will. I'd known SMI's since kindergarten and felt drawn to their life of prayer and service to others. I'd waited until I finished my degree so I might be more prepared to teach for the order.

Timothy's voice called me back to St. Lucy's Hall, where God's will for me seemed more vague than I'd gotten used to.

"I'm sorry," Timothy said. "I didn't mean that."

"I know."

"It's just that there I am, under the thumbs of Dad and Patty. She might as well be the nun. She's completely minus any understanding of normal sexual ..." Timothy's face turned red. "Well, it's tough, is all."

"I'm sure it is, Timothy."

I knew that my sister Patty felt an obligation to be the mother, as next in line when I left. I couldn't disagree that her life was nun-like. Twenty-six years old, keeping house for our father and Gabriella, who lived at home while she went to college. Patty never dated and spent her leisure time at novenas and helping out at the rectory of the parish church.

"And Gabriella doesn't get it, either," Timothy continued. "She doesn't have a care in the world. Her only goal in life is to make it to Italy where they'll know how to pronounce and spell her name without help."

I wanted to ask Timothy what all this had to do with his selling drugs. I was saved from that bad idea by the chimes of the grandfather clock in the main parlor at the end of the corridor. For the second night in a row, I heard the ten o'clock chimes from the main parlor.

"Where are you going to stay tonight?" I asked him.

"I hitchhiked here. Got left off on the Grand Concourse. I guess I'll just go back the same way."

"But we're not finished, Timothy. I'd really like to have a talk with you when we're both rested."

"Me, too, Sis. Maybe it would actually work without Dad around. Any room here?" He grinned at my exasperated look. "Just kidding. I can probably crash in the lounge on St. Alban's campus."

"Crash?"

"Uh, sleep. Stay overnight."

"What if they're not open? I doubt you can wander in at any hour."

"There's always the lawn."

I shook my head. "You can't sleep outside."

"It wouldn't be the first time."

I pictured the wide flashlight beam of a St. Alban's security officer landing on Timothy's cold cheeks as he lay sprawled on the campus lawn. The vision was enough to convince me that God wanted me to use whatever resources I had to help my brother.

"I'll be back in a minute," I told Timothy. "Let me make a call."

"You already know somebody here?"

"Yes, there's a young man in my department ..."

"A young man is it?" he said, faking an Irish brogue, and with a look that sent a crimson rush to my face.

"He gave everyone his business card, Timothy," I said, leaving the parlor at the same time as if to lessen the sin of the slight exaggeration I'd come up with, making Sister Ann William and me sound like a crowd.

Outside the parlor, the only sound I could hear in St. Lucy's Hall was the ticking of the clock. Unlike the steady stream of cars during daylight hours, traffic on the street was minimal at night, and I felt as though I were breaking a rule merely by being awake at such a late hour. In fact, I was.

I went upstairs and dug around in the bookstore bag where I'd put Aidan Connors's number. It was on a small business card advertising his part-time job at Lloyd's Used Cars.

"I'm not a salesman," he'd assured us, as if that would have been grounds for excommunication. "I'm the one under the car making sure it runs, hopefully." At the time, I thought Aidan's smile was warm enough to inspire trust in any customer.

He'd written his home telephone number on the back. In case we ever needed it, he'd said.

As I walked to the phone in the middle of the hallway, I questioned what I was about to do, calling a lay man I'd just met to ask a favor. I wrestled with conflicting admonitions from our Holy Rule. Was I justified in bending rules for Timothy just because he was my brother?

I remembered the New Testament gospel story of Jesus refusing to help his own mother because He was busy ministering to someone else. *Who is my mother?* Jesus had asked, when he was criticized for choosing a stranger over his own flesh and blood.

In the end, I settled on *whatsoever you do for the least of my brethren, you do unto me,* and dialed Aidan's number. I tried to remember the last time I'd handled a telephone. I recalled using it only once in the last six years, when our assigned parent didn't show up and three of us from my community needed a ride home from teaching Sunday School.

"Hello."

I heard Aidan's voice, surprisingly soft for such a large man.

The telephone was on the wall outside the bathrooms, which were empty at that hour. I kept my voice down, afraid of waking the Sisters in the nearby rooms, and worried about someone overhearing my conversation and misinterpreting it.

"Aidan, this is Sister Francesca. From the Theology Department at St..."

"I know who you are, Sister."

Aidan's laugh was warm and friendly, putting me at ease and giving me a nervous twinge at the same time.

"I hope I didn't wake you."

"Not at all. What's on your mind?"

"I need a favor. I hope to be able to repay you some time, but at the moment—"

"I'd be happy if I can help, Sister. What is it?"

By this time, I was resigned to an evening of incomplete sentences.

"My brother—Timothy Wickes—dropped in unexpectedly this evening. He's only nineteen, and he came down from Potterstown to visit me."

"Does he need a place to crash?"

"I'd be so grateful, Aidan," I said, making a mental note about this new meaning of *crash* that everyone but me seemed to know.

"It turns out I have more room than I need right now. My roommate left last week. He transferred to NYU and moved downtown. Does your brother have a car?"

"No. He hitchhiked."

My whisper was softer still as I described the unseemly mode of transportation.

"I'll come and get him."

"We're at 323—"

"St. Lucy's Hall, right?"

"Right."

"I'll be there in about fifteen minutes."

"He's been on the road, he's … kinda dirty," I said, adopting Timothy's self-description.

"No problem. Really, Sister. I'd be glad to help out."

Aidan seemed ready to hang up and jump in his car. But I had one other thing I needed to tell him. I cleared my throat and prepared to hear shock in Aidan's voice.

"There's something else." I'd rehearsed the next sentence on my way to the phone. "Timothy is on parole. He was in jail for a minor offense, but I thought you should know."

Aidan didn't pause a second. "All the more reason I'm glad to help."

I hung up even more impressed with my new classmate.

A half hour later I stood on St. Lucy's concrete steps and waved good-bye to Timothy and Aidan, who'd arrived wearing faded jeans and a wrinkled sweatshirt with holes in the sleeves. He didn't look much better than Timothy, I mused. Since I'd declined Aidan's invitation to breakfast in his apartment the next morning—there was no confusion in my mind about that rule—we'd made plans to meet at the campus cafeteria.

"How dumb is that?" Timothy had asked. "She can't go to a private home with friends and family, but she can go to a lousy cafeteria and eat in front of zillions of strangers."

Aidan smiled and ushered Timothy to his car.

"Not everything is perfectly logical in this life, Timothy," Aidan said, taking the words right out of my mouth.

I turned to go back into St. Lucy's, confident my brother was in good hands. In the back of my mind was the hope that Timothy might be impressed by Aidan Connors, who looked more like a football player than a theology graduate student. I was sure Timothy thought religion and theology were for old men like his father or ninety-eight-pound weaklings like his sister. I imagined Aidan's pale blue rosary in plain view on his coffee table.

Halfway up the steps to the building, I heard someone call my name. I'd seen a car pull up behind Aidan's, the occupants remaining inside. The sound came from that direction.

"Francesca, hold the door."

I saw Sister Teresa leaving the car, a black Ford Fairlane, like the fleet of vehicles I'd seen behind the priests' campus residence. The driver looked to me like Father Malbert, but I couldn't be sure it wasn't my overactive imagination that led me to that conclusion.

Sister Teresa came running toward me, up the stairs.

"Thanks, Francesca. Lucky you're here," she said. "I tried to reach Veronique to get her to open the door for me but couldn't get through on the phone. I didn't know what I was going to do next. Throw rocks at the window, I guess." She laughed. "Thank God you propped the door open."

Sister Teresa, who seemed to have given up on religious titles, was somewhat out of breath, and in the dim light over the front door, I could see her face was flushed.

"Sister Felix is having keys made, so this won't be a problem much longer," she said.

I rolled my eyes. "How handy for you, Sister."

Inside the building, Sister Teresa and I went separate ways. As I headed for the stairs up to my room, she went downstairs where there was a laundry room, a ping pong table, and a telephone booth. I wondered which equipment she needed at nearly eleven o'clock at night.

Thanks to my late evening visit with my brother, I'd been privy to nighttime activities I wouldn't have dreamed of—Jake Driscoll's meeting with Sister Felix, Sister Teresa's return from what looked suspiciously like a date, and Aidan Connors in his casual clothes.

I marveled at the night life at St. Lucy's Hall.

CHAPTER 8

I was on the third step up to my room when a bright flash caught my eye—headlights from a passing car reflecting off the brass plate on Mother Ignatius's office door. I paused for a moment, surprised that her name was still there, considering how quickly her adversaries had moved in on her territory.

A sudden, strong force pulled me in that direction, as if the shiny metal had become a powerful magnet attracting the chain links on the rosary around my waist. At that moment, I was ready to admit what had been nagging at me since Mother Ignatius's death. Life at St. Lucy's had already changed drastically with her out of the way. What if she hadn't died of natural causes or even stress? What if she'd been murdered?

Here's where I should stop, I told myself, and find some other wild fantasy to chase before my classes provided me with enough to do. But even as I had that thought, I approached the door to Mother Ignatius's office.

My ears alert for sounds from upstairs and down, I pretended to be casually walking by, and brushed my wide sleeve against the knob. The protruding sides of my bonnet were a distinct handicap as I tried to determine if there was anyone else in the hallway.

I spun around and approached again from the opposite direction. I stood with my back to the door, facing the foyer. With a rapid-fire prayer—Jesus, Mary, and Joseph!— I turned the knob and opened the door.

My breath came in short, rapid pulses. What did I think I was doing? Trespassing, for one thing. Did I expect to uncover proof of murder by finding a gun or a bloody knife? As if Mother Ignatius's body had been found with gunshot or stab wounds. More likely poison would have the weapon. I sniffed the air. As if I knew what poison smelled like, if it had an odor in the first place.

And who was this new person I'd become? A talker, a rule-breaker, a snoop. At least I'm not invading a crime scene, I told myself, since no one else thinks there's been a crime.

My belief in Mother Ignatius's murder grew as I remembered her note to me and her troubled look, hours before her death. Just this one bit of investigation, and I'd be ready to declare either a grand coincidence, or a sin against the fifth commandment.

Thou shalt not kill. I shivered as I entered the room.

Moonlight from a small window behind Mother Ignatius's desk illuminated its surface, almost bare except for a blotter and a few accessories. For the first time I found myself wishing a flashlight were standard SMI equipment.

The office was about ten feet square, approximately the same size as our dormitory rooms. A door on the side wall opened to a small bathroom, connected in turn to a bedroom. The entire suite was probably not more than a ten by twenty rectangle. I walked the length of it, aided only by the Marian Avenue street lights.

Besides a narrow cot wrapped tight as a mummy in white sheets, Mother Ignatius's bedroom held only a chair and a light oak armoire, slightly larger than the one in my room.

At the foot of the bed was a chenille bed spread, folded to a narrow rectangle. I was surprised at its frayed condition, marked by tears and pulls in the fabric, the only flaw in an otherwise perfectly ordered room. I suspected Mother Ignatius had a hard time asking for anything new for herself.

I walked up to the armoire, leaning so close that the edge of my bib touched the handle that held its doors together. Somewhere in my consciousness I hoped they would fall open at the touch so I might be judged innocent of breaking and entering a closet.

No such miracle occurred, however. I held my breath and turned the knob. The doors swung open. I let out my breath and looked at the empty space. My eyes wandered over the entire cabinet as if it were possible for me to miss something in the small volume. A shelf along the top was bare, a rod just below it held nothing, not even empty hangers.

I closed the doors, tempted to wipe my fingerprints off the handle, until I reminded myself that no one but me considered this a crime scene.

I walked back through the bathroom. A loud noise startled me. I pressed my back against the wall.

False alarm.

I'd inadvertently brushed against the switch that turned on the fan. I turned it off quickly and blew out a heavy sigh. I screwed up my mouth in annoyance. Agitation, I thought, the wages of sin.

I left the bathroom, which was empty of everything but standard fixtures, disappointed that there was no medicine cabinet, the better to hold poisons.

The office held the best opportunity for information about its recently deceased occupant, I decided, rummaging in the desk. But either it wasn't used much or had already been stripped of interesting material, I thought with displeasure.

Until my fingers bumped into a small packet of letters stuck in a crevice at the back of the center drawer. Another moral dilemma. I solved it quickly, stuffing the bundle into my pocket, and willing myself not to examine my conduct.

I was about to walk away from the desk when I noticed an object that seemed out of place in the small glass dish that held paper clips. I picked it up and turned it over in my hand. A cuff link. A single onyx cuff link with an elaborate silver letter D.

That's enough, I decided, I have two things to work with. But then a third presented itself with no effort on my part. Against the wall, behind the door to the corridor was a credenza, and on it a tea set. In a leap of logic that would surely have rattled my hero, Saint Thomas Aquinas, I was able to jump from the lovely blue and white china pot with matching cups, to a nighttime habit that got Mother Ignatius killed—someone poisoned her tea.

I had only a moment of exultation at this striking discovery when I was discovered myself. Before I ever heard him enter the dark office, I stood face to face with Father Malbert. Nearly knocking me over as he opened the door, he seemed as surprised as I was.

We said "Sister" and "Father" at the same time, stepping back from each other, like an odd couple in an old-time family comedy routine.

"I came to pick up some altar linens and candelabra that Mother Ignatius was keeping for me," Father Malbert said, in a tone that had an undercurrent of, *it's your turn to explain.*

"I needed information to send to my Mother Superior," I said, hardly proud of how quickly a lie came to lips that were only a few hours from receiving Holy Communion. On the other hand, I hadn't seen any altar linens or candles in Mother Ignatius's suite, either.

We nodded to each other, and parted, as if our meeting had happened under the most normal of circumstances, instead of in the late Mother Ignatius's office during the midnight peals of the clock down the hall.

On my way upstairs, I said an act of contrition and forced all secular matters to the back of my mind.

As I undressed for bed, I came upon the letters and cuff link I'd confiscated. Overcome with disgust for myself, I put both in the back of my desk drawer, determined to find a way to return them without giving them further thought.

In my dreams that night, my desk burst into flames that followed me out the door, up Marian Avenue, all the way to Potterstown where Mother Julia tied me to a stake.

———————

Walking to campus for the first day of classes on Tuesday, I was only briefly tempted to tell Sister Ann William about my adventures in the late hours of the night before. I decided it wouldn't be prudent, especially since I didn't know what any of it meant. If I'd learned nothing else in my brief graduate school career, I'd come to understand the wisdom of a rule of silence. As Mother Ignatius had admonished, it was indeed a slippery slope from simple "flexibility" to a complete relaxation of religious discipline.

I was guilty of a string of transgressions, more serious than any I'd ever reported at a Saturday night Chapter of Faults. In my calmed-down state I judged that the lie I'd told Father Malbert was only a venial sin, not of the more grievous, mortal variety. Even so, I resolved to go to confession at the first opportunity.

If I'd been following the rules of my order, I wouldn't have received a visitor, even my brother, after hours. And I certainly wouldn't have invaded Mother Ignatius's suite. If I'd been guarding my eyes as I was taught the first day in the Novitiate, I wouldn't have seen Jake Driscoll leave Sister Felix's office and Sister Teresa's late-night return. My soul seemed as weighed down as Saint Christopher carrying the Christ Child across the river.

Thinking of Mother Ignatius made me sad, and I said as much to Sister Ann William.

"I wonder what's going to happen at St. Lucy's now that Mother Ignatius is gone."

She shrugged her shoulders and raised her eyebrows. "Did you see the notice about the meeting tonight? Not something she would have approved of."

"A meeting?"

"There's a memo tacked to the bulletin board by the mailboxes. A meeting after dinner to discuss new house rules."

"We haven't even had Mother Ignatius' memorial services yet."

"I know," she said. From Sister Ann William's lips, it sounded like "ah now."

For some reason, I reached my limit of self-control at that moment. Perhaps I was reacting to the Bronx Botanical Gardens across the street. Its countless varieties of plants, trees, flowers, and shrubs reminded me of Sister Ann William's plant pathology class and the poisons we'd talked about. My resolve to give no more thought to the mystery of Mother Ignatius's death vanished on a light breeze that ruffled my long skirt.

"How hard would it be to poison someone and not have it be obvious?" I asked the pharmacist-to-be at my side.

"Well, of course, I'll know more after I've had this class, but it's not that difficult if you know what you're doing. For example … "

Sister Ann William stopped mid-sentence. "Sister Francesca, whatever are you thinking?" She let out a long breath and shook her head from side to side, then lifted her briefcase and clutched it to her bosom, as if to shield herself from frightening thoughts. Her pale skin turned even whiter, giving her the look of the young St. Maria Goretti, martyred at an early age.

"I'm thinking someone may have poisoned Mother Ignatius." With my thoughts—ugly as they were—out in the open, a wave of relief swept over me, carrying almost-sweet perfume from the massive gardens on my left. "She was afraid of something. She was going to tell me what it was, and then …"

"So you think whoever was with her on Sunday night might have killed Mother Ignatius?"

"What do you mean 'whoever was with her'?"

Sister Ann William's steps faltered as she tried to keep up with my questions. I realized my excitement was intimidating her and forced myself to calm down. "I'm sorry, Sister, but this could be really important," I told her in as soft a voice as I could manage.

She took a breath. "I heard Mother Ignatius, in her office that night, and I heard another voice—I'm sure someone was in there with her."

"A man or a woman?"

Sister Ann William paused and tilted her head to the side, as if straining to hear the sounds again. She shrugged her shoulders. "I can't be positive. I'd say either a man or a woman with a low-pitched voice. They were definitely arguing, however."

"What time was that?"

"Well, it was after Compline. I went to watch an eight o'clock news program in the parlor. But then I got these guilty feelings, since we're not allowed television at my Motherhouse except for occasional documentaries. I probably left about eight-fifteen."

I made a quick calculation, figuring that eight-fifteen was exactly between the time Mother Ignatius wrote the note at eight o'clock and my arrival in the parlor at eight-thirty. I wondered why I hadn't heard anything when I passed the office myself, but Sister Ann William cleared it up for me.

"The door wasn't quite closed when I walked by to go upstairs. Once they closed it, I couldn't hear a thing. Not that I was listening."

"But why didn't you tell anyone? I mean, she was dead the next morning."

"She was an old woman who died in her sleep, Sister Francesca. Why would I think of mentioning that she was talking to someone so many hours before?"

I took a deep breath to calm myself. "You wouldn't, Sister. Of course not. Did you by any chance catch word or a glimpse through the crack in the door? Did you hear what they were arguing about?"

"No. I wasn't paying attention. I just vaguely remember there was a conversation. It's not as if they were really yelling or anything. I might even be wrong that it sounded confrontational. And I could still hear the television set down the hall."

Sister Ann William shuddered, and I knew the crisp air was not the reason. I felt responsible for her agitated state, and without thinking I put my hand on her shoulder. I removed it immediately, hoping she didn't notice. While Christian comfort was a virtue, a physical expression of it was forbidden a person with a vow of chastity. I looked around the wide boulevard that led to the campus, as if I expected to see Mother Julia's disapproving look from the window of a passing car.

"I'm sorry if I've upset you, Sister," I said.

"It's all right, Sister Francesca. But what do you think happened to Mother Ignatius if it wasn't a peaceful death?"

"Well, suppose Mother Ignatius served tea or coffee to the man—or woman—in her office. And suppose he had something with him, some poisonous liquid, or powder, and he put it in her drink. Suppose it was timed so it would take effect while she was sleeping …"

I didn't need Sister Ann William to tell me that was a lot of supposes.

"If there were anything strange about Mother Ignatius's death, wouldn't the police have noticed?"

"But that's just it. As far as we know, the police weren't called in. The murderer probably counted on everyone's assuming the death was natural, but I'm guessing he took precautions anyway. That's why I need you to find out what kind of poisons wouldn't leave an obvious trace."

Sister Ann William let out a long breath. I could tell she was struggling to process the scenario I'd presented. I pictured her writing to her Superior at the Holy Charity Motherhouse in Texas about a crazy Sister of Mary Immaculate from upstate New York who thought up murder plots as a hobby.

"Tell me again. What makes you suspicious in the first place?" she asked me, her briefcase back down at her side.

I respected Sister Ann William's need for reinforcement. I told her again about Mother Ignatius's distraught state, her request to meet me, and the note she'd left in my mail slot. Leaving out my observations of the night before, I recounted the suspect list I'd built up in my head. A real estate developer who needed more property, an Albanite Sister who wanted a promotion, and a few others who wanted their own keys. It didn't seem like much when I laid it all out, even after I threw in a chaplain who might be dating a nun.

Sister Ann William didn't think much of the list, either.

"First, Mr. Driscoll's rich and powerful. He could have gotten that contract broken easily. I know the type. My older brother James is a lawyer and he's always doing that kind of thing for Houston oil men."

"He makes illegal transactions?"

"Not exactly. James explains it a little differently. He says no contract is impossible to break. There are always extenuating circumstances a good lawyer can find."

I nodded, trying to absorb the facts of the real world. "And in this case, I suppose Jake Driscoll could have claimed Mother Ignatius was too old to be responsible."

Sister William nodded. "Or that the original signers didn't foresee future needs of the local community. So, for suspects, that leaves us with Sister Felix and the other Sisters, and Father Malbert." She clucked her tongue. "I can't believe a religious person would ever commit murder, let alone over some silly rules."

"I can't, either," I said. "Let's forget about it."

"Did you read a lot of Sherlock Holmes before you entered?"

"Agatha Christie."

We shared a much-needed laugh and turned onto the campus path.

As we approached the pharmacy building where we would part for the morning, Sister Ann William brought her briefcase to her chest again.

"It would still be interesting to find out what kind of poisons might not leave a trace," she said, with a conspiratorial grin.

"Yes, it would."

"Just from the scientific point of view."

"Of course."

Maybe it wasn't so awful to have friends.

CHAPTER 9

I walked on to Aquinas Hall, where the Theology Department was housed, and made a ten-minute visit to the small chapel on the first floor. I looked for a priest in the confessionals but found none. Except for a repetition of formal prayers and a prayer for Timothy, I was unable to focus on spiritual matters. The Case of the Dead Mother Ignatius, of concern only to me and Sister Ann William, it seemed, flooded my brain.

What would the police do if they had my suspicions, I wondered? Although I was helpless to do anything about it, I came up with a list. Canvass the neighborhood. See what cars were in front of St. Lucy's Hall on Sunday evening after eight o'clock. Talk to every Sister in residence, especially the ones on the first floor watching television — ask if anyone remembered a stranger arriving in the evening. Determine whether doors and first floor windows were kept locked routinely. Dig into Mother Ignatius's past for anyone with a reason to kill her. Find out what her habits were with regard to drinking tea at night. Determine whether she made it herself or had someone bring it to her.

I'd have asked Sister Felix some of these questions if she hadn't aborted our interview.

I wondered if I could get the china set I'd seen in Mother Ignatius' office to a laboratory surreptitiously. Maybe I could also mail the packet of letters and the cuff links to the Bronx Police Department. I sighed at the realization that it would be entirely inappropriate for me to carry out any of this.

I thought about Sister Felix. Had she lied to me about Mother Ignatius's not having a meeting or did she simply not know? Her suite was two doors down from Mother Ignatius, with a coat closet in between. It was impossible to know if she'd been in a position to hear her Superior's last words. Or if she herself had been the combatant my friend Sister Ann William had heard.

The strange behavior of Father Malbert also came to mind, though I had to admit it was no stranger than mine. There were certainly no altar linens or candelabra in Mother Ignatius's suite when I'd snooped around in it, but that didn't mean they hadn't been there—they might have been removed without Father Malbert's knowledge.

Or maybe he'd gone to her office for the same reason I did. Just to snoop. Something to consider.

Since Mother Ignatius was at least in her late seventies and died without signs of struggle, I assumed no autopsy would have been conducted. I consoled myself with the thought that at least it wasn't too late for that, since the Church didn't allow cremation. How could our souls rise and join our bodies on the Last Day if we'd permitted ourselves to be turned into a pile of ashes beforehand?

I heard the warning bell for my ten-thirty class and offered a quick genuflection as I left the chapel, no more at peace than when I entered.

My first class was in Church history and liturgy, a last-minute substitution for a cancelled comparative religions class. I was surprised to find myself looking around for Aidan. Wondering about Timothy's night with him, of course.

I took a seat near the middle of the large, sloped lecture hall, dominated by a long counter-like desk across the front, and dozens of rows of student chairs bolted to the old wooden floor. The only adornments were an American flag in one corner and an enormous crucifix centered over the blackboard.

I tried to judge the political leanings of our professor, Father Glanz, by his looks as he walked in and sorted through his books and notes.

Tall, with a weathered face and enough gray hair and thickness around the middle to be in his fifties at least. That should be old enough to be sensible, I thought.

I knew it would be impossible for any professor to teach a class in liturgy without entering the debate sparked by Vatican II. The Roman Catholic mass, a commemoration of the Last Supper, was a central controversy. One faction wanted to keep the traditional ritual—Latin for the essential parts, the priest celebrant with his back to the congregation, Holy Communion place on our tongues. Liberal Catholics wanted the liturgy more accessible to everyone—using the local language and modern translations of scriptural passages. In the new liturgy the priest would face us and encourage us to add our own individual prayers and concerns.

As a result, clergy and laity were encouraged to make the mass a social as well as a spiritual event. Halfway through the service, we were expected to turn to our neighbors in the pews nearest us and give them "the greeting of peace," which meant anything from a kiss to a handshake. As if we'd gathered for the annual parish spaghetti supper. Not what I thought Jesus had in mind for the Holy Sacrifice of the Mass.

I didn't wonder for long where Father Glanz stood on the issue, his sober appearance notwithstanding. One look at the syllabus he'd handed out told me I was in for more internal conflict. An expert in Semitic languages, Father Glanz had listed as one of his objectives "to understand the rational and historical bases for changes in the liturgy."

"Uh-oh," said the person slipping into the seat next to me.

With a bonnet extending six inches out from my face, I had to turn a full ninety degrees to see who was talking. I found myself eye to eye with Aidan Connors. He held the syllabus with two fingers of one hand as if it were evidence in a crime. With the other he pointed to the same line of text I had just read.

"I hear he consecrates brownies and milk at home liturgies," Aidan said. He wore a broad smile and a considerably better selection of clothing than the night before. His blue crew-neck sweater, which matched the color of his eyes, looked as new my own bib.

"Good morning," I said, laughing in spite of the near blasphemy. "Did everything work out all right with Timothy?"

"Absolutely fine, Sister. We talked for a while, made plans for him to meet us for lunch in the cafeteria between eleven-thirty and noon. He was still sleeping when I left."

"I'm so grateful, Aidan."

"No problem. It was interesting, actually. I learned a lot about you last night."

My eyes widened as I tried to think of what Timothy knew about me that shouldn't be broadcast to the world at large. Other than my baptismal name and my tomboy past, I couldn't think of anything.

I had a sudden recollection of my high school days when I'd sit around with my girlfriends and talk about the nuns who taught us. We had so many questions that seemed fascinating at the time. What color was Sister Dorothy's hair? Black, probably, to match her eyebrows. Did the nuns swim in the pool after we'd gone home for the day? More interesting, what did they wear when they did?

Now a nun myself, I wondered if Aidan had the same questions about me. Just in time to distract us both from my reddening face, Father Glanz let out a loud cough and banged his heavy notebook on the desk. If that didn't get everyone's attention, his opening words certainly did.

"If Jesus held the Last Supper today," he said, "He might not have chosen bread and wine to consecrate." Father Glanz cleared his throat, as if to prepare us for the punch line. "More likely, He would have used pizza and beer, or brownies and milk."

By the time my first graduate school class was over, fifty minutes later, I longed for the days when I'd walked the paths of my Motherhouse, wrapped in a black wool shawl, oblivious to the winds of change swirling around me. My meditations then had been on the sufferings of Christ and the teachings of the Church, undistracted by the notion of consecrating fast food or chocolate dessert. I'd thought of *heresy* as a word that applied to the non-believers of earlier centuries, like Luther, Manicheus, and Jansen. Not to a priest/professor in a Catholic university.

I said as much to Aidan as we walked toward the cafeteria.

"I know what you mean," he said, in a way that was more relaxed than I was ready for.

I persisted. "Doesn't he have to follow the Cardinal's guidelines?"

"I'm sure there are ways around them."

I seemed to be learning a lot about loopholes lately, in contract law and in the Church. I wasn't sure I wanted to know any more.

"What do *you* think of the new liturgy?" I asked Aidan, hopeful that a man who prayed the rosary held on to traditional views all around.

"Well, Sister, at the moment, I'm open. To a certain extent, I mean. A lot of this so-called new stuff, like using the language of the people instead of Latin, is really old. Goes way back to the early days of the Church."

"I'm aware of that argument."

"Of course. You would be. I'm sorry." Aidan sounded more contrite than the occasion called for.

"No need to apologize. I did ask you."

"It's a strange time in the history of the Church. In the country, actually. Everything seems to be in turmoil."

"I agree."

Ordinarily I would have stopped there, satisfied our conversation had been a necessary follow-up to our class together. But the sharp fall weather and my new life as a student overtook my better judgment, and I was moved to pursue the topic.

"I believe if you choose to be a Catholic, you know what you're getting into. It's not like joining a club. You should accept the Church for what it is and not try to change it."

"It sounds a lot like love it or leave it," Aidan said.

"So?"

"So? Haven't you been reading the papers?" He paused. "No, I guess you haven't. It's the slogan these days. It's what we hear from people who refuse to think for themselves or question our government's practices."

I had the urge to poll the students we passed along the pathway. Could I tell from what they wore where they stood on these issues? I constructed a chart in my head—a patch made from a faded American flag meant thumbs down on our government, a neat cardigan symbolized loyalty to our elected officials.

My correlation fell apart when I tried to tie Aidan's words to his classic blue sweater.

We walked in silence for a few minutes while I adjusted my opinion of Aidan Connors. I had no hard evidence, but I put him in the group of Catholics who now would take the Host into their own hands at Holy Communion if offered it by the priest. As for me, I approached the Communion rail with my hands in a prayerful attitude and my tongue ready to have the priest lay the Host on it, just as I'd been taught when I was seven years old. But the tiny Susan Marie Wickes in the second grade at Immaculate Conception Grammar School in Potterstown seemed very far away.

I walked up the path to St. Alban's student union building, feeling nostalgic for the past.

———————————

One night with Aidan Connors seemed to do a lot for my brother. When he joined us at lunch he was in a good mood, and, to my relief, made no sarcastic remarks to Sister Ann William. The old Timothy might have offered her a beer or told her a joke of questionable taste.

After lunch, Aidan left to put in a few hours at his part-time mechanics job at Lloyd's shop.

"Time to get my hands dirty," he'd said. He won a look of approval from Timothy, who'd seemed to hang on Aidan's every word during lunch.

Sister Ann William walked with Timothy and me back to St. Lucy's. I was proud of my brother's graciousness as he asked Sister Ann William about Texas, telling her he'd like to visit someday. It was the first I'd ever heard of his desire to explore the south.

By one-thirty that afternoon, Timothy and I were alone again in the small parlor.

"Aidan's really nice," he told me.

"I'm glad you got along."

"He likes you, too."

"I thought we were going to talk about you."

"Yeah."

"Have you thought any more about what you'd like to do in the next year or so?"

"Yeah. I talked to Aidan, and he says I should go back to school when my suspension is up." I gave Timothy my most attentive look as he explained his current thinking. "It's not that hard, and I might as well get it over with. I'll be glad later." I nodded and uttered weak sounds of approval, afraid too much agreement from me might work against his good plans. "And about Melody. Aidan says if our love is so strong, it will last through a couple of years while we get our studies behind us."

Aidan this and Aidan that. Difficult as it was, I refrained from reminding Timothy that his father and all his sisters had already given him the same advice. Still, I knew I should be grateful if one *crash* with Aidan Connors did more for my brother than all my years of counseling. It might have been my imagination, but I thought his clothes looked cleaner, and I wondered if Aidan had also done Timothy's laundry.

"So you're going to get a job for the next couple of months until you go back to school?" I tried to sound casual, lest enthusiasm from his nun-sister have an adverse effect.

"Yeah. I could go back to the one I had in Potterstown. But there's a little problem. The job is what got me suspended in the first place."

"You mean selling drugs?"

He frowned and picked at his sweatshirt. "Yeah."

So much for the easy solution. I sat quietly, squinting against the bright sunlight coming through the parlor window, while Timothy told me about his alleged friend, Joey Riley—a much older man, thirty-one at least, he said.

"See, I thought he was doing me this big favor. He owns a pizza parlor on the west side of town, and he said I could probably make it to manager in no time, no college degree needed. All I had to do was these special errands for him. That's how it started. I was just delivering."

"Not pizza, I take it."

"Not pizza."

Timothy looked at me and I sensed he was trying to decide how much to tell me. I'd seen that look often on visiting days while my father and siblings struggled to stay with happy talk. I didn't enter a convent to be kept from their troubles, I'd tell them, but I often wondered how true that was.

"Joey gave me a lot of money, compared to what I could make anywhere else. But then, I was good, so he gave me more responsibility, you might say."

"So you started selling the drugs yourself?"

"Yeah. Not for long, though. Just long enough to get arrested. Jeez …"

Timothy banged the coffee table in front of him, a substitute for a curse, I guessed.

"Timothy, you're very young. And if you're determined to … "

"Go straight."

"Right," I said, aware of my limited crime vocabulary. "I know you'll be able to do it."

Timothy cleared his throat in the way that usually meant there was more to come, and it might be touchy.

"Aidan said I could stay with him for a couple of months," he said. My suspicions about *touchy* confirmed and then some. "He has a bigger place than he needs now, and he could use a roommate. What do you think?"

"Does he know …?"

He nodded. "I told him why I was arrested and all. I am clean, you know. I never used that much myself in the first place. I didn't like feeling weird, believe it or not."

"I do believe you, Timothy. What about your parole conditions?"

"I'd need permission from my PO, but if you said it was OK, I'm sure that would go a long way."

I took a deep breath while I ran the scenario through my mind. Timothy living down the street from me—I knew I'd feel more responsible for him, being right here, with my father and sisters upstate. So, what about the two-hours-a-month visiting rule, I asked myself. With all the time I'd spent with Timothy in the last couple of days, I'd already used up my family visit quota through Christmas.

And while I was assessing the impacts of Timothy's request, I threw in the notion of having Aidan Connors connected to my family in a way that bordered on intimacy. I wondered what Mother Julia would say, but I had a pretty good idea. I tried one more diversionary tactic.

"You'll have to deal with Potterstown eventually, Timothy. You can't hide from it forever."

"But I'll have a chance to get on my feet first. Earn some money legitimately." In a sudden movement, Timothy stood up, a frown taking over his face. "Sis, you're sounding like you don't want me around here."

I leaned over and took Timothy's hand, pulling him back to his seat. The sadness in his eyes displaced any thoughts of putting him off or calling my Motherhouse for approval.

"That's not true, Timothy. You know I'd do anything to help you."

"You think your order would have a problem, because you might see me a lot. Is that it?"

I remembered Timothy's remark the night before, about my being allowed to eat with the entire student population of St. Alban's U. but not at my own father's table. I realized that if a homeless stranger asked for my help, my superiors would encourage me to be selflessly charitable. Why should it be any different if the person needing help is my brother?

"There's no problem, Timothy. Welcome to the Bronx!"

CHAPTER 10

Timothy was on his way by three o'clock on Tuesday afternoon. He'd laid out his plan for the immediate future—he'd take the evening bus to Potterstown to pick up "a few things," and return to the Bronx in a couple of days with a form for me to fill out, vouching for his housing arrangements. Meanwhile, I should keep my eyes open for a job for him.

"Timothy, you know I have no experience finding employment even for myself," I'd told him. "The only jobs I've ever had were for pin-money—babysitting, stuffing envelopes, camp counselor …"

"I know. But that's all I'm asking for right now. Not a career or anything."

"I haven't the slightest idea where to look."

He grinned at me. "Just, you know, pray."

Ordinarily I'd have been annoyed at my brother's flip manner, but I was so relieved that he'd come out of his depression, I let it pass.

I stayed in the parlor for a long time after Timothy left, the closed door muffling the sounds of Sisters checking their mail slots, coming and going through the front foyer. My whole body was tense, and my head ached. I sat on the edge of the soft chair, my back as stiff as the long pole of a candle snuffer. I rehashed every intense moment of the day, from my unorthodox liturgy professor to my radical decision about helping Timothy move to the Bronx.

I wondered why Aidan hadn't told me about his offer to take my brother in. The only reason I could think of was that he wanted

Timothy to be free to make the decision on his own and to tell me himself when he was ready. Maybe I should take counseling lessons from Aidan Connors, I thought.

Besides all of this, I reminded myself, I had homework to do and a possible murder to solve. I realized with an unexplainable feeling of guilt that I hadn't thought about Mother Ignatius since early morning in Aquinas Hall's chapel.

I shook my head as if to reorder my priorities. I seemed to have forgotten my first obligation was to my religious duties as a Sister of Mary Immaculate. I'd already fallen behind in my spiritual reading. SMIs were required to do at least a half hour of reading daily, from a spiritual book other than our prayer and meditation texts. Mother Julia had given me a book of poetry written by an early SMI, for the new semester, but I hadn't opened it since Sunday evening, when I'd sat in my room and looked out over the garden—now Jake Driscoll's garden, I thought with a grimace.

No matter what other work we did as SMIs, the total time we spent in religious devotion each day amounted to at least four hours, including mass, rosary, meditation, spiritual reading, and community recitation of parts of the Holy Office. Without a prescribed time for spiritual activity at St. Lucy's, I was on my own to be faithful to each ritual. So far I hadn't done well. That's what get-togethers filled with punch and small talk will do for me. Three days away from my Motherhouse, and I was acting like a person with no attachment to a religious community.

I was still uncomfortable about my decision not to first ask Mother Julia about sponsoring Timothy's move to the Bronx. But my only other choice was to send my brother back to the criminal element of Potterstown and the likes of Joey Riley. And Mother Julia would not want that, I reasoned.

It turned out to be easier than I expected to skew Mother Julia's wishes in my favor from a distance of a few hundred miles. I thought how easy it was to abandon discipline when the old structure was missing.

I left the parlor and stepped into the small foyer just as the front door opened. For the second time in less than twenty-four hours, I bumped into Father Malbert.

"Excuse me," we said in unison, in a strange repetition of our encounter of the night before.

"Sorry, Sister," he said, smoothing back his disheveled light brown hair. "I'm running late."

After nervous laughs on both sides, Father Malbert headed for the chapel. As he walked away from me, he removed a narrow purple stole from the pocket of his Irish knit cardigan. He seemed to have a large wardrobe of sweaters, I noted.

In spite of the unusual combination of purple silk and khakis, I recognized that Father Malbert was preparing to hear confessions. Just what I needed—a confessor—lay clothes or not. I turned and followed him into the chapel, taking my place in the front pew where several other Sisters already waited. I guessed I'd missed an announcement about the hours for confession at St. Lucy's.

I sat on the hard bench and stared straight ahead at the altar—two altars, I mused, with a sigh. Like many parish churches and convent chapels, St. Lucy's had a makeshift, free-standing altar in front of the communion rail, to allow the celebrant to stand behind it and face his congregation. In the pre-Vatican Council days, the priest stood with his back to the people, offering the sacrifice of the mass to God in our name. It made sense to me.

I looked past the new wooden table to the beautiful marble altar on the back wall of St. Lucy's chapel. Carved into the marble was the Repository, the vault-like housing where Christ was kept at all times in the form of the Holy Eucharist. I focused my thoughts in that direction and considered my recent behavior. Examination of conscience, the Church called it. Without a Chapter of Faults in my near future, I decided to lump my transgressions in with my sins—it was hard to distinguish between them this week, anyway.

I was happy to see Father Malbert followed custom and entered the confessional booth at the side of the chapel. I was aware some chaplains were now hearing confessions face to face in the light of day, and others were recommending group confessions, where an assembly of people recited a general admission of sinfulness out loud and received absolution together.

Would I ever feel comfortable with such a radical change of custom? I hoped I'd be prepared if the time came when I had no choice.

When my turn for confession came, I was ready. I moved the curtain and stepped inside the small booth. Kneeling, with my hands on the tiny shelf in front of me and my eyes cast down, I recited the formula.

"Bless me, Father, for I have sinned. It has been three days since my last confession, and these are my sins."

"Go ahead, Sister Francesca."

I looked up with a start. Good-bye to another staple of Catholicism, I thought—the anonymity of the confessional. Father Malbert had turned in his chair and looked at me. Although there was a grille between us in the dark booth, enough light got past the curtain, and I knew he could see me clearly.

I considered leaving the booth and finding a confessor on campus who would follow the rules as I'd learned them. Instead, I calmed down and reminded myself that no matter how *au courant* our chaplain tried to be, he was still God's representative on earth. As long as he pronounced the words of absolution at the end of my confession, my sins would be forgiven by God Himself.

I cleared my throat and began my list.

"I have been careless in carrying out my religious practices. I have …"

"What do you mean, Sister? Can you be more specific?"

"I'm behind in spiritual reading, Father, and also I've been distracted at mass and at meditation, not giving my full attention."

"This is a distracting time, Sister. A new living situation, new people. Don't be hard on yourself. You may have to make adjustments to practices that were prescribed for nuns who did little else but pray all day." As if that were a life to be scorned. Just the kind of worldly advice I expected. "Continue, Sister."

I went on. "I've made decisions without consulting my superior."

"Again, Sister Francesca, don't expect to live the way you did at your Motherhouse. You have new responsibilities here. You're a graduate student. As long as you act with thought and care, you're being faithful to the spirit of your vows."

I almost asked how this would make me any different from a lay person, but I knew Father Malbert's answer wasn't the one I wanted to hear.

"Yes, Father," I said.

"Anything else?"

I'd saved the big one for last, having worked carefully on the phrasing. "I've been unnecessarily inquisitive about a matter that doesn't concern me."

"Specifically?"

Father Malbert required more specifics than any priest I'd known. I was used to confessors who were content with general categories. I struggled to come up with a truthful, but not incriminating, answer.

"I've been ..." I still couldn't bring myself to use the word *investigating*. "I've been trying to learn more about Mother Ignatius' death."

Father Malbert shifted in his seat, and for once I wished there were more light so I could see his expression. Maybe there's something to these new degrees of freedom, I thought.

"We all miss her, Sister," he told me, lowering his voice to the level of a mourner. "But what good can come of probing into her death? She died a faithful servant of God. Let her immortal soul rest in peace."

"Yes, Father. Thank you, Father."

"Is that it?"

"Yes, Father."

"Good. For your penance, say the sorrowful mysteries of the rosary for the repose of the soul of Mother Ignatius. Now let's hear your act of contrition." He raised his right hand and said the words of absolution, while I recited my part.

Oh, my God, I am heartily sorry for having offended Thee ...

I finished my prayer and left the booth, feeling less cleansed than usual after confession, maybe because Father Malbert had absolved me in English instead of Latin. But I had the firm belief my soul was back in the state of grace.

The door to Sister Ann William's room, directly opposite the stairway, was open. She sat at her desk, which she'd wedged under her window so she faced the street. Though my room was on the garden side of the building, with a much better view than the brick fronts of 198th Street, it hadn't occurred to me to rearrange my furniture.

"What a good idea," I said, hardly aware that I was speaking out loud.

"Sister Francesca, I've been waiting for you." Sister Ann William came to the door and waved her arm in the direction of her bed, which had books and papers spread out like an altar to the gods of graduate studies. "I gathered up some literature from the department office this morning. I didn't want to talk about it in front of your brother on the way home. I thought he might get the wrong idea."

What's the right idea? I wondered, as I picked up a colorful pamphlet. Its cover was dominated by a photograph of a lovely shrub with purplish flowers and bright red berries clustered about the stem.

I read the caption. *Daphne contains mezerein, an acrid resin, and daphnin, a bitter, poisonous glycoside. Consumption of even a few berries can put a person into a coma, and death can ensue.*

I gulped and picked up another booklet. Not much cheerier. This one lumped potatoes, jimsonweed, and angel's trumpet into one family and warned about convulsions, coma and death from the alkaloid toxins they contained. *Less than five grams of seeds or leaves could be fatal to a child.*

I wished I knew how big a gram was.

I was astonished at the juxtaposition of photographs of magnificent flowers next to warning labels. Laurel, rhododendron, azalea, and foxglove on the same page as stomach upset, mental confusion, diarrhea, paralysis, and death. The array of literature on Sister Ann William's bed was enough to make a person afraid to walk through a garden. I'd barely passed science classes in high school—now I realized my life might be in danger from lack of botanical knowledge.

"This is amazing, Sister," I said. "It looks like it's even easier than I thought to poison someone. Just bring her flowers!"

Sister Ann William laughed. "It's not that bad." She pointed out the small print in the pamphlets and technical memos—voluminous details about which part of a flower is poisonous, and under what conditions. I noted that in some cases it would take a very large, unlikely dose of leaves or berries to do serious harm. "Merely handling flowers is different from actually consuming them," she said. "But you're right, there's a lot of potential for disaster if you don't know what you're doing with plants."

"Or if you do know."

She nodded. Her expression told me she was probably thinking along the same lines I was. "A lot of these symptoms are consistent with a heart attack or a stroke in an old person. We should find out which of these flowers might be here in our own garden."

"Also, we need more medical knowledge, like what are the symptoms that a doctor might miss without an autopsy."

"And there's more than just plant poison to consider. I walked by the pharmacy lab today and noticed the cabinets that are kept locked—chemicals and pharmaceuticals—all controlled substances for one reason or another. I'm going to try to get some kind of inventory of what's in there and a list of who has access to it."

Sister Ann William's face was animated and flushed with the excitement that comes with a research project. At that moment a group of Sisters came up the stairs, chattering about their classes and professors. Sister Ann William and I stopped talking and looked at each other. We both seemed to feel the impact of what our research was about—a possible homicide in our own convent dormitory.

A sudden wave of guilt came over me. I pictured myself at a Chapter of Faults accusing myself of being a bad influence on an otherwise trusting religious from a small town in Texas.

"I hope you haven't felt forced into this ... project, Sister."

"Oh, not at all. It's been very interesting to me. We don't have to think of it as—well, anything but academic. That other matter probably has nothing to do with this, anyway."

"Right," I said, with no more conviction than I'd heard in Sister Ann William's voice.

I walked to my room and took stock of my afternoon. At three o'clock I'd cleansed my soul in the confessional, and at three-thirty I was back in the same spiritual quagmire.

CHAPTER 11

My napkin ring was at a different place when I walked in to dinner at six o'clock that evening. At our Motherhouse that usually meant a Sister had left the order—she'd have been ushered out the back door in disgrace while the rest of us were sleeping. On such occasions, everything would be changed to disguise the fact that there was an empty seat in chapel or at the table. Chore lists and places in study hall would be scrambled, dormitory rooms reassigned. If we did figure out who had left, we were forbidden to mention it or to ever speak of the defector.

I doubted this was the reason my place at St. Lucy's table had been changed. I was now next to Sister Felix, immediately to her right. I glanced around— Sister Teresa was on my right, Sister Veronique across from her. I wondered if a random placement of napkins could have resulted in this pattern. However, when Jake Driscoll entered the refectory and took the seat opposite me, to Sister Felix's left, the thought crossed my mind that the new arrangement was not arbitrary. More like an ambush. Had I become a troublemaker to be reckoned with?

A general buzzing sound went through the large, hollow room when Mr. Driscoll appeared just behind Sister Felix. Not conversation, since we hadn't yet said grace, but significant coughing, clearing of throats, and muffled gasps echoed from the plain walls and uncarpeted wooden floor. Apparently, I wasn't the only one who'd never seen a lay person at dinner in a convent refectory.

After grace, Sister Felix, still standing at the head of the table, formally welcomed our guest. He had dressed for dinner in a shirt, tie, and navy blue jacket. An image flashed across my mind, and I looked at Jake Driscoll's wrists. A twinge of disappointment—I'd hoped for the sight of one sleeve neatly tucked together with a gold and onyx cuff link bearing the letter D, and the other sleeve hanging loose, missing its partner. As it was, Mr. Driscoll's pinkish shirt wasn't the kind that required cuff links.

Sister Felix continued to fulfill her duty as hostess with a final remark before signaling the server.

"I hope this will be the first of many meals we'll share with our neighbors and benefactors," she said.

Which category does Jake Driscoll come under? I wanted to ask. He doesn't live in this neighborhood and what benefit is it that he's taking away most of our grounds?

"Good evening, Sister Felix, Sister Francesca, Sister Teresa, Sister Veronique," he said, mercifully not addressing the whole length of the table. "This is quite an honor."

The server for the evening approached Sister Felix and handed her a heavy white platter of broiled chicken over rice.

St. Lucy's Hall employed young women from the Academy of St. Catherine of Sienna, a few blocks away, as housekeepers and servers at meals. I'd seen this evening's waitress dusting the benches in chapel on my first day. She looked like a younger version of myself as a teenager—tall and skinny, with freckles and red hair that drew attention even if all you did was set bowls of vegetables and baskets of dinner rolls on the table.

Sister Felix took a portion of meat and passed the dish to Mr. Driscoll.

"Please, Sister," Mr. Driscoll said, turning the utensils to me before taking a serving for himself. "After you."

I took a small piece of chicken and about a tablespoon of rice, having once again lost my appetite in the face of stress.

As he took a healthy serving of meat, Mr. Driscoll made a teasing remark to the server, comparing her hair to the carrots she'd offered

Sister Felix. He pointed to his own shock of straight white hair and said, "Rice."

The server and many of the Sisters joined in his laughter, as if he'd told a hilarious, original joke. I smiled weakly and said nothing, hoping my face didn't betray either my feelings of irritation or the color of my own hair.

If I'm going to have to sit here and talk, I thought, it might as well be about something I'm interested in.

"How's work on the new contract progressing, Mr. Driscoll?" I asked.

"Very well, Sister, and how are your studies?"

"Fine, thank you."

Before I could say more, his loud voice broke in, continuing his new line of discussion.

"I've heard great things about the new Theology faculty. One of the most important departments at the University these days, wouldn't you say?"

Hard to argue with that. One round for Jake Driscoll. A glance at the frown on Sister Felix's face had thrown me off track and dissuaded me from making another unwelcome comment, at least for the moment.

Sisters Teresa and Veronique held up their ends of a conversation about their classes in the English and History Departments. Both spoke freely of current events. They seemed well-versed in data—the death toll in Vietnam and the chemical makeup of the weapons. It seemed neither of them needed their superiors to filter the daily news for them.

"Did you read about Father Ellison's program to help clean up the streets of Harlem?" Sister Teresa asked.

"We're going down to 125th Street on Saturday," Sister Veronique said. "Father Ellison has arranged for anyone who's interested to be part of the crew. We're going to sweep the streets, paint over the graffiti, whatever." Sister Veronique swept her fork through the air in a breezy, cleansing motion, dropping bits of rice on the table.

"I'm in," said a Sister whose name I didn't know.

"Me, too," said another.

It was the first I'd heard of the event, although Mother Julia had told us about the famous Father Ellison, a Jesuit priest making a name for himself by preaching a social gospel. He and his followers had already been arrested several times. They'd been pulled from doorways and from the steps of administration buildings where they protested government policies in Vietnam, civil rights violations, and other causes that Mother Julia referred to as "worldly." According to her, Father Ellison would have us believe that Jesus was a social worker—as if appearing on earth as the Son of God was not enough—and that we should follow suit.

Lax as I'd been since my arrival at St. Lucy's Hall, one rule I'd held to was abstention from newspapers, television, or any other source of worldly news.

"Do you read newspapers at your home convents?" I asked. I looked past Mr. Driscoll, addressing the question to all Sisters within earshot.

I heard a variety of overlapping answers—"of course," from Sister Teresa, "not yet," from Sister Veronique, and "some of us do," from the unnamed nun next to Sister Veronique.

Jake Driscoll hadn't participated in the conversation about cleaning up Harlem, and I wondered where he stood on the political spectrum. After a bite of chicken, I was ready for another round with him.

"What do you think of the reforms of Vatican II, Mr. Driscoll?" I asked.

"I'm afraid I'm going to have to plead the Fifth, Sister. I try to stay away from controversy."

"You seemed to have some with Mother Ignatius—controversy, that is."

"Sister Francesca."

Sister Felix's voice was full of reproach. If my own Mother Julia had said my name that way I would have immediately fallen on my knees in front of her and begged forgiveness.

But Sister Felix had already shown herself to be less than admirable—in my opinion, she hadn't waited a decent amount of time before undoing Mother Ignatius' legacy to St. Lucy's Hall. In the two days since our old Superior's death, we'd acquired a new property contract with the University, the promise of keys for every Sister, and entertained a lay man in the refectory. And these were just the things I knew about.

My stomach lurched at the thought of what might be decided later at the community meeting. I'd finally seen the notice Sister Ann William had told me about. "Come to the main parlor at eight o'clock. Important issues to be voted on," the announcement read. As if God's will were to be found in majority rule or consensus.

The situation was strange enough to spur me on. After all, I told myself, Sister Felix has not been declared my superior yet. I ignored her warning look and pressed the issue.

"Perhaps I misunderstood, Mr. Driscoll. I was under the impression that Mother Ignatius stood between you and your goals for this property."

"Sister!" Sister Felix made a motion to stand up, the better to make herself clear, I assumed, but Mr. Driscoll interrupted her.

"No. It's all right, Sister Felix," he said. "Sister Francesca is a resident, and she has a right to know what's going on."

I felt my face heat up, knowing we had the attention of at least the first five sisters on each side of the table. Eating came to a halt, and even the carrot-topped server seemed unwilling to approach us. She kept herself busy filling water glasses at the far end of the refectory.

"Mother Ignatius was an extraordinary religious," Mr. Driscoll said. "But she had no understanding of the unstable fiscal condition of the University and this house. Her ideas were not necessarily good for the Church of today."

Sister Felix gave him a smile of approval, as if she wished she'd said it herself.

"So now St. Lucy's and the University have more money than they did three days ago, and you have their property. Is that necessarily good for the Church?"

"Good question. You have a point, Sister. I admit I'm talking about money, not the spiritual realm. I know you'd like to think the religious life has nothing to do with money, but that's not realistic. Someone has to pay for this." He swept his arms around in a large circle, embracing the refectory, floor to ceiling. "Whether it's here or in your own convent, there are bills to be paid. Everything from your basic food and electricity to medical care and your long-term needs. Where do you think that money comes from?"

"God provides, Mr. Driscoll."

He nodded his head and looked straight at me. "Maybe I'm the way God provides, Sister Francesca."

I paced the tiny floor of Room 25 until I was nearly dizzy, running through the dinner conversation in my head. Intimidated a second time by Jake Driscoll, I'd excused myself from the table and gone to my room. I was distressed I hadn't been a better spokesperson for Mother Ignatius on the one hand, and a more exemplary representative of my community on the other.

Finally, I pulled my chair to the window and looked out over St. Lucy's garden, as if I could protect both the yard and Mother Ignatius by the sheer power of my staring.

Drawn by the soft colors of the setting sun, I allowed my glance to move upward. I found an unlikely source of inspiration in the imposing yellow and gray brick buildings of the Bronx, and I was able to ground myself once again. Although the campus was beyond my range of vision, I strained my eyes, focusing past the tenements of Marian Avenue and 198th Street, and imagined I could see the Gothic tower of St. Alban's administration building.

Homework. The sight of the campus, real or imagined, reminded me I needed to do my homework. That was my mission and that's what would free me from the confusions of my new environment.

I took up my text on Church liturgy, ready to read the chapters Father Glanz had assigned. The first few paragraphs were more thought-provoking than I'd expected.

From time to time, we need to re-examine the roots of our customs and laws. And if the reason for a particular rule has disappeared, then perhaps the practice of it ought to follow.

I took a breath as I considered the logic of the statement. I had no trouble accepting it in theory, but I was suspicious of applying it to cherished rituals and mandates of the Church. I read further.

Deep into an argument in favor of women as priests —*we now know that women weren't excluded at the Last Supper. They simply weren't reported as being present, due to the custom of the times* —I heard a soft knock at my door. Once again Sister Ann William appeared at my threshold with food. This time it was dessert.

"I noticed you left early," she said, offering me a slice of almond tart with an attractive topping of strawberries and blueberries in a thin layer of whipped cream. It looked both patriotic and delicious.

"I wouldn't have left if I'd known this was coming. Thank you."

Sister Ann William laughed and handed me the plate, a napkin, and fork. I wondered if she'd been a full-time server in a former life.

"Are you going to the meeting?" she asked. "It starts in about ten minutes."

"I haven't decided. Are you?"

"I haven't decided, either."

"We could both go and cause trouble."

This time Sister Ann William's laugh was loud enough to attract the attention of a Sister entering a room halfway down the corridor. Sister Ann William put her hand to her mouth, and I had another twinge of guilt that I was a bad influence on her.

While Sister Ann William went to get a notebook, I took the time to eat the tart in the comfort of my room. Immediately afterwards, I wished I could transport myself to Potterstown to convene a special Chapter of Faults.

"I allowed myself worldly pleasures," I'd say to Mother Julia and the assembled community. "I ate in my room twice, and found comfort in food, friendship, and privacy."

Disgusted with myself, I rolled up my sleeve and wrapped my spiked chain around my upper arm, pressing the barbs into my flesh as I fastened the hook. Then I headed for the parlor, to resume my role as troublemaker.

CHAPTER 12

Sister Ann William and I entered the parlor as Sister Felix finished her opening remarks.

"… and since Sister Teresa Barnes is the most senior member of St. Lucy's Hall," she said, "I've asked her to chair this meeting."

Sister Felix's smile reminded me of a proud high school principal introducing the new student body president. She was going against custom by mentioning Sister Teresa's surname, which ordinarily would be used only in legal contexts like registering to vote or obtaining a driver's license.

Arriving late, Sister Ann William and I were forced to take seats in the front row of folding chairs that had been added to accommodate the thirty-nine residents. The room was filled to capacity, with some Sisters perched on the arms of easy chairs and on end tables. Most were fully dressed in their habits, but I noticed several nuns without their veils and a few with brightly colored sweaters or jackets.

The atmosphere was more like a political rally than a convent assembly. The undercurrent of chatter and the plates of cookies were a stark contrast to the utter silence and spirit of abstinence at any community meeting I'd ever attended. I looked around at the walls of the parlor, expecting to see a pagan banner draped over the large oil painting of St. Lucy, patroness of the blind, that hung over the mantel. Fortunately, the image of the fourth century virgin and martyr was undisturbed. In silence, I invoked the aid of the woman whose eyes were torn out by secular authorities, then miraculously restored. I prayed we would all see clearly.

Sister Veronique distributed an agenda, typed on onion skin paper with a thin red stripe along the side, like the kind required for theses. She wore a grin, giving her face a victorious look. The sight reminded me of the battles fought by the late Mother Ignatius, who seemed to me the loser in an undeclared war.

I bristled as I read down the numbered list of topics. Nestled between item number one, *Keys to the front door*, and number three, *New refrigerators*, was number two, *Changes in the Liturgy*, as if the most sacred rituals of the Church were only slightly more important than the availability of a midnight snack.

As the muscles in my arms tensed, my penitential chain tightened and a stab of pain from the spikes went through me. Good. Something to offer up, Mother Julia would have said. Sister Teresa had stepped to the front and faced the assembly, standing to the left of the television set. For once I would have chosen the evening news over a community meeting.

Sister Teresa shook a box full of keys, causing them to jingle like the bell at Benediction. "Here they are," she said. "Sister Felix, soon to be Mother Felix, we hope, has taken care of one of our main requests with great speed. Thank you, Sister."

Sister Veronique led a round of applause. She'd assumed the role of acolyte, her plump body spilling over the sides of a chair directly in front of Sister Teresa. Sister Ann William's clap was nearly soundless, while I kept my hands folded on my lap and turned slightly to get a measure of the response of others. I was looking for allies, should the need arise, and located several potential supporters.

"Of course, this means an end to the curfew also," Sister Teresa said. "We're all adults and we can make our own decisions about what time to come home. Any comments or questions?"

I had a few. What was this about "adults?" I wanted to ask. Had they forgotten Our Lord's admonition in Matthew's Gospel? *Unless you become as little children, you shall not enter the Kingdom of Heaven.* That was the idea behind our vow of obedience. To become childlike and, therefore, closer to God. I considered commenting on the breakdown of discipline that personal keys represented but decided to wait and fight a bigger battle.

One came soon enough.

"Number two. Changes in the liturgy." Sister Teresa's announcement was accompanied by a deep sigh, as if she'd been waiting for centuries to get her hands on the way Mass was celebrated. "We'll no longer need those little boys from St. Mark's Prep. Father Malbert is happy to work with us so we can be his servers. Altar Sisters, you might say."

Another round of applause, as Sister Teresa made a show of folding her hands, prayer-style, in front of her chest, and nodding, imitating the movements of altar boys in parish churches everywhere.

"What about receiving the wine—drinking the Blood of Christ?" a Sister in the row behind me asked. "I hear they're doing it at Marymount."

Sister Teresa nodded. "We've talked about everybody drinking from the chalice, and a few other things, like taking the host in our hands. Father Malbert is planning to introduce one thing at a time, with homilies to explain each change."

How considerate, I thought. My head was pounding from the strain of keeping my opinions to myself. I weighed the idea of bolting from the room in protest. Instead, I raised my hand and Sister Teresa acknowledged me.

"Sister Francesca?"

"I just want to mention that the Mary Chapel on the north side of campus offers a Latin mass every morning at eight, and an extra one at ten on Sundays. In case anyone's interested." I heard my voice quiver at the end, and I dared not glance at anyone, lest they read uncertainty in my face.

Sister Teresa looked surprised but recovered quickly. "Uh, thank you Sister. Did everyone hear that?"

She repeated my information in a neutral tone, with no sign of mockery or displeasure, making it difficult for me to justify an angry exit. I wasn't sure how to deal with such courteous, rational opposition. For the moment, I decided to stay put.

The remaining topics were matters of housekeeping. A small refrigerator for drinks and snacks would be placed on each floor. Guests would be welcome at dinner, as long as we gave reasonable notice to the kitchen staff. Sister Felix was looking into having more phone lines brought into the house. And Jake Driscoll, our favorite guest, had made arrangements for the Sisters to have private time at a local gym to make up for the loss of our yard.

None of the changes was earthshaking, but each one represented a departure from normal convent rules, and that saddened me. Our vows of obedience seemed useless. I seemed to have given up my family and my own dear friends only to become buddies with the rest of the world.

"That's it for now," Sister Teresa said. "But watch this spot, as they say. Sister Veronique and I will continue to work with Sister Felix and Father Malbert. We'll be reporting to you regularly via the new bulletin board in the laundry room, and we'll have another meeting next month. Now let's have tea and cookies."

"The last time I'd heard a speech like that, the person was running for office," I said to Sister Ann William.

"Me, too, Sister. Shall we leave now?"

"Definitely. They'll never miss us."

Our exit was masked by the general hubbub of the room—metal chairs being folded, excited babble about the cookies and the effort to improve the quality of life at St. Lucy's Hall.

Sister Ann William and I walked up the stairs and into our rooms in silence, our hands buried in our sleeves, as if we were clinging to at least one of the customs that had been breached in the past few days.

Alone in my room, I tried to devise a strategy for dealing with my new situation. If I did nothing, Sister Teresa and her followers would take over the management of St. Lucy's Hall, and our lives would be practically indistinguishable from that of any other female graduate student.

To make matters worse, the only two priests I'd met—our chaplain, Father David Malbert, and my liturgy professor, Father Leo Glanz—

didn't inspire confidence as counselors. Vatican Council II was not yet over, and already both priests had bandied about the directives as if Pope John XXIII had given us free reign to reinterpret the constitutions of the Roman Catholic Church. *Open the windows of the Church to let in a new spirit*, the bishops had said, but I was certain they hadn't meant to tear down the walls at the same time.

A few minutes after I took out my bedtime prayer book, ready to give up thinking for the night, the message bell sounded. Two rings, a pause, five rings. My signal. Another late night visit? I put on my robe, bonnet, and veil, and walked down the hall to the intercom.

"Telephone call for you, Sister Francesca," Sister Felix said. I wondered why she sounded cheery so late in the evening. I also wondered who could be calling me at nine-thirty.

I picked up the telephone next to the intercom grille, hoping there was no emergency in Potterstown. I thought of my brother Timothy in a bus crash on his way home, my father with another heart attack, one of my sisters the victim of a tragic accident.

A call from Mother Julia from the Motherhouse was not on my list.

"Good evening, Sister Francesca." Mother Julia's voice sounded anything but cheery. My stomach spun around, the taste of berries and whipped cream turning sour in my mouth.

"Good evening, Mother Julia."

"I'm concerned about a report I've had on your first few days away, Sister."

Mother Julia was not one to beat around the bush. "Please may I ask what it's about, Mother?"

"Sister Felix tells me you've not shown the spirit of cooperation and obedience I would expect of you, Sister Francesca." Mother Julia paused. If she was waiting for me to comment, she was disappointed. My mouth was dry and my mind reeling. She continued. "And I've learned of other deviations as well."

I was glad Mother Julia couldn't see my widening eyes and tense muscles. It was out of the question for me to defend myself—a breach of the vow of obedience to do anything but accept blame, just or unjust. In fact, we'd been taught that accepting an unfair accusation without question earned us far more merit in the eyes of God.

"Please pardon me, Mother Julia." Although I spoke softly, my voice seemed to echo through the empty, otherwise silent hallway. I envisioned a Sister in a white broadcloth nightgown behind each door, eavesdropping, hearing my humiliation.

"I'm sending Sister Magdalene to see you, Sister. She'll be taking an early bus in the morning. Do you have class tomorrow?"

"Yes, Mother Julia. I have Modern Philosophy at ten. I'll be back at St. Lucy's by eleven-thirty."

"I'll have Sister Magdalene go directly to St. Lucy's. Expect her around noon. Perhaps you could arrange for her to have lunch in the refectory."

"Yes, Mother."

"You've been such an exemplary religious thus far, Sister Francesca. I hesitate to bring you home until I learn more about the circumstances. Do you understand?"

"Yes, Mother. Thank you, Mother."

I hung up the phone, my heart beating rapidly, my stomach unsettled. I went over Mother Julia's words in my head as if they were scriptural text and I'd been asked to write a treatise on the passage. I was frustrated by a list of questions I wasn't allowed to ask. I knew I'd shown unwillingness to embrace the St. Lucy's Hall community, but I was sure Mother Julia would take my side if she knew what I was being asked to do.

To my dismay, I could think of many instances of deviant behavior for an SMI in any circumstances—committing myself to further involvement with my brother's life, having company in my room, not honoring the Great Silence, even snooping in Mother Ignatius' office.

And I thought it ironic that Mother Julia probably hadn't learned about my worst violation—strong feelings of friendship and affection for Sister Ann William and Aidan Connors.

I recited each prayer in my bedtime book three times before I fell asleep. The picture in my mind as I dozed off was of old Sister Magdalene, her teeth cracked and yellow, bent over in a St. Lucy's parlor chair, shaking a crooked finger at me.

CHAPTER 13

A t mass the next morning, I was struck by how well the Second Reading, from the Letter of Saint James, suited me. If I didn't know liturgical readings were fixed by the Church calendar, I'd have been sure Father Malbert had chosen the passage with me in mine.

For every kind of beast and of bird and of serpent is tamed, but the tongue can no man tame; it is an unruly evil, full of deadly poison.

I was so busy resolving to curb my own tongue, I didn't notice Jake Driscoll until I turned to pick up my hymnal. Out of the corner of my eye, I saw him sitting in one of the back pews. If he can eat with us, I guess he can pray with us, I thought, hoping his privileges wouldn't be extended to the upper floors before I graduated.

Sister Veronique served mass for Father Malbert, bobbing up and down the steps in the sanctuary, unlike any altar boy I'd ever seen. I was afraid she was going to trip over her long white habit in her enthusiasm as a ground-breaker—the first Sister to assist a priest during a formal liturgical service, at least in my experience. I left the chapel immediately after the blessing, although most Sisters went into the sacristy, presumably to congratulate Sister Veronique.

My head down, my thoughts in another century, I walked right into Jake Driscoll.

"Good morning, Sister Francesca. I hoped I'd bump into you."

He laughed at his pun, and I joined him before I could stop myself. Was there no end to the man's corny jokes?

"Good morning, Mr. Driscoll."

"If you have a minute, Sister, I'd like a word with you."

"Certainly," I said, wondering if he'd planned to give me another lecture on Church finance.

He followed me into the small parlor and sat opposite me. "I think I can be of some assistance to your brother."

I stifled a gasp and folded my arms across my chest as if to protect my privacy, and my family. "Timothy?" I asked him, in a voice made weak by surprise.

He nodded. "Yes, I hope I didn't overstep my bounds, Sister, but I had a call from Steve Rooney, and I told him—"

"From whom?"

"Steve Rooney. Your brother's parole officer. From the Review Board upstate." Mr. Driscoll sounded as though he were prompting a second grader who didn't know the name of the saint whose feast day it was.

I leaned against the door jamb and felt like I'd swallowed loudly enough for the whole house to hear. How could Jake Driscoll know the name of Timothy's parole officer when I didn't even know it?

To his credit, if he noticed my discomfort and display of ignorance, he didn't let on.

"Steve's a friend of mine from years ago. I guess when he approved your brother's plans for relocating down here for a while, he thought of me. He asked if I might be able to help out. It turns out, I can use a strong young man like Tim right now. Most of our summer crew has already gone back to school."

I was still too stunned to respond, so he continued.

"Nothing too exciting, but good, honest, construction work can sometimes be therapeutic for a guy."

Honest, indeed. Now what? I asked myself. What was that line about agreements with the devil? I considered this new option—getting my family involved with a manipulative real estate developer who was still on my list of murder suspects. And here was one more thing to explain to Sister Magdalene, at this moment on her way to the Bronx and a judgment of me.

"I think we can handle Timothy's employment without—"

"Sister, I'm not asking your permission." Jake Driscoll smiled, but his voice was emphatic. "I just thought I'd let you know."

"Thank you, Mr. Driscoll. That's very kind of you," I said, and rushed up the stairs to my room.

I had time to spare before class, having decided to skip breakfast—I couldn't bear the idea of rehashing Sister Veronique's performance as stand-in for a real altar boy. My stomach growled and I turned my ear to the door, selfishly hoping for another room service visit from Sister Ann William.

I opened my Modern Philosophy text, an anthology of Alfred North Whitehead, and read the description on the back cover. Another twentieth century non-Catholic, I noted, frowning at phrases like 'God is in flux' and 'the relevance of God to the evolving world.'

I let out a heavy sigh and looked out the window. Longing for an image of stability, I focused on the powerful old oaks and the weathered multi-story tenements lining the streets of the Bronx. I thought of St. Patrick's Cathedral, the stately monument to the glory of God, only a subway ride away on Fifth Avenue, with spires that reached toward heaven and the red hats of deceased Cardinals floating above its massive altar.

As my eyes drifted to the garden two stories below me, a more worldly sight came into view—Sister Teresa and Father Malbert sitting on a bench, their heads bent low, almost touching. Was this an outdoor confession? I wondered. I wouldn't have been surprised if neither of the pair saw the need for a purple stole or the formal atmosphere of an authorized confessional. Sister Teresa was without her veil, her fine brown hair an easy mark for the slightest breeze.

Much as I knew I should look away, I was fascinated by their gestures. Father Malbert waving his hands, then putting them together as if in prayer. Saying please? Sister Teresa first shaking her head, then nodding. No, then yes?

After a few minutes, they stood and embraced, certainly longer than they would have during the newly instituted Kiss of Peace at mass. Another perfect example of the slippery slope, I thought, as I watched Sister Teresa's flirtatious walk away from Father Malbert. I stepped back from the window, feeling like the voyeur that I was.

Sister Ann William came through with a plate of toast and jam. I hoped she couldn't tell what I'd been doing before her light knock. Discreet as she was, she never asked why I wasn't at breakfast.

"I don't have class until two o'clock this afternoon," she told me. "So I won't be going with you this morning. If you're still around campus about three, maybe we can walk back together?"

I shook my head. "I have a visitor coming from my Motherhouse. I'm to meet her here at eleven-thirty, right after my class."

Sister Ann William raised her eyebrows, the only way I could tell she was surprised. "Is something wrong?"

I had an urge to confide in her, to help relieve the tension of Sister Magdalene's visit. I swallowed the impulse.

"Nothing's wrong," I said, as if it were perfectly normal to have a visit from my Motherhouse less than a week into my assignment.

On the way to campus, I prepared myself for the interview with Sister Magdalene. I remembered she'd celebrated her golden jubilee the year before—fifty years as an SMI. I wondered what she'd think of my comfortable room at St. Lucy's. Besides my own sink and desk, I had a door that closed and locked, instead of the thin curtain that separated the tiny cells at the Motherhouse. I had no chores, and decided on my own when to pray, when to study, what to eat.

Would that alone be enough for Sister Magdalene to recommend my removal from graduate studies? I hoped not. I wondered if I should tell her how liberal I found most of my new community. Or my suspicions regarding Mother Ignatius' death. Each step on the way to St. Alban's seemed to bring a new question, and no answers.

In spite of the crystal-clear fall day, I felt a cloud over my head all along Southern Boulevard.

I was distracted also by Jake Driscoll's job offer and what motivated his interest in Timothy. I tossed about theories that he was generous on the one hand and wanting to control my family on the other. A caring, Catholic gentleman? Or a conniving murderer trying to buy my loyalty?

I told myself a man wouldn't commit murder and then talk about being the instrument of God's will, as he had called himself at dinner. However, it didn't take long for me to remember stories of the Crusades and the Spanish Inquisition—killing in the name of God was not a new concept. From the philosophy he expounded, I wouldn't have been surprised if Jake Driscoll thought he was doing the Roman Catholic Church a favor by eliminating a fiscal innocent like Mother Ignatius. For the time being, I'd keep him on my list of suspects.

By the time I walked into my Modern Philosophy class, only two things were clear to me. One, I was the only person in the city of New York who didn't think Mother Ignatius died the peaceful death of a seventy-five-year-old nun. And two, I'd started my new mission with a bad attitude.

My less than optimistic mood was not helped by Father Walters' opening lecture on the process philosophy of Alfred North Whitehead. Together, Walters and Whitehead set the stage for a new theological definition—a Creator who was evolving right along with the human species. What happened to St. Thomas Aquinas' Unmoved Mover and Uncaused Cause? I tried to picture myself praying to a God who was no more permanent than the trends of each new era, blowing in the wind like Sister Teresa's dark, uncovered curls.

"What do you think of Whitehead?" Aidan asked me as we stood to leave the classroom.

"Interesting."

"Interesting as in, you'll consider his ideas? Or interesting as in, it's a heresy and you wouldn't give it a moment's thought if it weren't on the final exam?"

I laughed at the choices Aidan came up with. "Just interesting," I said, not wanting to prolong our discussion.

I'd rationalized enough conversations already—telling myself chats with Aidan and the residents of St. Lucy's Hall were a necessary part of my new academic life.

An unpleasant scene flashed before me— a reprimand by Mother Julia a year or so earlier. She'd met me as I entered the front door of the Motherhouse. I'd just been dropped off by the parent of a Sunday School student.

"Sister Francesca, did I see you talking to that young woman— walking up the driveway as if you were particular friends?"

"Yes, Mother Julia. She's John Shaunessey's mother. We were talking about his First Communion next Sunday."

"It did not look to me like strictly business."

"No, Mother."

"You were laughing."

"Yes, Mother. She told me John's worried about hurting the Baby Jesus when he takes the Host in his mouth. He thinks his teeth ..."

"That's not really funny, Sister, is it?"

I bit my lip, as if to punish it for attempting a smile. "No, Mother Julia."

A voice cut into the memory.

"Sister Francesca? Is everything all right? Who's Mother Julie?"

I drew in my breath at Aidan's question, realizing I must have muttered at least part of my memory aloud. I turned to see a troubled expression on his face.

"I'm sorry. I was distracted for a moment. I'm fine," I told him with an embarrassed smile.

We'd reached the front door of Aquinas Hall, at the top of a large stone staircase leading to the grounds one floor below.

"I'm the one who's sorry, Sister," he said, touching my arm. "I didn't mean to pressure you into a position on Whitehead or anyone else. It's none of my business."

I drew my arm away with a quick movement that almost caused me to lose my balance. "Excuse me. I have to go."

I swept up my habit and hurried down the wide steps. What's wrong with him? I asked myself—a Catholic boy who says the rosary with beads from his First Communion, and he doesn't know enough not to touch a nun?

Walking back to St. Lucy's, I rubbed the spot on my sleeve where Aidan's hand had been.

CHAPTER 14

I was happy to see Sister Magdalene had not yet arrived at St. Lucy's. I went to the chapel and opened my prayer book, adding my own concerns to the formula for renewal of vows. I prayed in silence, my fingers gripping the pages as if the text would otherwise flee from an unworthy subject.

Lord, keep me faithful to my promises to you as a Bride of Christ. Strengthen my resolve to remain poor in spirit in spite of my comfortable life, obedient to all my superiors whether I agree with them or not, and chaste in the face of new temptations.

I sat back on the dark wooden bench, my eyes wandering across the altar, from the statue of St. Lucy on the left, to the Blessed Virgin on the right. I had disappointed them and all the saints in heaven. And Mother Julia. Clearly I'd proven myself unable to handle the charges of a professed nun away from her community. I had about decided to respectfully petition that I be returned to the Motherhouse, when I heard my bell signal.

Time to face Sister Magdalene.

I genuflected and went to the small parlor.

"Praised be Jesus Christ," Sister Magdalene said.

"Praised forever. Amen."

I got another taste of my breakfast jam as Sister Magdalene's customary SMI salutation caused a slight turmoil in my stomach. I realized I'd almost forgotten how we greet each other. At St. Lucy's, the Sisters used secular salutations—they said "Good morning" or "Hi" as we did when we were part of the world. I had little doubt I'd see a "Merry Xmas" sign on the bulletin board, come December.

"Sister Francesca, as you know, Mother Julia asked me to help her evaluate your suitability for this assignment."

Sister Magdalene sat in the only straight-backed chair, forcing me to take one of the easy chairs. I blamed myself for the tired look in her eyes. My irresponsibility had prompted a four-hour bus ride for a nun almost as old as the late Mother Ignatius. As I struggled to keep my back straight, the soft velour padding on the seat increased my feeling of inferiority as the servant of a suffering Master.

"Yes, Sister Magdalene."

"Mother Julia had a call from Sister Felix. She says you're having a difficult time adjusting to St. Lucy's strict regulations."

I took a large gulp of air and swallowed my surprise. Sister Magdalene's words seemed to be in a foreign language, like the Latin of the old missals, her shaky old voice exaggerating my feeling of disconnectedness. I'd expected Sister Felix to have reported on my impertinent behavior—questioning her regarding Mother Ignatius' last hours, prying into legal matters about St. Lucy's contract with the University, exhibiting borderline rudeness to her and Jake Driscoll at dinner.

Why had Sister Felix omitted those transgressions? Why had she insinuated instead that St. Lucy's environment was more austere than my Motherhouse?

"Sister Magdalene, I—"

Sister Magdalene held up her hand. "Sister, no explanation, please. Permit me to return to Mother Julia the news that you've kept your vow of obedience and haven't offered a defense." Her frown sent a shiver through my body.

"Yes, Sister Magdalene."

"I spoke to Sister Felix while you were in chapel, and we agreed you should be allowed to stay in school, your willfulness notwithstanding. It will be good for you to practice the discipline of St. Lucy's, however strict it seems to you. Your request for extra bedding, for example, showed a great weakness."

I breathed deeply, and invoked my patron saint, but not even recollections of Saint Francis of Assisi could quiet my mind. The pillows that had been my excuse to query Sister Felix about Mother Ignatius had provided the perfect basis for a reproach.

The small parlor had windows on both Marian Avenue and 198th Street. I looked out first one, then the other, seeking a place of refuge beyond the walls of St. Lucy's.

I tried to fathom the motive behind Sister Felix's report to Sister Magdalene. I came up with one scenario that fit my suspicions: she wanted to stifle my curiosity regarding Mother Ignatius' death—but instead of opening up that topic, Sister Felix had convinced my superiors I was lax in religious practices. To protect herself? To protect someone else? It also crossed my mind that she simply wanted to intimidate me into behaving myself.

"Are you ready to take this on, Sister Francesca?" Sister Magdalene asked me. "We are moved to give you another opportunity to grow in religious fervor."

I imagined how stunned Sister Magdalene would be if she knew what went on at St. Lucy's. My head felt dizzy with explanations I wanted to provide Sister Magdalene. I couldn't believe there was nothing in the outward appearance of St. Lucy's that would alert her to the true situation—nuns and priests socializing, Sisters coming and going as they pleased, eating and talking at any hour of the day. A most unorthodox interpretation of the Liturgy.

To me the laxity was palpable.

From all my studies, I knew in theory it was all the more noble to suffer for transgressions I hadn't committed. It was hard to deal with in practice, however, and I found it nearly impossible to hold my tongue.

I prayed for guidance as I considered my options. Tell the truth and be disobedient to one rule or withhold the truth and violate many more.

My final decision was driven by a separate consideration—with enormous guilt, I admitted to myself I wanted to stay at St. Lucy's. I wanted to study theology and also to learn what had happened to Mother Ignatius.

Sister Magdalene sat straight, her hands in her sleeves, the essence of patient waiting. I knew what to say to ensure I wouldn't be returned to the Motherhouse.

"Thank you, Sister Magdalene. I'm grateful for another chance to strengthen my spirit of obedience."

Sister Magdalene smiled, the wrinkles on her face rearranging themselves into a pleasant pattern. She stood and walked to the Marian Avenue window, as if to signal a shift in the conversation. As she faced me, her starched white bib reflected light from the garden.

"There's another matter, Sister." She paused and her face returned to its somber expression. "It's your father."

My heart jumped, my insides turning queasy. "Yes, Sister Magdalene?"

"He's had a heart attack. He's in the hospital in Fishkill."

How is he? When did this happen? Who's with him? I caught my questions in time to avoid another breach of SMI rule. Sister Magdalene would tell me all God wanted me to know, in her own time. I gulped and waited for her to continue.

"Your sister Patricia called us this morning. Since I was coming here, anyway, Mother Julia thought it best if I told you in person. I'm sure you'd like more details, Sister."

"Yes, Sister Magdalene. If I may, please."

I went back to chapel as soon as Sister Felix came to take Sister Magdalene to lunch.

"I've had a long journey, Sisters. And I have another one ahead of me," Sister Magdalene had said. "So, if you don't mind, I'll take my meal alone."

Gladly, I'd thought, wondering how long it would be before I'd be able to eat again.

I'd sat quietly in the parlor while Sister Magdalene told me what she knew. My father and Patty were about to leave for five-thirty mass at St. Leonard's, as they did every weekday morning. Timothy and Gabriella were asleep. In my mind, I could hear my father cry out in pain as he fell over in the driveway. After things had settled down in the hospital, Patty called the Motherhouse. My father was stable as of the time Sister Magdalene left for the seven-fifteen bus. Mother Julia would call me if there was any change.

I knew Patty would have prevented anyone from contacting me directly at St. Lucy's. She'd respect Mother Julia's position as intermediary between me and my family. Timothy's right, I thought, Patty might as well be the nun. She follows the rules more closely than I do.

I'd always felt Patty—two years younger than me—would have entered a convent if I hadn't. But I chose first, leaving Dad and my younger sisters and brother four years after my mother died. My father was thrilled, although it meant my earning power was lost to the family. Timothy was thirteen at the time, Gabriella fourteen, Kathleen sixteen, and Patty twenty.

A trained welder, Dad worked for the railroads. He maintained and repaired all the cars passing through the Potterstown station. It was a steady income, but not one that provided frills for a household of seven. Patty left college soon after I entered and took a job as a receptionist for a Potterstown optometrist. If her motive was economic necessity, as I suspected, the family kept it from me.

Not everyone in my entering class was as lucky as I was. I thought of Elena Russo, a young woman who'd entered with me—an Italian American whose parents disowned her when she chose religious life. Following old school Italian beliefs, Mr. and Mrs. Russo considered convent life an embarrassment, to be embraced only by women too ugly to attract a husband and too stupid to have a career.

It occurred to me that if God Himself weren't enough inspiration, my family's sacrifices should motivate me to keep my vows with great diligence. All the more reason to use great caution before accepting a modern way of life that might just be the Devil, exercising a temporary hold on the leaders of the Church.

Sister Magdalene brought permission from Mother Julia for me to send a note to my father and reminded me I'd be permitted to attend his funeral if he died. SMIs could choose to be present at the services of one family member only, but I was in the world when my mother died, so I was free to return to Potterstown if …

I had difficulty completing the sentence in my mind. Although it had been ten years, it seemed too short a time since we'd lost my mother to leukemia.

I prayed to Saint Francis. *Consoler of the sick who ask thy prayers, turn thy compassionate eyes upon my father, Brendan Patrick Wickes. Grant him the grace to accept God's will. Help him to turn his pain into a spiritual bouquet to secure his place beside thee in heaven.*

The call bell interrupted my prayers. Two, pause, five. My signal. This time it was a phone call.

"Sister Francesca? Tim called and told me about your father," Aidan Connors said. "I'm so sorry."

I tightened my grip on the phone. Had something else happened? Had my father …? "How recently did you speak to him?" I asked in a shaky voice.

"Just got off the phone. Evidently he's doing as well as you could expect. Tim's going to stay a few more days, though. I guess Patty's pretty upset and wants him to hang around Potterstown."

"I'm glad he's with them," I said, wondering how it happened that a near stranger knew more about my family than I did. One of the peculiar consequences of the Holy Rule, I realized.

"I can drive you up there if you like, Sister. It's only about three hours by car, and we don't have class till two o'clock tomorrow afternoon."

I drew in my breath. "Thank you, but I can't do that, Aidan. I can't just drop in on my family." Let alone arrive in Potterstown with my veil blowing out the window of a man's car, I added to myself. I pictured Mother Julia, one hand on her hip, the other holding out my dismissal papers.

"I could have you back in plenty of time for class."

I clenched my jaw. "That's not the point. It's against the rules."

"Well, I thought I'd offer. My aunt's a Sister of St. Joseph, and she's able to visit when someone's sick."

"I'm not a Sister of St. Joseph. We all have different rules. You're starting to sound like my brother, Aidan. He's never understood the religious life."

He laughed. "Tim did go on a bit about that. You can take phone calls at St. Lucy's, but it's strictly forbidden at your Motherhouse. You can …"

I grew impatient. "It's God's will, Aidan. It's not to be questioned."

"I understand."

I hung up, annoyed that he'd persisted, and—even worse, that I'd understood his logic also.

CHAPTER 15

A tray of food in front of my door told me Sister Ann William had come to my rescue again. So far she was one of only two people of recent acquaintance who hadn't annoyed me—and the other was dead.

I arranged the neatly wrapped sandwich, small carton of milk, and package of chocolate cookies on one half of my desktop, leaving the other free for writing a note to my father.

My plans for a stress-free lunch were thwarted, however, when I found a reminder of my recalcitrant behavior—lying on the box of note paper in my desk drawer were the cuff link and packet of letters I'd found in Mother Ignatius' office. I put the jewelry aside and examined the correspondence. The envelopes were white, all the same size, and pressed into a bundle about a quarter-inch thick. I ran my fingers along the edge and counted six letters.

Only a thin rubber band stood between me and a venial sin. My own lessons to my Sunday School students came to my mind. *A violation of the standard prescribed by the moral law in a matter less serious than mortal sin*, I'd told class after class. Certainly not as grave as breaking a commandment, but not to be taken lightly. I thought of Saint Augustine's words on venial sins:

Tremble when you count them ... a number of light objects makes a great mass; a number of drops fills a river; a number of grains makes a heap.

I walked around the room, waving the small bundle, talking to myself, as if I were a canon lawyer arguing a point of theology before a Roman synod. These letters don't belong to me, I told the imaginary jury of Cardinals. They nodded. But at the moment, they belong to no one else, either. They nodded again. The late Mother Ignatius had no family. Since I found them, might they not be considered mine? *Hmm*, they said.

I knew nothing of civil law, so I was free to use Thomistic reasoning without regard for the fine points of the secular legal system. The concepts of breaking and entering, theft of property, and obstructing justice were vague in my mind, and I didn't think they applied to my circumstances.

The smell of ham and cheese filled the tiny space that was my room. I reached for my sandwich and continued my debate. What if reading these letters helps me solve a crime of murder? Surely righting the wrong of a mortal sin would justify a venial sin. If I find nothing useful, I'll destroy them, and no harm will be done. In either case, I'll say my Act of Contrition and go to confession as soon as possible.

During the final round of internal questions and answers, I slipped the rubber band from the letters. The sound it made when it snapped out of my hands seemed as loud as a whip cracking against the back of an infidel in the Middle Ages.

I sat on the bed, within stretching distance of my lunch, and flipped through the stack of mail. The letters seemed to have been written by the same person, someone as old as Mother Ignatius by the look of the script. Return address—Convent of the Sacred Hearts, Albuquerque, New Mexico. Postmarked between July and September, the latest one a week before Mother Ignatius' death. So recent, they could be significant. I told myself if the letters had been decades old, I wouldn't intrude on the privacy of the sender or the receiver.

I took a cookie and washed it down with a mouthful of milk, as if physical nourishment could compensate for the spiritual weakening I brought on myself. I pulled the letters from their envelopes and laid them out on my white chenille bedspread in chronological order. The stationery was heavy white stock with plain letterhead—The Order of the Sacred Hearts of Jesus and Mary. The signature on each was difficult to read—*Mother Consiliatrix*, I guessed—followed by her order's initials, S.H.J.M.

She had written to Mother Ignatius every other Sunday since July 4, an unusually high frequency. In most communities, Sisters wrote to their immediate families each Sunday, and once a month to non-family members, with special permission only. From her use of letterhead, I knew Mother Ignatius' correspondent must be Mother Superior of her convent, but even so she would have kept the rules unless urgent matters were being discussed.

I ran my eyes across the pages, reading only a phrase or a sentence here and there. I was reminded how, as children, my friends and I peeked through our fingers at the scary parts of a movie. Was I trying to lessen the impact of reading someone else's mail by this same, casual approach? At my Motherhouse, I wasn't even allowed to read my own mail until it had been screened by Mother Julia or Sister Magdalene.

You've already committed a sin, I told myself, go ahead and finish the task. I took a deep breath and read the first letter, skipping past the preliminary greetings.

The matters of which you speak—D, E, and F—are serious indeed. It's always a strain on our faith in Holy Mother Church when one of its own is seen to be all too fallible. I understand your reluctance to be specific, but perhaps if I had more details, I could be of more assistance.

Remember the words of Saint John: "the world and its desires shall pass away, but the man who does the will of God shall live forever."

I reread the beginning.

D, E, and F.

D for Driscoll, E for someone whose name began with E, and F for Felix? Or just three letters of the alphabet, part of a longer list that began with A? Maybe Mother Consiliatrix simply wasn't interested in matters A, B, and C. I thought of the cuff link with the letter D. Just as likely as not, a coincidence.

Mother Consiliatrix's reference to *one of its own* could mean any Roman Catholic. Unfortunately, all my suspects fit that criterion.

I moved on to the other five letters, hoping for something more specific. Mother Consiliatrix offered Mother Ignatius prayers, support, and advice, but continued to be vague about the exact nature of the problems causing the stress. I felt as if I were trying to learn a new hymn, while missing every other note. And of course, that was true—I didn't have Mother Ignatius' side of the correspondence.

In the last communication, written on September 12, Mother Consiliatrix seemed to have made up her mind regarding what Mother Ignatius should do.

If what you've told me is true, you are certainly correct in assessing your obligation. Difficult as it may be, I urge you to follow your inclinations and go to the authorities. Two of the issues seem to be matters for the secular courts, the other should be taken to the Chancery. I pray to the Sacred Hearts of Jesus and Mary …

Three issues. Two secular, one religious. What I had was one real estate deal and one case of a flirting nun. I was missing one secular issue, and a person with the initial E, among other things. And which so-called issue got Mother Ignatius killed? All of them? None of them?

At the end of a half-hour, I'd finished reading each letter twice. I'd been so engrossed, I was sure I'd have missed my own call signal if it had rung. The correspondence deepened my conviction that Mother Ignatius' death was related to something she knew but gave me nothing concrete to work with.

Thoughts about going to the police with the packet crossed my mind, but I couldn't imagine they'd perceive anything suspicious. They hadn't seen the look on Mother Ignatius' face when she told me how frightened she was, and the letters alone could be dismissed as the chatter of two elderly nuns, perhaps old friends, separated by thousands of miles.

I stood up for what was becoming routine pacing and glanced at the remains of my lunch. My heart lurched. Next to the last cookie was the card for the note to my father. I uttered a disgusted grunt—what sort of person is distracted from writing to her critically ill parent by a potentially non-existent crime?

As soon as I sat at my desk to address my father, images of our life together flooded my mind and pushed out thoughts of murder and religious mayhem.

I remembered my favorite time of day as a child—Patty and I would go to our living room window at precisely four-thirty in the afternoon. My father would round the bend of Firth Road in

Potterstown, on his way home, taking a short-cut through the field across from our house. Day after day, he'd pretend to trip and fall, each time in a different spot. Then he'd get up and take a bow, swinging his old striped railroad hat in front of him. The smile on our faces would still be there when we'd greet him at the door.

I struggled to suppress tears as I wrote. In letters to our families, we were never allowed to discuss details of our daily customs, nor share any news of other Sisters, good or bad. In spite of the restrictions, I'd always found enough to write about—rehearsals for a Christmas pageant, classes in Sacred Scripture, a visit from the Bishop, a Silver Jubilee celebration.

But this time it was hard to fill a page with news that would cheer my father. My new Superior had died, my old Superior had to send her delegate to manage my behavior, my classes were unsatisfying, St. Lucy's Hall was a den of reformers, and I'd launched a one-nun murder investigation.

Nothing fit for the resident of an intensive care unit.

I looked out my window for inspiration and came up with a few words about the lovely fall weather in the Bronx and the splendid flowers and bushes in the garden. I was happy to add a paragraph about the positive changes in Timothy's life and closed with a promise of my loving prayers. It felt strange to lick and stamp the envelope. For the first time in six years, I'd be mailing an uncensored letter. I placed a *Saint Anthony Guide* sticker on the back, as if to take the curse off an unsupervised communication.

A knock on my door startled me. My eyes darted to the incriminating evidence spread out on my bed. I scooped up the pile of Mother Consiliatrix's letters and stuffed them into my drawer along with a few tufts of chenille.

"Yes?"

"It's me. Sister Ann William."

"Yes, Sister. One minute." I brushed my habit, as if to clear it of signs of my transgressions before I opened the door. "Thank you for lunch, Sister. I'm going to have to do your chores for a month to make up for all your service."

She laughed. "Too bad we don't have any chores here. I kind of miss them."

"I know what you mean. It's strange to live as though we were in a hotel. I keep looking for the lists and charts. Scullery duty, dormitory floors, laundry room …"

"And don't forget the plum job—starching the altar linens!"

I smiled and nodded. We shared a moment of silence in which I suspected Sister Ann William, like me, revisited her Motherhouse and its familiar, comforting routines.

"Are you on your way to class?" I asked her.

"I am. I'm going to stop at the campus store first, to order a medal of Saint William for my brother. He's entering the seminary in Houston next week." Sister Ann William's broad smile told me she was proud of the young man whose name she'd chosen as her own in religion. Seeing my questioning frown, she added a quick explanation. "I have permission from Mother Clarisse to use the discretionary money I have for snacks and supplies."

"What a wonderful idea. I'm sure he'll appreciate it."

"Is there anything I can pick up for you while I'm at the store?"

I started to shake my head, when my eyes landed on my desk drawer. "I think I'll come to campus with you," I said. "I'd like to go to confession."

CHAPTER 16

O n the way to campus, I added two more "firsts" to my list—I dropped the note to my father in a mailbox on Southern Boulevard, and I told Sister Ann William about his heart attack. In Potterstown, I wouldn't have been allowed to mention such a personal matter—Mother Julia would inform the community whenever there was a special occasion for prayers. I was sure she'd already put a notice on the bulletin board in the assembly room, asking the Sisters to remember Brendan Patrick Wickes at mass and Benediction. She'd also remind them at grace before dinner.

Thinking of Mother Julia gave me a sudden longing to be back with my community and the ordered, regular life of the Potterstown Motherhouse. I regretted manipulating Sister Magdalene into leaving me at St. Lucy's. I thought if I made a list of all the recent departures from my normal SMI life, it would stretch from the Bronx Zoo to St. Patrick's Cathedral in midtown Manhattan.

Sister Ann William was solicitous, stopping in her tracks to make the sign of the cross. "I'm glad you told me, Sister. I'll make a novena for your father to Saint William, starting today."

"Thank you, Sister. I know that would mean a great deal to him."

"A daily communicant, I'll bet."

I nodded. "Only a stay in the hospital can keep him away. And I'm sure he asked for Communion as soon as he could speak."

Sister Ann William was such a reasonable religious, I considered sharing the information I'd learned from Mother Consiliatrix's letters and asking her advice. Should I mail the letters back to Albuquerque anonymously? Mail them to the police? Tear them to shreds? Toss the cuff link in the fountain by the University library? I ruled out the idea of sneaking back into Mother Ignatius' office and restoring everything to its original place.

In the end, I was dissuaded from confiding in Sister Ann William—I couldn't bring myself to admit to her how I'd come upon these items in the first place.

We parted ways at the Mary Chapel. I checked the schedule at the door and was happy I'd remembered correctly—confession daily at two o'clock. The priest on duty was the chairman of the History Department and Sister Veronique's "very important person on the faculty," Father Joseph O'Neill. I hoped there was a chance he wouldn't want to give me a lesson in social consciousness.

I'd seen Father Malbert talking to him in the hall near the chapel and worried it was Father Malbert's turn in the confessional booth. I didn't relish the idea of having to report specifics of my behavior to him again. Nor did I want to be let off easy, as I'd expect him to do. After waving to me, Father Malbert entered a doorway several yards away.

As it turned out, Father O'Neill was cut from the same cloth.

"Don't be hard on yourself, Sister," he told me in the confessional. "Did you intend any harm to the person whose letters you read?"

"No, Father."

"Did you read them from concupiscence, hoping for pleasures of the flesh?"

I winced at the suggestion, and shook my head, as if he could see me in the darkness behind the grille. "No, Father."

"Did you hope for some personal gain?" He leaned closer to the grille and laughed. I smelled alcohol on his breath, and hoped it was sacramental. "Are you going to blackmail the good nun in New Mexico?"

Another flip Albanite. "No, Father," I said, without a trace of humor.

"Then, say three Our Fathers and three Hail Marys, and make a good Act of Contrition. God bless you, Sister."

Oh, my God, I am heartily sorry …

I pushed aside the heavy maroon curtain and left the booth. I wondered if there was a priest anywhere in the Bronx who'd take me to task and give me a decent penance. Not wishing to assume the "holier than thou" attitude Mother Julia warned us against, I restricted myself to the meager propitiation Father O'Neill had prescribed.

I'd just finished the five sorrowful mysteries of the rosary for my father when Father O'Neill exited the booth and came over to the pew in front of me. Unlike the dashing, fair-haired Father Malbert, Father O'Neill was dark, squat, and balding. His large nose had the red glow of someone who drank more than his share of non-sacramental wine.

"Sister Francesca, you're new at St. Lucy's. I've been wanting to meet you." Another surprise. Had Sister Veronique talked about me? I wondered. Described me? I imagined her reporting on my rudeness, and thus awakening interest in knowing me. All to my chagrin. To my further dismay, Father O'Neill addressed me in normal tones, though we were in the presence of the Blessed Sacrament.

"How do you do, Father." I tried to whisper without seeming to reproach him for his loud voice.

"Do you have time for a cup of coffee?"

I shook my head and shrank back, nearly falling off the kneeler.

"Uh, no. Thank you, Father."

"Some other time, then."

I nodded and collapsed on the seat.

St. Alban's was the friendliest place I'd ever been to, as a nun or otherwise.

I'd told Sister Ann William I'd be going straight home to St. Lucy's after confession. I took comfort in the long walk, no longer sore from my adventure on Southern Boulevard. I thought of my sisters and brother, who were most likely camping out in the Fishkill General Hospital waiting room.

I could picture them: Patty leading the rosary for the family and friends who'd gathered in the hospital waiting room. Timothy sitting with his arms folded, lips unyielding. Kathleen, now Mrs. Neal Mooney, would be bringing cups of coffee to everyone, and trying to comfort Gabriella, who'd be sobbing quietly. At least two of our neighbors on Firth Road would be standing by at the Wickes home ready to serve a meal to anyone who walked in the door.

By now the route between the campus and St. Lucy's was familiar, and I was able to lose myself in Potterstown and Fishkill.

If I hadn't been so engrossed, I might have been aware of the vehicle bearing down on me from behind.

Before I heard it, I felt it. Just as I turned the bend in the boulevard, where the sidewalk sloped downward. A wallop on my right side. I was knocked to the ground, the wind sucked out of me. I fell on my back, my legs thrust into the air, so it was impossible to see who or what went spinning down the sidewalk after the impact. Faster and noisier than a bicycle. Not as big as a motorcycle.

"A motor scooter," someone said.

"Are you all right, Sister?"

"What a jerk."

"It was a guy in a blue jacket."

"We should call an ambulance."

"There's a phone booth on the corner."

"I think it was a woman, not a man. And it was a brown jacket."

More startled than injured, I straightened my bonnet and opened my eyes. I focused on two young women kneeling beside me, concern on their faces. I could tell they were reluctant to touch me, except to pull the skirt of my habit down over my legs. Aidan wouldn't have had a problem, I thought.

A man standing to one side pointed to a vehicle at the curb. "I have a car. I can take her to a hospital," he said.

"No. Thank you. I'm fine. I was just surprised."

After a few more minutes of fussing and opining as to what the reckless driver looked like and what he or she was wearing, I realized we'd never know for sure. Once I stood up, pains raced up my spine, and I agreed to a ride home. One of the women, a slim blonde who identified herself as Mary Margaret showed her Catholic upbringing by offering to accompany me so I wouldn't be in a car alone with a man.

"St. Stephen's, White Plains," she said as she climbed in the back seat with me. She smiled broadly. "Twelve years with the Augustinian nuns. I know the rules."

"Thank you, Mary Margaret."

———————

It was only ten minutes by car from where I'd been sprawled on the sidewalk, to St. Lucy's Hall. I learned the driver of the car was Mark Dealy, a graduate student in business administration. With my new freedom as an uncensored letter writer, I decided to get his address so I could write him a thank you note.

I stepped out of Mark's car in front of Sister Teresa as she approached the steps to St. Lucy's front door. I didn't realize the extent of my disheveled appearance until I saw the look on her face.

"Francesca! What happened to you?"

A sharp pain shot through my head as I twisted around to look at my skirt, soiled in the back. My bib was askew, my rosary broken. Apparently a protuberance on the bike got caught in a loop of the large beads that hung from my waist. One section of ten beads was detached from the rest, swinging well below my knees, like a renegade incense holder.

"Some creep ran her down with a motor scooter," Mary Margaret told her, shaking her head. "She could have been a lot worse off."

Sister Teresa gasped. Her hands flew to her face, her fair skin turning red, as if she herself were the culprit.

"She didn't want to go a hospital," Mark said. "But I think someone should make sure she's all right."

"I'm fine. Just a little shaken," I said, tired of the third person references.

"I'll take care of her," Sister Teresa said. She straightened her shoulders as if to assume a position of command, and in doing so pulled the front of her habit even tighter across her chest. I tried to dismiss an uncharitable image of her small silver cross disappearing into the horizontal fold at her bosom.

I sat up in my bed, my head resting against extra pillows Sister Teresa had brought me. So much for joining myself to the sufferings of Christ in the Garden of Gethsemane, I thought.

To my chagrin, on the way to my room we'd passed several Sisters, including Sister Felix. They offered in turn tsk-tsks for the offender on the scooter and good wishes for me. Sister Felix had put a note about my father's heart attack on the bulletin board and all assured me of their prayers for his recovery. The Wickes family was getting its share of attention from the residents of St. Lucy's.

Sister Felix also stopped in to visit me—the first time I'd seen her since Sister Magdalene's visit. An awkward moment.

"Take care of yourself, Sister Francesca," she'd said to me, with no warmth at all in her voice. From her manner, I wouldn't have surprised if it had been she who'd run me down, except I didn't think anyone would miss a nun on a motor scooter.

I couldn't help wondering what her motive was in lying to my Superiors—painting a false picture of life at St. Lucy's. If her intention was to stop my meddling, why hadn't she broached the topic directly? I yielded to common sense and put all unpleasant thoughts aside until I felt well enough to deal with them rationally.

Sister Teresa checked in often during the afternoon, asking about my bruises and inquiring about the accident. Did I see who did it? Would I recognize the vehicle? Should the police be informed?

I shook my head. "It wouldn't do any good to report it since I didn't see a thing. It happened very quickly."

On one of her visits, Sister Teresa proposed soothing music to help my recovery. "Veronique has a portable radio in her room," she told me. "She's not back from campus yet, but I know she'd be happy to have you borrow it. Some nice chamber music might help you relax."

"No, thank you, Sister," I said. "I'll probably fall asleep from the hot tea and aspirin."

I wished Sister Magdalene could have heard the suggestion—a radio in my room. In spite of her lack of religious decorum, however, Sister Teresa proved to be a gentle and attentive nurse. She'd taken the skirt of my habit to the laundry room and cleaned it, adding a promise to have my rosary repaired by morning.

"Father Malbert is good with his hands," she said.

I groaned inwardly at surrendering my rosary to a priest who probably could no longer name its fifteen mysteries.

"Did you ever wear a large rosary around your waist?" I asked Sister Teresa, for some reason unknown to me.

She nodded. "We're still supposed to, but ..." She shrugged her shoulders. "Anyway, don't worry. I'll take good care of yours."

I knew I'd have to rethink my assumed correlation between Sisters who wanted change, and rude or uncaring behavior.

I'd thought of trying to negotiate the three flights of stairs down to St. Lucy's dining room, but when Sister Ann William appeared at my door with a dinner tray, I was relieved. We laughed about the turn of events as I cut into a piece of pot roast with some difficulty. Although my right arm was sore, my unbecoming fall seemed to have done nothing to curb my appetite.

"I may be destined never to eat in the refectory again," I said between mouthfuls of soft, boiled potatoes.

"Don't say that, Sister Francesca. You're going to be up and about in no time."

Instead of music to relieve stress, Sister Ann William suggested we say Compline together. I accepted gratefully, acknowledging that a round trip to the first-floor chapel sounded like an exhausting journey.

After I'd finished a large portion of butterscotch pudding, we read our evening prayer out loud. We decided to omit the customary hymn to the Virgin Mary at the end, since we both had voices that sounded best when buried in a choir. Instead, we recited the words of the *Salve Regina*.

... mater miserecordiae, vita dulcedo et spes nostra, salve

Hail Holy Queen, Mother of Mercy, Our Life, Our Sweetness, and Our Hope...

Once Sister Ann William had departed, I turned to the stack of mail she'd put on my tray—more mail than I'd receive in a month at the Motherhouse. I thought how delighted my father would be to see so many cards and notes from St. Lucy's Sisters, offering spiritual bouquets for him.

"I'm giving one daughter to God, and getting a convent full in return," he'd said to Mother Julia when I entered.

Considering the bounty of another house of prayer for my father, plus the solicitousness of Sister Teresa and Sister Ann William, I finally felt a sense of community with the Sisters of St. Lucy's.

Too bad it had taken Mary Margaret's designated "creep on a motor scooter" on Southern Boulevard to bring it about.

CHAPTER 17

Timothy called me from Potterstown at ten in the morning to report on our father's condition.

"He's stable, but not out of the woods." A pause. "Everyone's here. You should be, too."

I braced myself. Conversations with my brother were never easy, and I knew this one would be particularly difficult. We both had cause to be agitated, if for different reasons.

"Where I should be is where God wants me, Timothy. Every Sister in the house is praying for Dad."

"Huh. That's a big help. How come you're breaking the rules— talking to me? Patty said not to bother you, and you probably wouldn't pick up the phone, anyway."

"I understand you're upset."

"Has Driscoll called you yet?"

I leaned against the wall, to support both my aching back and my emotional swings. "Why would Mr. Driscoll call me, Timothy?"

"Steve Rooney, my Parole Officer, notified him about Dad."

Another inroad into the Wickes family. "I see. Why do you think he did that?"

"Makes sense. Officially Driscoll's my employer, although I won't be able to start as soon as I thought. I'm staying home until Dad's better." I remembered Jake Driscoll making it clear he didn't need my consent to hire Timothy. No matter, I thought, what my family does is out of my hands, as it should be. "He said he's going to arrange a ride for you to come up here."

"I can't do that, Timothy."

"I know you refused Aidan's offer, but I figured if a girl drove you up it would be OK. A ton of college kids do that—drive people around for pay. And Driscoll knows a couple of undergrads who'd be happy to take you. It's your father, for Christ's sake."

Thou shalt not take the name of the Lord thy God in vain.

My brother knew many ways to get to me. Breaking the Second Commandment was one of them. I took a deep breath. My whole body ached from my accident. Or what I hoped was an accident.

"This is not a good time to have this discussion. I'm standing in the middle of a hallway, and I have to leave soon for class."

"Yeah, well, life goes on, I guess. Except maybe for Dad."

When we hung up my brother and I were no closer to understanding each other than when he was twelve years old. My father and sisters, delighted with my vocation, had tried to explain it to Timothy. "Susan Marie is going to help God save souls," Patty told him.

Young Timothy shook his head, looked at me and said, "God doesn't need your help. We do."

Either my brother was right, or this past week was the greatest test of my vocation.

As for Jake Driscoll, I couldn't decide whether he should be nominated Catholic Man of the Year or Bronx Prince of Darkness.

I returned to my room, picked up my books, and met Sister Ann William for our walk to campus. On Thursdays we both had a class at noon. By then I was ready to face Southern Boulevard again, this time more aware of potential motor traffic on the sidewalk.

I needed to talk to a person who'd be objective as well as trustworthy. Sister Ann William was my best candidate. Between the front door of St. Lucy's Hall and Fordham Road I laid out the details of my week so far, beginning with my invasion of Mother Ignatius' private chambers. She was a good listener and took her time absorbing the synopsis. As I expected, she had a few questions.

I had some myself, and it was my story.

"Why do you suppose Sister Felix lied to Sister Magdalene?" she asked me.

"I think it was a cover-up." I checked her expression to see if I'd made sense.

At first, she twisted her mouth to the side in apparent confusion. Then her eyes brightened, and she snapped her fingers. "She wants you to stop investigating Mother Ignatius' death and the real estate deal, but she doesn't want to call attention to it. So she invents an excuse to have you reprimanded, sending a message to you, counting on you to back away. Otherwise, you get sent home. She doesn't care which."

I smiled, as if one of my students had just recited correctly the six laws of the Holy Roman Catholic Church. "Right," I said. "She knows I'm not the kind of religious who'd defend myself to a superior."

"What do we do now?" Sister Ann William asked me, with a look that furthered my perception of a teacher/pupil relationship.

"I don't know that there's anything we can do. We seem to have nothing but coincidences and intuition."

"We also have suspects and motives," she said, her voice inappropriately cheery, considering the topic.

"I guess we do."

Sister Ann William listed our imagined killers and their reasons. She might have been reading from a chart that hung from the clouds over Southern Boulevard, not far from the spot where I'd been flattened the day before. "We have Sister Felix who's ambitious for Mother Ignatius' job; Mr. Driscoll—Mother Ignatius stood between him and significant financial gain. Sisters Teresa, Veronique, and all the other Sisters impatient for change. For all we know Mother Ignatius had threatened to tell their Superiors. And Father Malbert qualifies, too, for that matter, for the same reason."

It was hard not to notice all our suspects were liberal thinkers. "Maybe we're too quick to accuse people who think differently from us," I said. "Or it could be we're manufacturing problems because we don't have enough homework yet to keep us busy."

"Maybe. Or …" Sister Ann William cleared her throat, as if to signal a new stage in the dialogue. "Remember our conversation when we talked about poisons?" She lowered her voice as two chattering students passed us. "We realized we lacked information on the medical aspects, like what would be found in an autopsy if someone were poisoned to death?"

I nodded, looking around at the placid scene. Students and faculty, some in habits and Roman collars, others in what appeared to be deliberately tattered clothing. A bright fall day smelling of freshly cut grass and new textbooks. The sun shone on majestic academic buildings. Who would guess the two young nuns walking with heads bent together were discussing a possible homicide in their convent?

"I remember the talk about poisons," I said, in a weak voice. I took a deep breath, wondering if I were the worst thing that could have happened to this sweet pharmacy student from the Sisters of Holy Charity in Texas.

"Well, I have some information," she said. A chill ran through me as I prepared myself for Sister Ann William's report. "I've been doing some research in the pharmacy library. First of all, there are many substances in the body naturally, in small quantities—like insulin—that would be toxic in large doses. So even with an autopsy sometimes it's impossible to tell if a lethal amount was ingested. It's hard to distinguish between what a murderer might have administered and what was there in the first place. Some chemicals decay quickly into breakdown products, and the original poison eludes detection."

"Interesting." *Confusing* was more accurate. But, as good a teacher as Sister Ann William might be, I thought it hopeless to try to repair the lack in my science education.

"There's more."

"I'm listening."

"Once I got started, I found it quite engaging. And it's all part of my pharmacy education, I decided."

"In case anyone asks?"

Sister Ann William blushed and looked over her shoulder. Picturing her Mother Superior Clarisse following a few steps behind us, I guessed.

"Anyway, I looked into the psychological aspects of poisoning. Did you know, for example, that it's the weapon of choice for highly intelligent people?"

"Such as our suspects."

"Exactly. The article I read said you have to be smart to locate substances and figure out doses and so forth. It's more intellectually demanding than simply shooting a gun or stabbing someone. Especially if you're trying to disguise the murder as a natural death."

"So that makes them more difficult to catch, I imagine."

She nodded. "Back to the autopsy—it only gives results if you know what to look for. The special tests—other than the usual screens for alcohol and common drugs—can be very expensive and time-consuming, so they're not done routinely."

"Fascinating as it is, what good does it do to know all this now? It's too late."

"Technically it isn't. Mother Ignatius hasn't been buried yet. You missed Sister Felix's announcement at dinner last evening. The wake hours were extended a day to give Sisters from her Motherhouse in Reedville a chance to visit. So there's a second wake tonight and the funeral is tomorrow."

"But it's not as if we can demand an autopsy."

"I have an idea about that, too," she said.

Innocuous as it seemed, the news was too much for me to absorb. I pictured us picketing outside the funeral home where Mother Ignatius was waked, insisting on an autopsy. Or stealing her body and performing one ourselves, with our scissors and candles in a dark corner of St. Lucy's.

I was glad we'd come to the point where we had to go separate ways to class. I needed to think about whether it would be wise to pursue this business. Not only was my own vow of obedience on shaky ground, but I had the uncomfortable feeling Sister Ann William would follow my lead. I didn't want that responsibility.

"We can talk about it on the way home," she said, apparently unaware of my quandary.

I gave her a wan smile. "I can hardly wait."

CHAPTER 18

I pulled my copy of *Summa Contra Gentiles* from my black canvas book bag. I'd looked forward to my first graduate theology class in the works of Saint Thomas, and hoped I wouldn't be disappointed. As soon as I heard Father Barrett's opening remark—how sad that students of today aren't prepared to read original Latin texts—I knew I was in the right place at last.

I thought back to my undergraduate Church Latin course. I'd written a paper using primary sources—on the proof that God is eternal, without beginning or end. Nothing was more inspirational than good, clean logic in the service of God, and Saint Thomas Aquinas—the Angelic Doctor and patron of Catholic colleges and universities—was the master of the genre.

Our first class, on how likeness to God may be found in Creatures, passed quickly, with no reminders of the struggles of twentieth century life. I briefly considered doing our assignment in Latin, but decided I'd better see if I could meet Father Barrett's expectations before trying to exceed them.

It was only when the hour was over, and I was heading up the stairs of the theater-style lecture room that I saw Aidan Connors. He waited for me at the top, near the door to the hallway. Due to my front-row seat, my eyes-forward bonnet, and my intentness on the thirteenth century, I hadn't seen him during class.

"Sister Francesca, how are you? I heard about your accident." The concern on Aidan's face wiped away the annoyance I'd felt at his earlier prodding—that I should suddenly appear at the Fishkill General Hospital.

"It was nothing. I'm fine, thank you."

"No bruises?" he asked, causing my irritation to reappear. No personal questions, I wanted to remind him. Did he expect me to discuss the enormous black and blue patch on my right hip? I was torn between wanting to know how he'd found out about my accident and a desire to end the discussion. The latter, I decided.

"Really, I'm fine. Thank you."

Apparently I made my point and Aidan changed the subject.

"I'll bet this class is more to your liking," he said. He tilted his head back toward the blackboard, still full of Father Barrett's doodling—enormous overlapping circles to encompass God and the world, sprinkled with Latin words and phrases.

Patrem omnipotentem, factorem caeli et terrae. Filium Dei unigenitum.

"I love it. It's what I expected from a master's program in theology."

"Me, too. More like seminary."

A tiny sound of surprise escaped my lips. "Were you in the seminary?"

There it was, before I could catch it. A personal question. No wonder Aidan Connors didn't know his place. I didn't know mine. I gave him no reason to behave himself.

He nodded and seemed to disappear into his adolescence. "The Jesuits. I went in right from high school in spite of my parents' advice. I lasted four years. Got my bachelor's and left. Way too young." Aidan turned and smiled at me. "Or maybe it was the Kadota figs."

I looked at him and broke into a laugh that was too loud for my liking. "Kadota figs! Did you have those awful yellow lumps, too?"

He nodded, wrinkling his nose as if the overly sweet smell had crossed a time barrier and reached his nostrils. "I guess it's a staple of religious life—canned figs in syrup every Friday evening for dessert."

"If you can call it that."

He laughed. "We used to transfer them to each other's plates when the Prefect wasn't looking."

We'd left the building together and stood talking at the corner of the large quadrangle known as the parade grounds. The day was warm enough to attract students to the massive lawn—they lay sprawled about in twos and threes, binders and textbooks beside them.

"They're tricky things," Aidan said. "Vocations, I mean. Not figs."

What now? I wondered. Am I supposed to counsel this man? Or does this come under the no-discussion-of-vocation-with-defectors rule? My relationship to Aidan Connors was becoming as confusing as Mother Ignatius' death. I had a sudden urge to tell him my suspicions about Mother Ignatius' death, but I stifled it. We had enough interaction already. I chose a neutral tone, back on the topic.

"I'm sure it was a difficult decision to leave the order."

"It was. I'd like to talk to you about it some time. You seem so sure of yourself."

I turned my head away in an effort to clear my mind before I responded. Another reality faced me, however, as I got a look at the enormous clock on the Administration Building tower. I gasped. "Sister Ann William's waiting for me."

"Another time, then."

"Yes."

"Take care of yourself, Sister Francesca." He smiled. "Walk slowly and watch the sidewalk traffic." Aidan's voice was soft—both concerned and friendly. I noticed he was wearing the same or a similar sweater as every other time I'd seen him on campus—a pale blue that matched his eyes. I wondered if he'd adopted a uniform out of habit from his days in seminary.

I brushed aside my curiosity about the rest of Aidan Connors' personal life, as well as the overly pleasant feeling I had whenever I interacted with him.

Sister Ann William was more animated than usual on our walk home, having browsed through a book on poisons while she waited for me.

"Did you know about half a teaspoon of nicotine can be fatal? From just three cigarettes you can extract enough to kill a person. You put the tobacco in a container, pour boiling water over it, let it steep, then strain it through cheesecloth." In spite of an armful of books, Sister Ann William used her hands to dramatize the process. "Put it over a small flame until it evaporates into a couple of drops and ..." She snapped her fingers. "... you have a lethal dose of nicotine."

"Then what?" I asked, unwilling to dampen her enthusiasm.

"You can apply it so many ways. For one thing, just rub it on someone's skin—it's absorbed through every pore of the body. It's very slow, however, so I doubt that's what killed Mother Ignatius. There'd be vomiting, nausea, convulsions, a little like strychnine poisoning."

"That's more than I need to know."

Sister Ann William finally noticed my shivers and squeamish expression.

"Sorry, Sister. I forgot not everyone's used to this sort of thing. I guess you were never a candy-striper?"

I shook my head. "My sisters Kate and Patty were. But I stuffed envelopes and answered phones in the rectory. Nice clean work." I relaxed my shoulders, hoping our graphic discussion was over. I almost wished she'd forgotten about the pending issue—how we could get an autopsy performed on Mother Ignatius' body.

Sister Ann William cleared her throat, and I knew my wish for a non-clinical topic was not to be granted.

"I talked to my Uncle Jeb, back home? He's a doctor?" Sister Ann William's accent was back in full force, I noted, apparently brought on by the allusion to her kin. "I didn't tell him the details, of course. I made it sound like I needed information for class." I gulped. We were both getting too good at white lies and mental reservations. "He said in the absence of family, anyone closely connected to the deceased can request an autopsy."

"I wouldn't say we were closely connected to Mother Ignatius."

Sister Ann William held up her hand. "Or someone of prominence who has an interest in the results."

I gave her a questioning look, wondering whom she had in mind. The Bishop? I wasn't ready to answer to Mother Julia for a spontaneous trip to the New York City Chancery Office. Even if he could have been persuaded, we didn't have access to him. Sister Felix? I'd already fallen from her list of favorites.

"Mr. Driscoll," she said, ending my mental quiz.

"Jake Driscoll? Your idea is that we ask Jake Driscoll to request an autopsy?"

"You said he offered your brother a job, so he must like you. Therefore, he's predisposed to help."

"We're to ask a suspect in a murder case to request an autopsy on his victim so we can determine if he's the killer?"

"When you put it that way it doesn't sound like such a good idea."

I blew out my breath. "Not hardly."

For the rest of the walk home, Sister Ann William and I discussed elements of Mother Ignatius' death. We might have been two partners in the Bronx Police Department, Homicide Division. Or two logicians arguing the merits of a syllogism.

"Assume we persuade Mr. Driscoll to request an autopsy. I see at least two problems," I said, preparing my fingers for the count. "One— he may not get approval, and two—even if there is an autopsy, it may not help us. You said the standard screens for poisons are limited."

Sister Ann William nodded. "Uncle Jeb says they typically look for so-called normal drugs—alcohol, barbiturates, opiates, marijuana. But I've thought of a way to expand the tests." I gave her a questioning look. "We could make a list of the likely sources of poison—what someone around here could obtain easily—and ask for those specific tests."

I remembered the shed in what was left of St. Lucy's grounds. "Gardening supplies!" I said.

Sister Ann William gave me an approving smile. "Or the plants themselves. I suspect the rhododendron and azalea. There would have been evidence of vomiting and …" I gave Sister Ann William a look that prompted her to cut short her description. She ended with, "… and other external signs of abdominal upset."

"We don't really know what condition her body was in when Sister Felix found her," I said, reminding myself how ill-equipped we were to discuss the forensics of the case.

"That would be good to know. Say she was in a convulsed position, with early rigor mortis. A clear indication of strychnine poisoning. With cyanide, on the other hand, asphyxiation is very slow. The victim thrashes about as if she's struggling with herself. The bed would have been a mess, and someone might have heard screams or sobs while she was choking."

I cleared my throat. Sister Ann William's clinical manner—like that of a doctor coaching a freshman in medical school—was getting to me. "You seem to know a great deal about this."

"Uncle Jeb," she said, with a laugh. "He really wanted me to go medical school. He's adjusting well to my being at least in a related field."

My family's wishes for me seemed much simpler than that—that I be an exemplary Sister of Mary Immaculate—but lately I wasn't so sure I measured up.

Handicapped as Sister Ann William and I were, with no information on the condition of Mother Ignatius body, and no Uncle Jeb nearby, we managed to release a litany of possibilities, picking up the pace of our walk in our enthusiasm.

"You can buy arsenic in any mineral store," Sister Ann William said.

"And there's insulin. Maybe Mother Ignatius was diabetic."

"Or what if she had a heart condition? There's foxglove in our garden—the pharmaceutical source of digitalis. Poisonous in overdose, of course."

"Rust remover, cleaners, antifreeze. Things you can buy in a hardware store." My contributions were the less technical candidates.

"And we need to think seriously of the Pharmacy Department supply room. Everything we've mentioned is in there in several forms … from pure grade to complicated mixtures."

"Aren't they locked up?"

Sister Ann William nodded. "But so many people have keys, it's almost a joke." I shuddered as my companion gave me a list of possible offenders. Janitorial staff, undergraduates, graduate students, professors, administrators, clerical personnel.

"Oh, dear," was my only response.

By the time we reached St. Lucy's front door we'd come up with more murder weapons and suspects than we needed. All that remained was to find Jake Driscoll and ask him to request an autopsy on Mother Ignatius' quietly waked body.

The first part—locating our murder suspect/co-investigator—was easier than we thought.

Jake Driscoll stood at the door of our residence, rocking on his heels, one hand in the pocket of his neat navy trousers, the other carrying a thin brown attaché case. He looked as if he'd been waiting to keep a scheduled appointment with us.

"Good afternoon, Sisters," he said. "Glad to say you beat the rain home."

Sister Ann William seemed to recover before I did, addressing him while I was still checking the overcast sky. "Yes, we did." She cleared her throat. "Mr. Driscoll, do you suppose we could have a word with you?" she asked.

He gave us a little bow and extended his arm toward the small parlor off the foyer. "I thought you'd never ask."

When Sister Ann William tipped her head slightly toward me, I took it to mean she was abandoning her short-lived leadership role. I straightened my shoulders and mustered as much formality as I could in the presence of Jake Driscoll's unruly white hair and cavalier smile.

"Mr. Driscoll, Sister Ann William and I have been discussing the circumstances of Mother Ignatius' death, and ..." I paused, hoping for internal guidance, but received external help instead.

"You'd like to see an autopsy on the good Mother's body."

Sister Ann William and I leaned forward, our eyes wide, our heads bobbing like surprised schoolgirls.

"Done." He pulled a long manila envelope from his briefcase. "I have the preliminary report right here."

"You do?" I attempted a detached, professional attitude. "Is there any sign of …?" I lost my poise and my nerve before I could complete my question.

Jake Driscoll shook his head briskly, causing a spray of fine hair to cross his brow. He made no attempt to repair his grooming, but instead leaned his whole body toward us. "No poison."

A tingling sensation traveled up my spine. I looked at the image of the Sacred Heart over the doorway. For a moment I thought the case was over, and I half-expected to see the sad eyes of Our Savior replaced by a smile and wink.

Sister Ann William shifted in her seat. "How did you know we were interested in an autopsy?" she asked him.

Jake Driscoll sat back and crossed one leg over the other. "*I* wanted one. There's a lot of money at stake here, and you're not the only people who think something funny might be going on. Frankly, I felt I had to cover my … investments. So, I persuaded her Mother Superior in Reedville to authorize an autopsy."

"And that's the real reason the funeral was delayed," I said. "Not to allow travel time from her Motherhouse." I suddenly realized Reedville was closer to the Bronx than Potterstown, not a long trip at all.

He nodded, a self-satisfied smile spread across his face.

I searched my soul for the relief that should come at the end of a long investigation. But a little corner of my mind suggested it was closer to the beginning.

CHAPTER 19

Jake Driscoll watched as I pulled page one of the autopsy report from its envelope. Sister Ann William and I held opposite corners and read silently. *Case Number 65-994.* I wondered if Mother Ignatius' was 994th death of 1965. Numbers seemed easier to focus on than the medical details. *Regarding the circumstances involved in the demise of the decedent ...*

I found it hard to understand language I hadn't seen since high school biology with Sister Perpetua. Neatly typed paragraphs described the condition of Mother Ignatius' vital organs and the systems that had sustained her earthly life—gastrointestinal, pulmonary, endocrine, hematopoietic, cardiovascular. I was glad I was in our cozy parlor at two o'clock in the afternoon, and not in a dark coroner's laboratory at midnight.

Sister Ann William picked up the photographs, but I skipped that section and moved on to the more manageable, if useless, description of Mother Ignatius' clothing. Her attire had been logged in, in great detail—white terrycloth slippers, Grant's brand, size five and a half, medium wear. 100% cotton nightcap and long nightdress, both white, no pattern, no label, probably not commercial products.

The sleepwear was handmade by the convent seamstress, I was sure. I caught sight of more graphic language about Mother Ignatius' body fluids, organs, and genito-urinary system and longed for my theology texts—clean, crisp concepts like hermeneutics and the Hypostatic Union.

I studied Jake Driscoll's face, wishing I had better powers of discernment. I was vaguely distrustful of his boyish charm and overly cooperative manner. But neither could I imagine why he'd poison Mother Ignatius, then take it upon himself to request an autopsy.

Unless it was the perfect cover-up. For all I knew the New York state medical examiner was his brother.

In another scenario, I pictured Jake Driscoll using strychnine or arsenic to do away with Mother Ignatius, then ordering screens for everything else.

I gave a start when he appeared to be reading my mind.

"See, right there," he said, pointing to a long list titled Toxicological Screens. "They did tests for strychnine and arsenic, and a host of other toxins. Even phosgene gas, in case someone mixed some incompatible household cleaners under her nose."

My look must have told him I didn't appreciate his flip attitude. "Sorry, Sisters," he said. "I'm overreacting to what I see as good news." He pointed to the important line at the end of the autopsy report, the medical examiner's opinion. "Death by natural causes."

We handed the sheaf of pages back to him, and nodded as if we'd understood it completely.

"I hope this puts your minds at rest, Sisters. Remember what Our Lord said— 'Let the dead bury their own dead, but you go and proclaim the kingdom of God.'"

"Even the devil can quote scripture, Mr. Driscoll."

He gave me a sideways look that I suspected could turn angry at a moment's notice. Either he's guilty as the devil, I thought, or he thinks I'm crazy.

———————

Sister Ann William and I walked up the stairs in silence, as if the benign autopsy report had taken away our only topic of conversation. Before we parted to go to our separate rooms, I heard her heavy sigh.

"There's still the wake and funeral," she said. "The second night of Mother Ignatius' wake is tonight, and burial services are tomorrow. Remember?"

I let out a deep breath. "We go to ceremonies only for parents, but I plan to make a special novena for Mother Ignatius."

Sister Ann William looked around the empty hallway and lowered her voice. "They say the killer always shows up at wakes and funerals."

"Sister!" My voice came out in a hiss, but not enough to keep her from pursuing her thoughts.

She frowned, creasing her otherwise smooth, fair-skinned forehead. "Don't tell me you're satisfied with that one little autopsy report?"

I shook my head. I wished I could tell her I had no more doubts, but by now Sister Ann William was tuned into me enough to know better. "I guess not. I suppose there are other ways to murder people besides poisoning."

She nodded vigorously. "There certainly are. She could have been smothered, for example. Perhaps a tiny, untraceable bit of a toxic substance in her tea, just enough to weaken her, and then …" I grimaced as Sister Ann William brushed one palm across the other in a rapid motion, causing the books under her arm to fall to the floor with a thud.

We scanned the corridor, expecting doors to fly open, but no one seemed curious about the rumpus.

"Maybe we shouldn't talk about this out here," I said in a whisper.

"You're right." Sister Ann William reclaimed her books and turned toward her room, halfway down the hallway from mine. She paused, running her fingers along her chin. "We're allowed to go to wakes and funerals, if it's someone we're close to," she said. "I think I was close enough to Mother Ignatius, don't you?"

I swallowed hard. I felt responsible for the time she'd already spent entertaining thoughts of murder and researching poisons. But I desperately wanted to hear about the wake. "She was that kind of religious. Close to her charges," I said, calculating how many hours before I could get to confession again.

She smiled, apparently satisfied with my double-talk. "I'll join the group of Sisters from St. Lucy's. They're leaving after dinner, around six-thirty. Perpetual Help Chapel on the Grand Concourse." She paused. "You say the rosary every day, don't you?"

"Yes."

"Well, I'm sure there'll be a priest leading the rosary," she said, as if to urge me to bend the rules for the sake of public prayers to Our Lady.

"I really can't go."

She gave me another of her charming conspiratorial grins. "I'll report back what I see."

Not for the first time in my week in the Bronx, I wished SMI rules were different—I'd have been the first one at Perpetual Help Chapel to inspect the mourners. I imagined a sign on the murderer's forehead, clearly separating him or her from the ranks of the elect, like in the Book of Revelations.

A third angel followed them and said in a loud voice: "If anyone worships the beast and his image and receives his mark on the forehead or on the hand, he, too, will drink of the wine of God's fury."

I shivered and closed the door to my room.

With at least three hours before dinner, I began my homework for Father Barrett's class—a critique of the section of the *Summa Contra Gentiles* dealing with man's likeness to God.

That which is found to perfection in God is found in other beings by some manner of imperfect participation ...

In my case, the emphasis was on imperfect, I thought.

Since I'd studied the *Summa* in an undergraduate course, the assignment posed no challenge. I found my attention wandering, taking in other sounds and sights. A nearly empty bus lumbering down Marian Avenue, rain falling hard on the shrine of the Blessed Virgin in the garden, doors opening and closing in the hallway.

And a conversation in the room next to mine. Sister Teresa, in Room 26, had a guest.

The walls of St. Lucy's dormitory rooms were thin, and I couldn't help overhearing loud sobs mingled with the background noises.

"I don't want to leave school. I can't stand going back to Michigan."

"Well, you're going to have to, Teresa." I recognized Sister Veronique's voice, agitated, urgent. "He certainly won't leave. He'll never give up his career."

I considered running the water in my sink to drown out the sounds or knocking on the wall to alert my neighbors of their lack of privacy. I even thought of leaving the room.

Instead, I took off my bonnet and moved closer to the wall.

Much to my embarrassment, I was disappointed when the Sisters lowered their voices. Could they tell my ear was pressed to the wall? I could hear only phrases. "*... doesn't love you as much as he loves ...*" Muffled words. "*How ... Michigan ... far away from ...* " Choked sobs. "*... have to take care of ... He'll be here long after ...*"

I wondered who "he" was. Father Malbert? I didn't want to believe there was really a romance in progress between Sister Teresa and our chaplain. But I couldn't ignore the teasing about their friendship, their late-night return to St. Lucy's, their heads together in the garden. When Sister Teresa had brought my rosary back to me, she'd spoken of the handyman Father Malbert in terms bordering on intimate.

"He's so-o-o good with his hands," she'd said. The faraway look in her eyes seemed focused on the pair of them in a fixer-upper bungalow built for two.

Mother Julia's slippery slope arguments came back to me. "There's a reason for each rule, Sisters. Once you start taking liberties, all of religious life flies apart, like straw in the wind."

I remembered the foolish crushes most of us had on the priests in our parish. When I was in high school, a particularly handsome young prelate came to St. Leonard's. One of my friends, Joan Marie, claimed she'd found a way to marry him. We'd giggled when she announced her plan. "Well, since Father O'Shea is like God—he can forgive sins and all—I'll just marry God. I'm going to enter the convent and become a Bride of Christ. Then I'll be Father O'Shea's bride, too."

Whether from faulty logic or factors unknown to us, Joan Marie entered and left the convent within a year. Surely Sister Teresa's obvious affection for Father Malbert was no more serious than Joan Marie's for Father O'Shea? It was natural, if immature, to develop a crush on one's spiritual advisor.

The conversation in Room 26 had settled down to an almost inaudible level and I was left to my own imagination. If not Father Malbert, who? Did Sister Teresa love a man in a physical way? Then why wouldn't she just leave her community?

Liberals, I said under my breath. I paced my narrow floor, increasingly frustrated with nuns and priests who wanted change but couldn't deal with the consequences. I constructed a scenario in which Sister Teresa wanted to carry on an affair with a man and still put on her habit every day. Didn't they know they couldn't live in two worlds?

Or was it my own culpability that upset me? I'd been guilty of the same charge—keeping some rules and not others. Selective obedience, Mother Julia would call it. I'd encouraged friendship, not only with another sister, but even a lay man. I was convinced Aidan's recent attention to me stemmed from my initial call to him when my brother needed a place to stay.

I'd held fast to my rituals of prayer and Latin mass and thrown out the basic guidelines that made nuns different from women in the world.

I heard the door to Room 26 open and close—Sister Veronique leaving, I guessed. I sat down at my desk, my bonnetless, hairless head in my hands and wondered when life had become so confusing.

CHAPTER 20

St. Lucy's foyer was crowded with Sisters and guests on the way to dinner, and I found myself trapped in a round of introductions led by Sister Felix. More neighbors and benefactors, I assumed.

"Sisters, this is Mrs. Driscoll, whom some of you already know." She touched the shoulder of a woman with as much white hair as her husband, and a smile equally broad. "And Mrs. Pamela Edson, Father Malbert's sister." She laughed. "His blood sister, that is." Sister Felix linked her arm in Mrs. Edson's, and named us, one by one—Sister Ann William, Sister Miriam, Sister Emmanuel. When her eyes landed on me, she gave me a look that said *behave yourself*.

Both women looked prosperous, in professionally coifed hair, tailored suits, nylons, and pumps. I imagined they were both Catholic college graduates, though I had no evidence other than they had excellent posture and looked comfortable surrounded by nuns. Mrs. Edson seemed much younger than her priest brother, with the same attractive, thin features.

I smiled and slipped around the group, heading downstairs to the refectory. As I passed the recreation room on the basement floor I heard harsh voices—two men arguing it seemed to me. It wouldn't have surprised me if Sister Felix had welcomed in the neighborhood to use our ping pong table. I pictured two players arguing over a point, perhaps needing a referee.

I couldn't resist a glimpse as I passed the slightly open door.

Father Malbert and Father O'Neill. And they weren't holding ping pong paddles.

I tried to tune out the hubbub above me to concentrate on the priests' words. I slowed my step, lingering on the ball of each foot. The tiptoe method of eavesdropping. Not as indecorous as holding my ear to a wall?

The men were clearly at odds with each other, their voices angry. "*... get away with it.*" "*... dean's office ... not up for auction.*"

It was hard to hear more, with the noisy conversation on the landing. I knew the priests' altercation would end once the group started down the stairs. Not wanting to be caught, I entered the phone booth and pretended to make a call until a few people reached the bottom floor. Then I joined the small crowd and entered the refectory.

I took a deep breath. When and where had I learned all these techniques of subterfuge? At Saturday matinees with my sisters? Listening to mysteries on the radio, I decided. *Mr. and Mrs. North, Inner Sanctum, Mr. Keene—Tracer of Lost Persons.*

I wondered if justice would prevail as it did in those days, at the end of every half hour.

———————

With five guests—Mr. and Mrs. Driscoll, Father Malbert and his sister, and Father O'Neill, dinner went on longer than usual. On the one hand, I was happy to be sitting far away from Father O'Neill, lest he ask me for another date. On the other, I was curious about his quarrel with Father Malbert.

In the end, I found it a relief to be seated with Sisters I'd never talked to before. No opportunity for information, but none for rudeness, either.

I wanted to go straight to my room after grace, but the arrangement of stairs at St. Lucy's forced me to walk by a group of Sisters organizing the trip to Perpetual Help Chapel for Mother Ignatius' wake. The rain had stopped, but there was talk of umbrellas and rain hoods and keys for coming in late. The mood seemed more suited to an evening on the town.

"Are you coming with us, Sister Francesca?" asked Sister Jeanne d'Arc, a School Sister of Notre Dame from Michigan.

"No, I ..." I paused.

Sister Jeanne d'Arc gave me a questioning look.

Sister Ann William, who'd come up behind me, filled in the blank. "She has too much reading this evening. Sister Francesca is determined to get all A's," she said with a light laugh.

Grateful as I was for the rescue, I questioned my reluctance to admit my order didn't allow attendance at social functions. Even wakes. Was I suddenly ashamed of SMI customs? A fine martyr I'd make. Apparently I hadn't been helped much by years of reading about young women like Saint Agnes and Saint Maria Goretti, who'd upheld the standards of their faith, preferring death to dishonor.

"Too bad," Sister Veronique said, cleaning her thick glasses with the skirt of her habit. "We're going to a film on campus afterward. They're showing Fellini's 'Nights of Cabiria.' It's playing in the main auditorium at eight o'clock. If you finish your homework, maybe you could join us there."

"It's an old one that's been reissued." Sister Miriam from Room 24 sounded as though she were reading from a movie magazine. "An Italian prostitute with a heart of gold experiences many tests of her faith in human nature."

"Tragicomic," added another Sister.

"My English professor says it's spiritually enlightening," said another, pulling on clear plastic rain boots.

The last movie I'd seen was 'The Song of Bernadette,' in our Motherhouse assembly room. A film that deserved to be called spiritually enlightening. I wasn't ready to put a Lady of the Night on the same level of edification as the Saint of Lourdes. "We don't go to movies. SMIs, that is," I said, finally willing to speak up for my commitment.

Sister Miriam laughed. "Neither do we. Yet. But it's not stopping me. I know it'll change soon. Why miss an opportunity?" With a swift motion, Sister Miriam flipped off her veil, revealing short blond hair that lacked styling, as if she'd decided to let it grow recently.

"How are we to serve the world if we don't know what's going on in it?" Sister Veronique asked no one in particular. She tucked her black veil under the collar of a rain cloak, her white habit hanging below.

I felt my face flush. Now that I'd found my voice, I couldn't hold back. "We serve God, not the world. We pray for the world," I said. I sounded reproachful even to myself. Frustrated at my own inadequacy, I resolved to find a middle ground between pusillanimity and arrogance as soon as possible.

I made a visit to St. Lucy's chapel, offering all my night prayers for my father and for the other patients at Fishkill General, especially those with no one to remember them.

Back in my room, I couldn't keep my mind off Sister Ann William's impending adventure at Mother Ignatius' wake. I pictured her slithering through the crowd of mourners, looking for a killer. Perhaps he or she would be considerate enough to give an outward sign — throwing himself across Mother Ignatius' body, uttering a loud confession after the rosary, beating his breast in repentance. I doubted it.

It was time to bring a measure of reality and order to the ramblings of my mind. I took out a tablet meant to hold notes on the omnipotence of God and His essential goodness and began instead a case file on the alleged murder of St. Lucy's deceased Mother Superior.

What reasons did I have for postulating foul play? First, Mother Ignatius had been afraid of something or someone the night she died. Second, she'd had an impromptu meeting around eight-fifteen, a confrontation overheard by Sister Ann William, and denied by Sister Felix. Third, there were the contents of her desk — a cuff link and the letters from Mother Consiliatrix, about D, E, and F. Whatever they were.

I hesitated to add my personal experience — the motor scooter accident on Southern Boulevard — preferring to think it was unrelated. The alternative was too frightening.

My snooping hadn't turned up much, and my suspects were evaporating. Jake Driscoll was being too kind to think of him as a murderer. He was a family man I'd heard, a pillar of the Church. His wife looked like the model of the parish Sodality President. Sister Teresa seemed to have her own problems with an unnamed "he," and I had little more to condemn Sister Felix than her simple lie to me about Mother Ignatius' last meeting—which was none of my business in the first place. I wondered about her obvious attempt to discredit me in the eyes of my superiors, but I could hardly blame her, given my rude behavior.

My case against Father Malbert seemed to rest purely on his unorthodox theology. His entry into Mother Ignatius office was nothing more than I had done myself.

To further quench my wild imagination, I had an autopsy report and a professional opinion that made a lot of sense—a seventy-five-year-old woman had died in her sleep from natural causes. The many discussions Sister Ann William and I engaged in about lethal flower petals and a closet full of drugs on campus had been interesting, but nothing more.

Looking over my list, I realized the only possibility for further investigation lay with a nun in Albuquerque, New Mexico. Reviewing the dates of the correspondence I had in my desk, I calculated Mother Ignatius was due to write to her on September 19. She was dead by the next morning. Assuming she'd written in the afternoon, which was the custom for most orders, Mother Ignatius would have put her last letter in the outgoing mail before her evening meeting. Would the murderer have confiscated it from the outbox in the foyer? Did Mother Consiliatrix even know Mother Ignatius had died, or was she waiting for that next installment?

I had a powerful urge to contact Mother Consiliatrix and settle these questions. I was sure she could provide resolution for me—confirmation that Mother Ignatius' concerns were minor, having to do with small matters of housekeeping at St. Lucy's, or perhaps a worry about the budget and rising costs of food and altar wine. Then I'd be able to close the entire episode and return to the real reason I was in the Bronx, my graduate studies.

I had her return address in New Mexico, but the mail was too slow for my purposes. I looked longingly at the convent telephone number, also on the letterhead. Dare I think about making a long-distance call?

It was one thing to make a ten-cent local call, as I did to Aidan, quite another to dial across the country. I'd been allotted one dollar a day for expenses—a drink from the cafeteria at lunchtime or bus fare if I needed it. So far, I'd walked to campus every day and bought one glass of iced tea. I was four dollars ahead.

Not that Mother Julia had said, "Use the money for whatever comes up, Sister." But I was already past the point of scrupulousness in that regard.

If four dollars wasn't enough, I might have to walk to school through the winter months and stick to water at lunch on campus. Not a huge burden for the payoff of information from a person Mother Ignatius trusted.

Like most East Coast natives, I had a deficient knowledge of geography. I could only picture New Mexico very far away, right next to California. Was it earlier there or later? Earlier, if I remembered correctly from my seventh-grade class in time zones. It's only mid-afternoon there. All the better. As if waking up a nun was the worst sin I'd be committing this week.

The financing of the venture turned out to be the easy part. Once I dropped my coins in the slot, what would I say? "I'm a new friend of Mother Ignatius, and …" Or "I was so sorry to hear about the death of your friend, and I was wondering …" Every sentence I came up with trailed off. I gave brief consideration to posing as a policewoman. "I'm Officer Wickes, investigating the murder of your colleague."

In the end I decided to go with the simple truth, that Mother Ignatius had confided in me shortly before her death, and I was suspicious. I knocked on three doors before I'd converted all my small bills into coins. I passed up the wall phone on my floor and went down to the basement to the closed-in booth. I pulled the door shut and dialed New Mexico.

"Good afternoon. Sacred Heart." A young woman's voice, sounding too close to be in another time zone. I pictured a high school girl serving as all-purpose secretary/receptionist/server of tea and cookies/sweeper of the sacristy and sanctuary, like my job at St. Leonard's rectory at that age.

I swallowed hard and thought about hanging up. No harm done, just a few glasses of iced tea lost.

"Hello?" The sharpness of the tone shook me into action, less patient than I'd been trained to be in the same position.

"Hello. Uh, good afternoon. Is Mother Consiliatrix there, please?"

"She's not in at the moment. May I ask who's calling?"

The first tough question. But at least I'd read the handwriting on the letters correctly. I'd half-expected to hear, "You mean Mother Consolata?" Or even "Mother Cuthburga?"

I looked at the wall around St. Lucy's pay phone. Names, numbers, and assorted swirls decorated the top page of a note pad that hung from a small bulletin board. I focused on large, elaborate letters—NY—doodled in blue ink, styled like the logo of the New York Yankees, my father's favorite team.

"I'm calling from New York," I said, as if it mattered to the nuns in Albuquerque. "Sister Francesca." I gave my name in a way that implied I was an important person, perhaps the Cardinal's assistant.

"May I take a message? We expect her back this evening."

Another complication. After a pause—I was sure the young woman wondered why it took me so long to answer her simple queries—I left my name and the number on the phone in the booth.

"May I say what this is regarding?"

I drew a deep breath and cleared my throat to fill in the silence.

"Tell her it's about Mother Ignatius."

CHAPTER 21

B y eight o'clock, about the time my St. Lucy's Hall neighbors would
be watching "Nights of Cabiria," I was on my bed, fully dressed,
waiting for Sister Ann William. Although the hours for the wake
were seven to nine, I hadn't expected her to stay that long. Either things
were going very well for the amateur detective, or very badly.

I played mind games, predicting which would come first, a return
call from Mother Consiliatrix or the appearance of Sister Ann William.
I hadn't allowed for a third possibility. When I answered my bell
around nine-thirty, I heard Mother Julia's voice.

"Your sister, Patricia, called me," she said slowly, as if she were
keeping pace with a dirge.

I felt my knees weaken, my mouth go dry. I knew Patty would call
the Motherhouse so late in the evening for only one reason.

"Your father has gone to God, Sister Francesca. He died peacefully
about an hour ago."

A surge of sadness flowed through my body, blocking out the light
on the stairway, and I had to hold back tears. *Gone to God.* I tried to
summon an image of my father as part of a Botticelli painting, floating
to heaven, the Beatific Vision ready to embrace him, my mother
holding out her arms.

"Sister Francesca?" Mother Julia's voice was soft, gentler than I'd
ever heard it.

"Yes, Mother."

"You may use your September allowance for a bus ticket, Sister. Finish your week of classes tomorrow and plan to be here for confession on Saturday. Then you may attend the wake and visit your family on Sunday. You may also attend the funeral service, on Monday morning."

"Thank you, Mother."

"All our masses through this weekend will be offered for your father's soul, and for your family, Sister. And several Sisters have asked to accompany you to the services."

"Thank you, Mother."

I hung up the phone and leaned against the wall, my senses overloaded. I could see the tiny cracks in the ceiling paint, hear the ticking of the clock in the main parlor two floors below, taste the Communion wafer I'd had early in the morning.

My father's voice took over my brain as I walked back to my room, nearly bumping into a Sister on her way to the showers. From some trick of memory, I saw Brendan Patrick Wickes again as the star of a parish show one St. Patrick's Day. He'd stood front and center, in an ugly green costume that nearly made baby Timothy throw up. He'd sung with all his heart.

> *Here lies the Mick that threw a brick*
> *but he'll never throw another.*
> *For calling me a P.I.A.,*
> *he now lays undercover.*
> *On his tombstone you can read*
> *if you care to rub her:*
> *Here lies the Mick that threw a brick*
> *But he'll never throw another.*

I brushed away tears and saw my father as clearly as when I was ten years old, with his twinkle, his shuffle, his lumbering gait. As my father sang the ditty, never came out "niver" and he refused to tell us what a P.I.A. was.

Now, I'll niver know, I thought, and I cried as if that were the saddest thing about my father's death.

"Now I feel doubly sorry," Sister Ann William said when I told her of my father's death. She'd knocked on my door at close to eleven o'clock, explaining how she'd allowed herself to be talked into 'Nights of Cabiria.' "And afterward we went to a place called Jahn's for ice cream," she said, her voice repentant, as if she'd eaten roast beef on a Friday.

"No need to apologize, Sister. I'm fine."

"I'm sure you could be excused from class tomorrow if you asked."

I shook my head. "It's the first class in research methods, and I don't want to miss it. There's no reason to be in Potterstown tomorrow, anyway."

Except to be with my sisters and brother, I thought. But I'd given up that comfort when I took my vows. Only Timothy would have a hard time understanding my choice.

Sister Ann William and I stood on opposite sides of my threshold, whispering, although the hallway was noisy with Sisters returning from an apparently eventful evening.

"What about Mother Ignatius' wake?" I asked her.

"I didn't think you'd want to talk about it." She paused and gave me a sympathetic look. "Under the circumstances?"

The anticipation of a weekend with what was left of my family did put wakes in a new light. I shuddered to think of someone attending my father's services with the ulterior motive of observing the guests. On the other hand, Sister Ann William had already carried out that unpleasant duty, Mother Ignatius' killer was still at large, and we needed all the information we could get.

"Why don't you come in and tell me who was there."

Sister Ann William stepped into my room. I motioned her to my chair and sat on the edge of my bed, ready to hear evidence. "Well, the seven or eight of us from St. Lucy's, of course. Plus Mr. and Mrs. Driscoll and lots of priests. Sister Felix sat with a young woman who was introduced as Mother Ignatius' grandniece from Maine."

"I thought she didn't have any relatives."

"None close by. Just this one, I guess. It was nice that Father Malbert addressed her by name when he gave a little eulogy."

"Was he wearing khakis?" As soon as I said it, I regretted the uncharitable remark. Sister Ann William stifled a laugh and did me the courtesy of not answering the question.

"I was surprised at his talk—very touching and poetic. He said something like Saint Peter must have thought she was an angel, arriving in lily white, head to toe."

"That is nice."

She frowned, appearing to remember a distasteful aspect. "And then he said something almost embarrassing—he said, 'Of course, I have no firsthand experience. I'm just assuming Sisters wear only white at night' Everyone else seemed to think it was amusing."

Father Malbert's patronizing attitude bothered me, too, but I was able to resist a sarcastic retort. One of my pet peeves was how people often treated nuns as if they were children, prone to giggling at the slightest mention of personal or intimate matters.

"So you didn't see anyone suspicious?" I asked, although I was at a loss as to how I'd define suspect behavior.

She shook her head. "At least a dozen Sisters from Mother Ignatius' community were there." Sister Ann William held her hand a few inches above her head to represent the high white headpiece that characterized Mother Ignatius and Sister Felix's habit. "Very few lay people attended. We left right after the rosary. Then everyone but me was going to the movie, and I didn't want to walk home alone, so I gave in and went. I think my superior would understand. I closed my eyes at some unseemly parts, but on the whole it was an interesting story."

"I'm sure it was a wise choice, Sister, for safety reasons," I told her, as if I were any model of decision making lately.

"I wish I could go to Potterstown with you. Maybe if I call Mother …"

I shook my head. "No need, Sister, but I really appreciate your offer."

I thought of Mother Julia's most likely reaction to a "friend" arriving with me—not favorable. I could hear her as clearly as if she were perched on my sink watching us. "It's not appropriate for you to form a particular friendship with anyone, Sister Francesca, let alone a Sister of another order."

There was a time when I would have agreed wholeheartedly with her imaginary voice, but not this evening.

———————

While Mother Ignatius' body was being delivered to the earth, I attended my Friday morning class in theological research methods. Just the distraction I needed, although I didn't forget to pray for her.

Ashes to ashes and dust to dust. Would the souls of Mother Ignatius and my father meet? It was a question for a more experienced theologian than I was, but I thought they'd have liked each other if they'd met. Two old school Catholics.

No more than ten minutes into Dr. Baron's lecture, I realized the papers I'd written in college weren't worthy of the term "research." A small man, with a weak voice and thin graying hair, Dr. Baron was the only lay person on the Theology Department faculty. I wondered if, like Aidan, he'd dropped out of seminary. An image came into my mind unbidden—Dr. Aidan Connors, theology professor, a few years from now, wearing a pale blue sweater, standing before a class of graduate students.

This was the only one of my classes Aidan wasn't also enrolled in. I wondered what he'd chosen instead. Through with mental wandering, I sat up and tuned in, in time to hear our term assignment.

"A substantial research paper using a distinctive theological methodology," Dr. Baron said, hefting a pile of textbooks in the air. "This is graduate school, not an extension of your undergraduate studies. You may choose among textual, historical, and social methods, insofar as they contribute to constructive theology."

Clearly a well-organized seminar leader, Dr. Baron had advised us of the project in advance through a notice that came with our registration packets. I'd already decided to write my paper on Saint Augustine of Hippo, considered by many scholars as the first Christian theologian. When I entered the convent, I'd wanted to take the name of his mother, Saint Monica. Her prayers for her son brought him out of a worldly, sinful life into the Church and ultimately to sainthood. I had grand designs about my ability to do the same for my wayward brother Timothy.

However, there already was a Sister Monica, SMI, as well as a Sister Mary Monica and a Sister Monica Ann. I was too late. In the end I became satisfied with my religious name, my patron, Saint Francis of Assisi, and my connection to Great-aunt Francesca Sforzo.

"They all talk to each other up there, anyway," Mother Julia had said, her lips stretching into a rare grin.

Ten of us had enrolled in Dr. Baron's class: five Sisters and five young men dressed in the telltale black pants of seminarians. I noticed each man wore something distinctively not seminary garb—brightly colored socks, an elaborate ski sweater over a black shirt, and a few maroon sweatshirts with St. Alban's logo in gold.

I didn't recognize any of the Sisters as St. Lucy's residents and assumed they commuted from their local convents. I found myself wistful about living "at home," sure that all my difficulties of the past week were a direct consequence of residing outside my Motherhouse.

One of the nuns, who referred to herself by her full name—Sister Ruth Fitzpatrick—wore a habit modified in the extreme. Her street-length dark green dress appeared to be store-bought. A bronze cross hanging from a cord around her neck was the only sign of a religious affiliation. I wondered vaguely how long it would take to grow my hair to a length appropriate for public viewing. I'd never considered its wild shade of red natural in the first place.

The newly deceased Brendan Patrick Wickes slipped to the back corner of my mind as I involved myself in each person's preliminary ideas for a term project. The construction of arguments in theological disciplines. The relationship between theology and social theory. The discipleship of Saint Anthony of the Desert. All fascinating research topics.

To my surprise, I was impressed by Sister Ruth Fitzpatrick's proposal.

"I'd like to pursue the idea of a discipleship of equals," she said. Her voice was soft, her words revealing a thoughtful attitude. "I've been reading a collection of essays showing feminist methodology in textual interpretation… women who emerged as exceptions to the patriarchy. My tentative title is 'Feminist Critique of Prophetic Traditions.' I intend to stay within the bounds of Scripture."

"Should be interesting," Dr. Baron said.

I had to agree.

When I caught up with Sister Ann William in front of the student union building, she was talking to two other St. Lucy's residents—Sisters Teresa and Veronique had asked to join us on our trip home.

"I was so sorry to hear about your father," Sister Teresa said. "I've asked my Motherhouse to offer mass for him on Monday during his funeral service."

"Me, too," Sister Veronique said.

"Thank you very much," I said, happy that spiritual bouquets had survived the changes in the Church, at least so far.

We walked four abreast on the campus path, splitting up when faced with foot traffic from the other direction. Several times other pedestrians interrupted our conversation with greetings learned in grade school.

"Good morning, Sisters," from a group of three young women whose hair was longer than their skirts.

"Can I help you with your books?" from a construction worker who'd crossed the lawn with his arms outstretched, ready to ease our burden. I wondered if his coffee break was long enough to allow him to walk us all the way home.

We all agreed we'd have been disappointed if we hadn't heard the most commonly asked type of question—" Do you know Sister Grace Marie from St. Agatha's in White Plains?" As if everyone in a habit knew everyone else who wore one.

I had suppressed my strong desire to ask Sister Teresa about the drama in Room 26 the previous afternoon, but she brought it up herself.

"I hope we didn't disturb you yesterday, Francesca." Sister Teresa called to me from the end of our row of four. "Veronique and I were having a little disagreement." She laughed, as if to indicate it was just a silly spat between friends.

Veronique nodded her agreement. "I guess we've been seeing too much of each other," she said in a playful tone.

I suspected they'd arranged this ambush to dispel gossip or rumor I might be tempted to spread. I hoped they'd explain further what their argument had been about, perhaps naming the "he" they'd mentioned in unflattering tones. But Sister Ann William broke in with another topic.

"Wasn't that a nice little talk Father Malbert gave at Mother Ignatius' wake?" she asked.

Sister Teresa frowned and shrugged her shoulders. "He does have the gift," she said, her tone grudging.

A Gift of the Holy Spirit? Or the gift of blarney? I wondered, surprised at her attitude.

"He'll need it in his new job," Sister Veronique said with a touch of sarcasm. "His bright career ..."

"Veronique." Sister Teresa interrupted her with a tone meant to end the subject. I guessed this outpouring was not part of their original script.

"Oh, Teresa, it'll be out soon enough."

Sister Teresa sighed and shrugged her shoulders. "You're right." She turned to include both me and Sister Ann William who had fallen behind as we crossed Webster Avenue. "Father Malbert's been named Dean of Academic Affairs."

"I still can't figure Father O'Neill choosing him. He hates him," Sister Veronique said.

"That's a little strong," Sister Teresa said. "Anyway, the official announcement won't be out until tomorrow."

"But of course, Teresa got the news first. It's the little perk the new dean chose to give her," Sister Veronique said.

Sister Ann William and I seemed to be unnecessary to the conversation our companions were having. I had the feeling it was a continuation of the discussion that I'd eavesdropped on.

Sister Ann William, always the first to recover from awkward situations, offered a good cover for my uneasiness.

"How nice for Father Malbert," she said, leaving me to wonder if Texans had special training in social grace.

"Nice, all right. He doesn't care what he leaves behind," Sister Veronique said.

"So he's withdrawing as chaplain at St. Lucy's?" I asked, trying to keep the hopefulness out of my voice.

"No, he'll still be around for that. He's not about to give up anything that really matters to him."

I couldn't help feeling Sister Ann William and I had been listening in on a discussion that had started the day before in Room 26.

We turned up East 198th Street, holding down skirts that fluttered in unexpected gusts of wind. Sister Teresa walked ahead of us in silence. Behind her Sister Ann William and Sister Veronique shared anecdotes about their younger siblings.

I walked alone a few yards behind. I wondered what Father Malbert had done to alienate his biggest fans. With no effort, I created a scenario that named Father Malbert as the "he" who didn't love Sister Teresa as much as she loved him, who might be responsible for sending her back to Michigan, who'd do anything to save his career.

Including murder? I wondered.

CHAPTER 22

Sister Felix had posted a note on the bulletin board by the mailboxes. I was pleased to read that masses on Saturday through Monday would be offered for the repose of the soul of Brendan Patrick Wickes. Masses celebrated by Father Malbert held the same benefits as those by any other priest, including His Holiness Pope Paul VI, I reminded myself.

Sister Ann William knew I had only one suitcase, an enormous silver metal box, so she kindly suggested I borrow her new leather garment bag for my weekend trip. Without considering whether Mother Julia would approve, I accepted, and packed in it my Sunday habit, one clean chemise, stockings, and night clothes.

While I assembled my wardrobe, I tried to prepare my mind for Potterstown. I couldn't ignore completely the fleeting images of the past week's puzzle, but on the whole, I'd pushed Mother Ignatius' death so far back in my mind that even my mother's passing ten years ago seemed more recent.

My most vivid memory of that day was of Timothy, in a white shirt and little black tie, refusing consolation from any of us—especially Father Mulrooney, whom he seemed to blame for the loss of his mother.

"You said she'd be all right if I prayed," he'd told our pastor, his eyes red from crying. He seemed much too young to shoulder grief.

"I said *things* would be all right, Timothy, meaning we would all care for you. I didn't promise God wouldn't take your dear mother."

Father Mulrooney's meticulous logic worked for me— God's will was the best explanation for everything, good and bad in my life. But the reasoning was lost on my eight-year-old brother. He refused to continue his assignment as an altar boy at St. Leonard's, and had to be forced to attend mass from then on. I was fairly sure he'd never gone willingly since.

I picked up my missal and pulled out the card Patty had designed for the mourners at my mother's funeral. The only picture I had of my mother was the grainy black and white image on the two-by-four-inch holy card. On one side was her photograph, bordered in black, cropped from a snapshot taken on my parents' twentieth wedding anniversary. She died a month later. Under the photo, in an elaborate type of style, was the prayer of St. Francis of Assisi. *Lord, make me an instrument of Thy peace…* Important dates in Helen Louise Sforzo's life were listed on the back.

> *Born June 3, 1912*
> *Married to Brendan Patrick Wickes, October 5, 1935*
> *Mother of Susan Marie, August 20, 1937*
> *Mother of Patricia Catherine, June 27, 1939*
> *Mother of Kathleen Anne, July 15, 1943*
> *Mother of Gabriella, April 14, 1945*
> *Mother of Timothy Edward, December 3, 1946*
> *Died November 23, 1955*

I smiled as I thought of Gabriella and her whining. "I'm the only one in the family without a middle name."

"We thought Gabriella Wickes was enough of a mouthful," my father would tell her, pretending to struggle over the syllables.

To make up for it, she'd said, she chose *Bernadette*, the longest saint's name she could think of, at confirmation. I hadn't seen Gabriella Bernadette in a couple of months, since she'd been ill with a flu on my last family visiting day in Potterstown.

If I could change a single SMI rule, I thought, it would be the one forbidding Sisters to keep photographs except as they appeared on holy cards given out at funerals. I hoped Patty had thought to put our father's picture on his card. I looked out my window at the gold and red asters in front of Our Lady's shrine and drafted an amendment to the Holy Rule: Each Sister of Mary Immaculate shall be permitted one photograph of each member of her immediate family. The frame shall be simple …

Two rings. Pause. Five rings.

I abandoned my hypothetical role as Superior General of the SMIs and went down the hall to answer the intercom signal.

"There's a call for you on my line, Sister Francesca." Sister Felix sounded unhappy about the inconvenience. "Did you give this number to anyone?"

"No, Sister, I'm sorry. I don't even know your number."

"It's long distance. From New Mexico."

I sucked in my breath. "Thank you, Sister."

"You'll have to come to my office to answer it."

"I'll be right there."

I hurried down the stairs, wondering why the call had gone to Sister Felix's phone, in what was Mother Ignatius' office until that morning. I'd used the pay phone in the basement to contact Mother Consiliatrix. I'd left her secretary the number for the Sisters' line upstairs, since only those on the first floor could hear the pay phone ring. As far as I knew, neither of the lines went to Sister Felix's office.

Sister Felix was waiting at her door when I reached the ground floor. She motioned me to her desk, and stood next to me, arms folded. The frown lines crossing her forehead seemed to struggle against her tight headpiece.

I swallowed hard and picked up the receiver. "Hello. This is Sister Francesca." I turned my back to Sister Felix, brushing her wide veil.

"Hello? Sister Francesca? I have a message that you called me." Mother Consiliatrix's voice was high-pitched and shaky. She sounded so much like Mother Ignatius, I had the sudden image of my temporary Superior alive and well, living in Albuquerque, her alleged death a big out-of-season April Fool joke. "You said it was regarding Mother Ignatius?"

"Yes, Mother, thank you for returning my call." I put my hand over the mouthpiece and gave Sister Felix a pleading look, casting my eyes toward her door. She let me know by an intensified scowl she was unhappy about the arrangement. She took quick, angry steps out of the office, leaving the door ajar.

I told myself I'd worry later about Sister Felix's likely eavesdropping. Since she answered the phone, she already knew I'd contacted Mother Ignatius' friend.

My jaw tensed as I tried to remember what I'd rehearsed for my conversation with a nun I'd never met. A wave of embarrassment came over me as I realized I'd read her private correspondence. I wondered if policemen felt as guilty when they had to delve into the personal lives of victims and witnesses.

"Mother, I was wondering if you'd heard about Mother Ignatius' death."

"Yes, Sister. Her Superior General knows we've corresponded for years. She was kind enough to call me." She paused, then filled in the gap left by my tongue-tied silence. "Mother Ignatius never mentioned you." Her tone was more a question than an accusation.

"We'd just met. I'm a new graduate student. I live at St. Lucy's Hall."

She laughed. "I know where you live, Sister. I called Mother Ignatius' old number, to be sure I was indeed responding to someone at St. Lucy's. I didn't recognize the number you left."

Good detective work, I thought. Mother Consiliatrix is just the person I need to help solve this puzzle. I launched into my prepared presentation. "Mother, I'm sure it's hard for you to trust someone you've never met. But I assure you I have only the best intentions. I may have been the last person Mother Ignatius communicated with before she died." I struggled to keep my voice low, but loud enough to reach New Mexico.

The other end of the line was quiet, the long pause concerning me. I pictured Mother Consiliatrix pushing a button on the phone to call Mother Julia in Potterstown and have her dispatch Sister Magdalene back to the Bronx immediately. That, or the Bronx police to have me arrested. I cleared my throat to remind Mother Consiliatrix of my presence.

"What is it you want of me, Sister?" she asked. Her tone turned serious, as if she'd just realized I hadn't called to invite her to a memorial service for our mutual friend.

Time to get to the point. I took advantage of new noises in the hallway to drown me out in case Sister Felix was listening. "I know Mother Ignatius was concerned about something, and afraid of someone. I thought you might know more about it." I spoke quickly, in case the hall fell silent again. I left out the part about reading her mail.

I was breathing hard, as if I'd been running around the bases for Immaculate High's softball team. I thought I might faint from anxiety. What if Mother Ignatius' death was nothing more than it seemed? Then I'd bothered this old nun, costing her a long-distance call, for nothing. I couldn't decide if that would be better or worse than confirmation of a murder in my residence hall.

"I'm not sure I can help you, Sister. I haven't seen Mother Ignatius since a retreat we were on together nearly two years ago."

My turn again. Mother Consiliatrix was letting me do all the work. My only recourse seemed to be a lie. "I know about D, E, and F," I said, recalling the code in the letters I'd read. Only a partial lie, since I was convinced Mother Ignatius would have told me if she had lived. I heard Mother Consiliatrix draw in her breath. "Does that sound familiar to you?"

"This is very difficult for me, Sister," she said. "Mother Ignatius and I shared confidences."

"Please, Mother. I can't help feeling she wanted me to do something about what troubled her. She asked to see me that same evening, but before she could meet me, she was ..." I glanced toward the hallway. The edge of Sister Felix's habit and one shiny black shoe were visible, peeking from behind the door. I turned back to the phone, frustrated at the limitations of being virtually in front of Sister Felix as I talked. "Mother Consiliatrix, I promise you on the soul of my own mother, that I will not use the information you give me unless it becomes legally or morally necessary."

I heard a sigh that gave me reason to hope. "Very well, Sister. I can only trust my instincts. And you do sound sincere. Yes, indeed, Mother Ignatius was worried about her obligation to report something she'd learned serendipitously. It involved real estate, and ... some other goings on."

I bit my lips in an effort not to gasp audibly while my mind skipped over the connecting steps. From real estate deal to Driscoll & Sons. "Did she say who it was?" I nearly tripped over my tongue to avoid prompting her with Jake Driscoll's name.

"No, no names ever," Mother Consiliatrix said, as if I should know better.

"Is there anything else you can tell me? I think I know the deal in question, but it would help if I had even one more clue." And then what? I asked myself. Go to the police? I clenched my fists in frustration. After a long pause, she continued, speaking so slowly I thought she might stop altogether.

"She said only that a member of the St. Alban's community—I can't be more specific than that—was involved in a fraudulent real estate deal. Money was donated to the school in exchange for a favorable decision. I'm not sure of the details, but what should have been a sealed bidding process was made known to one individual so he would win a contract for new buildings on campus."

Mother Consiliatrix sighed. She sounded exhausted, as if speaking to me was a great strain. I couldn't blame her.

"No wonder Mother Ignatius was upset," I said, too loudly I realized, when I heard shuffling at the doorway. Sister Felix was making no secret of her impatience and her curiosity. Matter "D" for Driscoll was now clear to me, but I needed to complete my list. "What about the other problems, Mother?" I meant E and F, and I guessed Mother Consiliatrix probably had surmised by now I seen her letters. Good detective that she was.

"There were other burdens Mother Ignatius was carrying, Sister. A St. Lucy's Hall Sister and a priest violating their vows. Not illegally, mind you, but nevertheless ... Who is responsible for the integrity of religious life if not those who wear the habit?" I suspected Mother Consiliatrix didn't expect an answer. I uttered a sound of agreement and waited for her to continue. "And there was one other matter of manipulating the administration for personal gain."

I blew out a soft breath, wondering if Mother Consiliatrix was being deliberately vague. I couldn't blame her if she was. She had no reason to trust me with names and dates.

Still, I tried one last question. "Did you save Mother Ignatius' letters?"

"No, indeed, Sister," she said in a sharp voice, causing me to regret the final intrusion. "I thought it best to destroy them, but I doubt I would give them to you even if I could."

"I understand. Thank you, Mother. You've been a great help."

"I don't know what you plan to do with the information, Sister ..."

"I honestly don't, either."

"Do be careful, Sister Francesca."

I hung up the phone, chilled to the bone, in spite of a comfortable temperature in the room. Out of curiosity, I took a quick look around the office as I left, as if I'd hoped to find an incriminating piece of evidence. All I saw were partially unpacked boxes and a collection of spiritual reading filling one bookshelf.

From the look on Sister Felix's face, now staring directly at me from the doorway, she might have been the one Mother Consiliatrix warned me to be careful of.

I hurried past her.

CHAPTER 23

F riday, mid-afternoon, there wasn't much traffic through the foyer. Most Sisters were either on campus or doing research at the 42nd Street Library. I made a visit to chapel, then went upstairs.

It felt strange to be in my room with a bag packed, only a week after I'd arrived at St. Lucy's. Alone at my desk, things didn't seem as clear to me as they had while I'd been on the phone to New Mexico.

One confusing phrase was Mother Consiliatrix's "a member of St. Alban's community." Not the way I'd have described Jake Driscoll. Apparently he was a presence around the campus and St. Lucy's Hall long before Sister Felix invited him to dinner, so much that Mother Ignatius had thought of him as part of the community.

I tore a piece of paper from my Church History notebook, and made a list, matching the letters in Mother Ignatius' code with what I'd just learned. I had three issues, as the Mothers referred to them, and three letters.

D — Driscoll, real estate crime, owner of cuff link? Secular issue.

E — ?

F — Felix, sinner with E? I couldn't picture cold, steely-eyed Sister Felix, with her witch-like features, in a violation of the vow of chastity with anyone, but I had to allow the possibility. Religious issue.

Or

F — Father Malbert, sinner with E? Religious issue.

I looked at my chart. Who was E? There was a Sister Emmanuel in the house, but she seemed one of the more sensible nuns, among the few who didn't go to the movies. I certainly hadn't observed untoward behavior between her and Father Malbert. I wondered why the letters weren't D, F, and T for Teresa. Perhaps the two extra horizontal lines on the E were ink smudges, and the letter was in fact a T. I doubted it. Mother Consiliatrix's letter was neatly written, and I had the feeling from our brief conversation that she wouldn't have mailed a messy letter across the country.

The question marks in my chart left me unsatisfied. I had only the slimmest of evidence that what had bothered Mother Ignatius was related to people I knew personally. With great reluctance, I scribbled a more realistic list.

D — ?
E — ?
F — ?
Secular issue #1: real estate deal
Secular issue #2: ?
Religious issue: violation of chastity. Who?

I felt no smarter than a child just learning her catechism. I wished Sister Ann William were around to hear a review of my conversation with Mother Consiliatrix and help with the alphabet puzzle. She'd left immediately after our walk home, to join a study group at a lay student's apartment a block away—something I wasn't allowed to do. I wondered at my continual comparison of SMI rules to those of other orders.

I put my notepad with its scribbling in the desk with the other so-called evidence in the case—the cuff link and Mother Consiliatrix's letters. I added a mental record of my accident on Southern Boulevard, in case it was connected, and closed the drawer on the memory.

I settled down and organized the notes I'd take with me to Potterstown over the weekend. I wasn't sure how much time Mother Julia would allow with my family, but I expected I'd have a good amount of time for study.

A couple of hours spent in earlier centuries—the fifth with Saint Augustine and the thirteenth with Saint Thomas Aquinas—helped my mood considerably. I constructed a bibliography of Augustine's writings against heretics for my research seminar. Preparation for

Father Glanz's class sent me to texts on how the early Christian communities contended with their secular culture. Not much has changed, I noted.

I didn't think of Potterstown or Mother Ignatius until I heard the bell for dinner, when all the problems of the present century flooded back into my brain. At the same time, Sister Ann William appeared at my door.

"Anything new since I saw you?" She laughed at what she apparently thought was a silly question.

"A lot, in fact. I'll tell you after dinner." Sister Ann William frowned, as if she was annoyed she'd left my side, where excitement reigned.

"Just a quick tiny hint?" she asked, in her irresistible drawl.

"It's a long story. Do you mind being late for dinner?"

She smiled and shook her head.

We stepped out of line, into the small parlor. I was surprised how short a time it took for me to bring Sister Ann William up to date. To give her a meaningful timeline, I summarized the episodes: my snooping in Mother Ignatius office, reading her correspondence from Mother Consiliatrix, and the return call from New Mexico. Long and intense in real life, the events fit nicely into a four-sentence précis.

I finished the story in a soft voice after we attached ourselves to the back of the line for the refectory. The Sisters in front of us seemed too busy discussing the latest campus film to care about our conversation.

"So, there's definitely a real estate scam going on," I said. "She wouldn't name names, so I'm not sure who the corrupt developer is."

"We can at least eliminate one, just by asking. Remember how easy it was the last time?"

"With Mr. Driscoll?"

She nodded. I'd also thought about confronting Jake Driscoll. I envisioned the interaction—he'd be waiting for me, ready to hand over his financial records, with a caustic "I thought you'd never ask."

"But how would we recognize a shady deal even if he spread his bookkeeping at our feet?" I asked Sister Ann William, now holding the door to the refectory for me.

"I see your point."

We took places together at the end of the long table—Sister Felix had abandoned the custom of special cards to identify each Sister's seat. We'd been so busy whispering, with our heads together, neither of us noticed the guests at the head of the table. We made "hmpf" sounds in unison, asking each other if we'd ever have a meal again without lay people.

Jake Driscoll sat on Sister Felix's left, Father Malbert on her right, and his sister, Mrs. Edson, next to him.

Having little choice, Sister Ann William and I joined the conversation of the Sisters near us. None of the popular topics particularly interested me. Impossibly long papers assigned by Father O'Neill. Fascination with students at a downtown campus who were burning their underwear to make a point about the war in Vietnam. And the new Student Union Building, which would include a 1000-seat auditorium. Too bad it wouldn't be ready for the winter festival of Fellini and Bergman films, which were sure to be meaningful.

Sister Ann William and I made polite contributions whenever possible, but all the topics seemed to pale in significance compared to real estate fraud, infidelity to sacred vows, and murder.

I perked up my ears only once.

"I guess Sister Felix will finally be made Superior here," I heard from a Sister I didn't know.

"About time," said the Sister across from her, whom I recognized as an old-timer. "Sister Felix told us she expected Mother Ignatius to retire when I got here five years ago."

Retire how? I wondered.

———————————

After dinner I steered Sister Ann William toward the garden. "It's better to talk outside," I said, feeling like a Communist spy worried about her room's being bugged.

"I think we should just ask Mr. Driscoll," she said after she'd heard my whole report on Mother Consiliatrix's telephone call one more time.

"Ask him what?"

"You know, what his business policies are. Whether he follows the proper rules for bidding on a contract." Her voice was so sweet, she might have been discussing the recipe for honeyed corn bread. If we do approach Driscoll, I thought, Sister Ann William should do the talking.

I wasn't convinced it would do any good, however.

"We have no more competence in finances than in autopsy reports," I reminded her. "And this time we don't even have an Uncle Jeb to help out."

"You're right. We need something concrete but simple."

We'd strolled to the new limit of St. Lucy's yard, on the Marion Avenue side of the property. A long narrow trailer, big enough for a couple of offices sat where the lavender bushes used to grow. The steel-gray temporary building was just off the ground, with a two-step metal staircase leading up to the front door. A sign by the side of the door read, DRISCOLL & SONS.

Its low windows were uncurtained, tempting to two tall busybodies. We stood on our tip toes and peered in. Nothing surprising—file cabinets, worktables cluttered with a mixture of tools and office supplies, a typewriter and gooseneck lamp on a small table. The furniture seemed old and battered, as if it had endured many moves in its lifetime.

We looked at each other, and at the flimsy door. "What are you thinking?" I asked Sister Ann William, though I knew the answer. I'd been thinking along the same lines. Without waiting for an answer, I shook my head. "Not a good idea."

"Not now," she said. "But we could come back after dark."

I sucked in my breath, an ominous feeling creeping along my spine. We walked around the perimeter of the trailer in silence, hands in our sleeves, like other-worldly building inspectors on a stroll. For a former tree-house builder like me, and a spirited adventuress like Sister Ann William, the job seemed trivial. That it would be unlawful trespassing—a felony probably worse than anything my parolee brother Timothy had done—also crossed my mind.

We waited till eleven o'clock, when most lights in St. Lucy's were out, and left through the back door. The night was still and noiseless except for an occasional car on Marion Avenue. I could think of no precedent for what I was doing, except for the time I'd sneaked into Mother Ignatius' office. But her door had been unlocked, and the action had been spontaneous. Breaking into the Driscoll & Sons trailer was more like a planned operation by two seasoned burglars.

Sister Ann William had removed the white collar from her navy blue dress, and I'd turned my white bib to the back where it would be hidden by my veil. No reflecting surfaces on either of us. We both wore black gloves meant for walking to school on cold winter days, not for second-story jobs. I held a flashlight, borrowed from Sister Miriam—I'd told her I dropped something behind my bed—while Sister Ann William picked at the lock on the trailer door with a long thin instrument from her pharmacist's kit. It looked like a dentist's tool, and I didn't ask for further explanation.

I thought I heard my partner mutter a prayer as she fiddled with grooves and tumblers, and I hoped she wasn't wasting precious indulgences on this questionable project.

At a particularly quiet moment, the phone inside the trailer rang.

Sister Ann William jumped, causing her implement to slip along the metal door. Who'd be calling a work site at this hour? I wondered. Sister Ann William looked at me, her eyes an eerie yellow in the glow of the flashlight. The phone stopped after three rings.

"Wrong number," Sister Ann William whispered, as if to calm herself and remove the idea of a threat to our maneuvers.

After what seemed like hours, we heard a click, and the door gave way. We stood up and took deep breaths. We made motions with our heads and hands toward the inside of the trailer, and then toward our residence hall, as if to weigh our options. Perhaps only a venial sin if we turned back at this point?

Another long exhalation and we entered the office. I started to remove my gloves, a reflexive action on arriving indoors, and Sister Ann William put a hand out to stop me.

"Fingerprints," she mouthed.

In the next moment she made a move to pull the chain on the desk lamp, and I held her back. It appeared we were learning on the job.

We hadn't talked much about what we'd do once we were inside the trailer. Probably because we never thought we'd get that far. We stayed close together as we tugged at drawers, cabinets, and a storage box, all locked. We fingered rolls of blueprints leaning against the walls and a row of hardhats on top of the file cabinet, coming across nothing that looked like a ledger. Or evidence of shady dealings.

"Everything incriminating is locked up," Sister Ann William said, her voice a hoarse whisper.

I winced at her assumption of Driscoll's guilt but nodded in agreement. "Can't you use your tool?" I asked, pointing my flashlight toward her pocket.

She shook her head. "Not on those kinds of locks. I could try the padlock on the storage container, though."

"Let's try the desk first." I swung the flashlight toward the scarred gray metal desk, strewn with floor plans, correspondence, and to-do lists. My hope was renewed when the light landed on a half-completed letter in the typewriter. We bent over to read the text.

Memo: To the Property Committee, St. Alban's University

From: Driscoll & Sons

"Aha," I said.

"What is it?" Sister Ann William asked.

"Hold it right there," said Jake Driscoll, as the overhead lights rained down on us.

CHAPTER 24

Sister Ann William and I stopped in our tracks, like children in a game of "statues."

My flashlight was trained on Jake Driscoll. His gun was pointed at us. It didn't seem like an even fight.

"Well, well," he said, in a sing-song voice that sent a chill through my body. I thought I could hear my partner's breathing, coming in short spasms. "I saw you hovering around here after dinner. You have a lot to learn about criminal behavior."

The sides of my bonnet kept me from seeing where Sister Ann William's eyes were focused. Mine were on Jake Driscoll's gun. Neither of us had uttered a syllable since the lights went on. I couldn't imagine screaming even if I could reclaim my voice. No one was likely to be within earshot, unless a Sister with insomnia was taking a stroll in the garden. Or some real burglars lurked outside the trailer.

As if finally noticing our discomfort, Driscoll put his weapon in the pocket of his jacket. "Relax, Sisters. I brought this along, in case it wasn't you. Although I couldn't imagine any other thieves in flowing veils."

"We know we shouldn't be here, Mr. Driscoll," Sister Ann William said as I tried to recover my equilibrium.

"Let's have a seat," he said, ignoring her confession. He pointed to a small round conference table at the end of the trailer. Although he'd put his gun away, his tone didn't seem to allow a choice.

The three of us sat on uncomfortable swivel chairs covered in blue fabric that had seen hard labor. For a moment I was concerned that pieces of white plaster would stick to the skirt of my habit, as if that were all I had to worry about. Driscoll looked from one of us to the other, shaking his head. A parent preparing to discipline his children? A priest considering which penance to issue? Or a crooked real estate developer about to murder two sleuths who'd found him out?

"I don't know what to do with you two. You're trespassing here, and I could make a lot of trouble for you." We gave him vigorous nods. "If I wanted to. And I don't know why I don't. Anybody else and I would've searched them straight off. All those years of Catholic school, I guess. Taught me to respect the habit. Though I never had any nuns like the two of you."

Driscoll got up and paced the short width of the trailer, passing back and forth in front of us. He rubbed his forehead, like a man hoping for inspiration before an important decision. His collegiate outfit— well-pressed khakis and a navy blazer—did nothing to mitigate his hulking presence. I called up my special repertoire of prayers, that he wouldn't reach for his gun.

He took a seat again, hands folded on the scratched-up table. "I'm afraid I know the answer, but I'm going to ask you, anyway. What are you doing here?"

Driscoll's pacing had given me time to organize my thoughts, and I remembered the phone call from Mother Consiliatrix that prompted our illegal nighttime activity.

"It came to my attention that a local real estate developer has been engaging in questionable business practices," I said. I wasn't proud of my stilted explanation, but it was the best I could manage.

"Questionable business practices? What do you know about business practices, Sisters? When was the last time you even handled more than milk money from third-graders?"

Neither of us had ever taught grammar school, but we made no attempt to correct his impression. "We know what's right and wrong," Sister Ann William said, though I doubted she did in this case, any more than I did. If Jake Driscoll thought he could intimidate us, both by his expertise in economics and his powerful voice, he was right.

"You think you can apply your simple rules of ethics to the real world? Well, it doesn't work."

"So cheating is a normal way of life, even for a practicing Catholic?"

Jake Driscoll stared at me. "I won't dignify that Sister." I tried to inspect his eyes, as if I were a living polygraph machine. The light in the trailer wasn't good enough for me to see his expression, but his tone was unmistakably angry. "Unlike your sheltered life, the world is complicated."

"Bending the law is never the answer to complication," Sister Ann William said. It came out as if she were pouting, but I knew it was due partly to fear and partly to her accent. I wondered if I were the only one aware that, moments ago, two nuns had bent the rules to enter a trailer unlawfully.

Driscoll laughed, a low, condescending chuckle. "It happens all the time, Sisters. One hand washes the other." He elaborated by rubbing his hands together, then made a steeple of his fingers and pointed it at me. "I didn't interview a dozen twenty-year-olds for the construction job, did I, Sister Francesca? I gave it to your brother. As a favor, because I know you."

I crossed my arms over my chest. I felt my whole body redden when I realized my bib was turned around, exposing the straight pins I used to fasten the bodice of my habit. I jerked my bib around to the front in one quick practiced gesture. "Maybe you should have held the interviews, Mr. Driscoll. I didn't ask you for any favors."

"The point is, Tim can do the job. It saves everybody time."

"You don't know anything about his ability to do the job. And the analogy is weak from at least two other aspects ... "

He interrupted me with a long, exasperated breath. "I can't argue with you, Sister. You're a professional at Thomistic logic. But I'll tell you this—I wouldn't know about the twelve other guys, either, after an interview. And this way I get to help a friend."

While I bristled at his calling me a friend, Sister Ann William had clearly decided to move the discussion forward.

"We heard you ... someone ... obtained a contract from St. Alban's faculty committee illegally," she said, pointing to the letter we'd glimpsed in the typewriter.

Driscoll put his hand in his pocket—where the gun was, I noted—and turned to her. She cleared her throat and continued in a shaky voice. "This hypothetical person acquired information about the competing bids by giving money to the university."

In spite of the gravity of the situation, I smiled at Sister Ann William's attempt to sound proficient in the language of law.

"And you're in my trailer to find evidence about this hypothetical crook?" He pulled the sheet of paper from the typewriter and showed it to us. "Not that I'm obliged, mind you, but for your information, this is a legitimate memo to the faculty committee advising them of a change in tax status. It concerns a project that's at least fifteen years old." He flicked his fingers at the limp page. "But that's not the point. Apparently convent training hasn't changed much in fifty years. You two are just like Mother Ignatius—she thought she could stop the wheels of progress by her own will."

"So you killed her because she wouldn't conform to your values?" I asked, as surprised as he and Sister Ann William seemed to be at my outburst.

Jake Driscoll threw up his hands. "I've had about enough for one night."

I swallowed hard as he stood up and walked to the door. He pointed to the outside world. "Sisters, if you'd be so kind as to leave my office?"

Only then, as I brushed by him, did I notice his tie clip. A round onyx stone with an elaborate silver letter D.

Jake Driscoll's face was red, his eyes were stone cold.

We walked out without a word.

I woke up on Saturday after a restless night, still tired and relieved to be alive. In unspoken agreement after leaving the construction trailer, Sister Ann William and I had gone directly to our rooms, with a goodnight nod and weak smiles.

I'd put the last book into my travel portfolio when I heard my signal. I went to the intercom, thinking how I'd placed and received more phone calls in a week at St. Lucy's than in my entire religious life.

Timothy was on the line.

I leaned against the wall—and against SMI custom. A passage from our Holy Rule flashed before me.

The Sisters shall not lean for support on the backs of chairs while sitting, or other surfaces while standing, preferring instead to stand straight and lean on Our Lord.

I moved away from the wall and braced myself for Timothy's sarcasm. "How is everyone doing?" I asked.

"How do you think?"

"I'll be in Potterstown this afternoon. I'm taking a ten o'clock bus."

"I wonder how much time Mother Julia will allow you to grieve."

"Timothy ..." I swallowed my annoyance and resolved to allow my brother more leeway than usual. We'd lost our father. It would be worse for him, not even twenty years old, and without direction as far as I could tell. I looked at the wall around the phone, a soothing, pale green. "We'll all be together tomorrow, Timothy."

I heard a long sigh. "Right. Aidan will be driving up on Sunday for the wake. If he decides to stay over for the funeral, I might ride back to the Bronx with him on Monday."

"Aidan?"

"Aidan Connors, Susan. My friend, *your* friend. Can you get your head around that?"

I ignored the question. "Wouldn't you like to stay around Potterstown a little longer, maybe for the rest of the week?"

"Yeah, but the sooner I start earning some income, the better for everyone."

Whether he meant it to or not, the reminder of my lost earning power caused its usual twinge. I wondered if Gabriella would be able to finish school—and how I'd feel if she couldn't. My father had planned to work at least another ten years until he was sixty-five and all his children were well into adulthood.

"Maybe you could ride back with us," Timothy said, apparently not finished with his baiting. "Aidan says he'll have a girl with him, if that matters to your bosses."

"I'll stick to the bus. But thanks for the thought."

On the way back to my room, I speculated about the girl Aidan was taking to Potterstown. A girlfriend? A faculty member? They'd have to be pretty close, I thought, for him to take her to a wake upstate. His own family lived in New Jersey, so he wouldn't be combining the trip with a visit to them.

Why do I care? I asked myself. Here I am fingering my newly repaired rosary, dedicated to Christ by a vow of celibacy, and hoping Aidan doesn't have a girlfriend.

I blinked my eyes and prayed for the pitiful specimen of a religious I'd become.

I'd planned to skip breakfast and walk to the satellite intrastate bus station on the Grand Concourse, the wide tree-lined thoroughfare a few blocks from St. Lucy's Hall. A ten o'clock bus would get me to Potterstown around two-thirty, in time for the Saturday ritual of Confession, which I sorely needed.

Sister Ann William offered to walk to the bus stop with me. We carried my luggage past dozens of stately art deco structures—I remembered reading in the St. Alban's catalog that the Bronx had the world's largest concentration of residential buildings in the art deco style. Nearly three hundred of them had been built in the late nineteen twenties and thirties, many of them on the Grand Concourse.

As we talked about the narrow escape of the night before, the sleek lines and graceful curves of the tenements provided a safe, solid backdrop. I thought about more recent construction signs I'd seen— DRISCOLL & SONS development on St. Lucy's old property and EDSON & SONS new Student Union building on campus. I doubted either would provide much inspiration for the generations to come.

"I've never experienced anything like that in my life," Sister Ann William said, interrupting my pilgrimage into the neutral world of architecture. "We're lucky he didn't have us arrested. And after all that, we didn't find anything incriminating."

I shook my head and told her about the match between the cuff link I'd found in Mother Ignatius' office and the tie clip Jake Driscoll was wearing. I didn't need to have them side by side to know they were from the same set.

"But he could have lost his jewelry at any time, not necessarily the night of Mother Ignatius' death."

"True."

"On the other hand, he owns a gun. That makes him suspicious right off."

"But Mother Ignatius wasn't shot to death," I reminded her. "And I'll bet every construction manager in the city has a gun."

We seemed to be taking turns accusing and defending Jake Driscoll.

"I guess we're no smarter than before we broke and entered." Sister Ann William smiled in spite of the bleak assessment.

I smiled with her. There seemed nothing more we could do at the moment.

CHAPTER 25

Everything I saw through the wide window of the bus reminded me of Brendan Patrick Wickes. As we made our way through the small towns north of the Bronx, the general stores brought back memories of Saturday trips to the colorful, sweet-smelling candy barrels in our neighborhood. A red striped carnival tent took me back to county fairs with all of us girls in tow and Timothy in my father's arms. A white church steeple spoke of the faithful usher in his Sunday suit pushing long-poled baskets, collecting the offerings of St. Leonard's worshippers.

I pictured my family—Patty in one of her many black outfits. Kathleen on the arm of her new husband. Gabriella erupting into tears. Timothy straight-faced and stoic. Aunt Celia from my mother's side and Uncle Sean from my father's, arranging the casseroles and folding chairs in the Wickes family dining room.

By two-fifteen, when the bus stopped a few yards from the station parking lot, I'd come close to tears a half dozen times.

Two SMIs were waiting for me in one of the Motherhouse cars. Sister Rosemary, a tiny woman who was about my age and her much older companion, Sister Geraldine, wore somber expressions—the most they'd be allowed to do to console me. No outward expression of sympathy was permitted.

Sister Rosemary had on the special bonnet for driving—perforations along the side allowed part of it to be flipped back and pinned to its base. With our regular bonnets, we had no peripheral vision and could not legally drive wearing them.

It was much colder in Potterstown than the Bronx, probably in the low forties, but true to the October first Rule, the Sisters wore their summer shawls.

"Praised be Jesus Christ," the Sisters said in unison.

"Praised forever. Amen," I replied.

We rode in silence to the Motherhouse.

I was home.

Mother Julia's Saturday afternoon lesson seemed chosen especially for me.

"Poverty, my dear Sisters, does not begin and end with the renunciation of money." Mother Julia faced us in the assembly hall, her back the straightest in the room. I sat with my community—eight rows of Sisters, six or seven to a row. "Our Lord taught us to be poor in spirit, to shun worldly comforts."

I was certain she had in mind the extra pillows I'd requested from Sister Felix. I wanted to stand up and announce that I'd only used them as an excuse to approach Sister Felix on a delicate matter. I hadn't so much as rested my head on them. "Take nothing for your journey, no staff, nor bag, nor bread, nor money."

As Mother Julia quoted from the Gospel of Saint Luke, I thought of myself as the prodigal child, come back after a lifetime of debauchery.

When the lesson was over, we lined up for confession with old Father Harrington. Often as an SMI I'd had to struggle to think of something to confess, using small transgressions like a hurried step or a less than perfect mopping of the scullery to fill the gap. No such problem this time. My struggle was how to phrase my sins to attract the least amount of attention from the other side of the grille.

Besides excessive talking and snooping, I knew I'd have to confess my real sin against chastity—physical feelings for Aidan Connors. I couldn't deny the emotion was different from my affection for Sister

Ann William, which was itself forbidden by Holy Rule. It was just as well to face this head-on.

Father Harrington didn't seem as alarmed as I'd hoped.

"Have you acted on these feelings, Sister?"

"No, Father."

"Not even … uh, in the privacy of your cell?"

"No, Father!" I hoped my vehemence didn't persuade him I had something to hide.

"Then you've nothing to worry about, Sister. It's only natural. Ask Our Lady, virgin before, during, and after the birth of Christ, to guard your body and your soul."

"Yes, Father."

"Anything else?"

Undecided about breaking and entering, I engaged in the Thomistic logic Jake Driscoll had found so annoying. I argued with myself in the manner of the Angelic Doctor. Was every crime a sin? Not if you don't intend to loot or maim. Did Sister Ann William and I intend harm in any way to the occupants of the trailer or its contents? Not at all. Therefore, not a sin.

In the end, I talked my way around my activities in the Bronx. Father Harrington stayed awake longer than usual, and he gave me a strict admonition.

"Make the Stations of the Cross, Sister, and make a firm resolution to renew your religious discipline."

"Yes, Father."

I began my walk around the chapel, pausing at each of the fourteen reminders of Our Lord's passion and death.

At last, I thought, a proper penance.

———

We ate dinner in silence while a novice in the full habit, but with a white veil, read to us from a biography of an early SMI missionary. I listened to the trials of the women who underwent great hardship to set up the first SMI schools and felt pitifully lax at the thought of my full plate and warm bed.

At least the fare at the Motherhouse was simpler than meals at St. Lucy's. Sisters here were served a tin platter of food, each receiving identical portions of plain meat, vegetables, and potatoes. We were expected to eat everything put in front of us. No allowances for individual sizes or appetites. No leftovers. No second helpings.

Later, on the dormitory floor, not a word was spoken except an occasional "Praised be ..." I thought how quickly we form new habits, and just as quickly break them. I saw the wisdom of the rules, and at the same time questioned them as I never had before.

I'd expected Mother Julia to take me aside for private counseling. But other than an announcement before grace about my father's death, she paid no special attention to me until after mass on Sunday.

"How are your studies, Sister Francesca?" she asked. She'd invited me to take a chair across from her in the tiny, sparsely-furnished office overlooking the vast SMI property.

I'd anticipated this question and had my answer ready. Overly enthusiastic and I'd be brought home—too comfortable in the world to be trusted without supervision. Not sufficiently positive and I'd be judged a complainer, unworthy of the mission.

I'd have to be not too proud, not too humble—a tricky balance.

"Classes are interesting, Mother. They promise to be useful in whatever mission I'm called to when I finish my studies."

"And your adjustment? Did Sister Magdalene's visit help?"

"Yes, Mother. It was a great blessing to have her."

Mother Julia leaned back in her chair, but not so far as to touch the surface, and smiled. I'd passed the test.

"About your family visits, Sister ..." Mother Julia put her hands in her sleeves, a signal that the next words were to be taken as orders. "I've talked to your sister Patricia. A very holy woman, by the way."

"Yes, Mother." I bit back the thought that Mother Julia would have preferred the saintly Patricia in her community.

"Your family is coming here at one o'clock today for a private visit. Take the blue parlor. At four, you may ride with them to the funeral home. Sister Magdalene will accompany you. Patricia assures me there will be room for her."

"Thank you, Mother."

"Tomorrow you'll be able to attend the funeral and take the noon bus back to the Bronx. That should get you there well before dark."

"Thank you, Mother."

I wondered what Timothy would have to say about the non-negotiable mourning arrangements.

The blue parlor retained its name, though much of the reason had vanished. The new carpet was closer to a shade of teal and the furniture was a cream-colored living room set donated by a benefactor. The only true blue was in the robe of the Blessed Virgin Mary in a large painting that hung over the sofa.

Visiting days were usually full of laughter, my family showering me with armfuls of treats and gifts they knew I couldn't keep. A pile of school supplies, a dozen pairs of black cotton stockings, boxes of candy and cookies. All went directly into the common store.

This time my sisters were empty-handed, except for their grief.

Gabriella jumped up to greet me, falling into my arms. "Oh, Susan. What will we do without him?"

"We'll be all right," I told her, wishing I had a better answer. I found it strange to see Gabriella, usually in bright colors, in a dark dress—navy blue with long sleeves—and wondered irrelevantly if she'd borrowed it.

Patty and Kathleen took their turns hugging me, wrinkling my bib and trying to smooth it over.

"Don't worry about it," I told them. I took stock of the small room, then looked out into the hallway. "Timothy?"

My sisters had crowded onto the sofa, their different shades of red hair giving them the look of a chorus line for St. Leonard's fund-raising shows. They shook their heads. "He'll see you at O'Farrell's," Kathleen said. "He's so stubborn. Neal stayed behind so he wouldn't be alone in the house." Kathleen's husband and high school sweetheart Neal had been like a second brother to us.

"Timmy doesn't like Mother Julia," Gabriella said, earning a disapproving look and a stern "Gabriella" from Patty, whose black dress looked perfectly natural on her. I'd seldom seen her in anything but.

"Well, he doesn't," Gabriella said, choking back tears that I knew had nothing to do with our brother's quirky temperament.

I'd taken a seat opposite them, when Patty made the pronouncement she usually made at wakes and funerals.

"O'Farrell's did a very good job. Dad looks wonderful," she said, from her place in the middle of the sofa. Gabriella and Kathleen turned their heads to her and laughed in spite of themselves. Cliché though it was, Patty's comment helped us all settle down to normal breathing.

"He's in his Sunday suit, of course," Kathleen said. "Neal took care of getting the clothes down there."

"We should have put him in his ratty old slippers. He'd change into them, first thing every evening," Gabriella said.

"Dad would never let anyone replace those slippers," Patty said. "I don't know how many times he got new ones for Christmas, and he'd give them to St. Leonard's rummage sales."

"I think he wore them to bed," Kathleen said, sending Patty and Gabriella into more nervous laughter, and me into another realm of memory.

Mother Ignatius. The list of her clothing in the autopsy report. Nightgown. Night cap. Slippers. Who wears slippers to bed?

At the same time, I remembered the pulls in the threads of Mother Ignatius' otherwise smooth white bedspread. Slippers and pulls—to me it added up to a struggle.

My hands and feet tingled, as if I were just waking up. Mother Ignatius didn't die in bed, she was put there by whoever killed her, slippers and all.

"Sister Francesca?" Patty said, addressing me as usual by my religious name. I snapped my head up. Apparently my chin had fallen to my bib as I'd taken the mental trip to the Bronx, and they thought I was asleep.

Sister Rosemary's sudden entrance into the parlor saved me from having to explain my wandering mind. I'd missed her knock and wondered what else had gone on in my absence.

"Some tea and cookies. Right out of Sister Loretta's oven," she said, bending to place a large tray on the table in front of the sofa. She stood to her full five feet and faced my sisters. "I'm so sorry, girls. Our prayers are with you." She smiled at me and left the room, making no further sound.

I brought myself around to the present. There's nothing I can do about Mother Ignatius now, I told myself. And I still don't know who the killer is. Even a ten-year-old child could have overpowered Mother Ignatius.

The three teacups on the tray reminded me where I was—SMIs don't eat or drink in front of laity, even their families. After only a week at St. Lucy's, the rule seemed strange to me. I poured tea for my sisters, happy for once that Timothy wasn't present to try and tease me into having a cookie.

By the time Sr. Magdalene came to ride with me to the funeral parlor, I'd been back and forth between the blue parlor and the Bronx enough times to make me dizzy.

CHAPTER 26

I sat in the first row at O'Farrell's, with my sisters and brother. It took another two rows to hold all our aunts and uncles and cousins, many of whom I hadn't seen for years. Convent visits were limited to four relatives, not even enough spots to allow all my siblings to accompany my father every month. They'd all be able to come now, I realized, with great sadness.

Heavy brown drapes, drab carpet, cheerless paisley seat covers on black wooden chairs—O'Farrell's had a darkness about it that was probably meant to be soothing, but also intensified the gravity of the occasion. I looked around for my father's cronies to lift our spirits with their songs and skits. Brendan Patrick Wickes, laid out in his Sunday clothes, would expect a big send-off. I suspected the men had planned their program for after Sister Magdalene and I left. As if we hadn't attended our share of Irish wakes in our pre-convent lives.

All faithful Catholics, my parents' generation nearly genuflected when they approached me.

"Sister Francesca, God bless you," said my old Aunt Annie. She who'd slapped my bottom when I misbehaved as a toddler now addressed me as if I were her Superior. She ran her fingers over my large crucifix. "Such a wonderful thing you're doing. You pray for us, Sister."

I thought of Elena Russo whose parents had disowned her, and realized how lucky I was.

"I will pray for you, Aunt Annie. And your prayers are equally important."

She nodded, her eyes showing a respect I knew I didn't deserve, especially in the light of my recent conduct.

Even more so in the next moment, when I felt my face redden at Aidan Connors' approach to my father's casket. A slender young woman with blond hair to the middle of her back knelt next to him. The cascade of silky locks reminded me of the reason we shaved our heads. As Saint Paul told us, *if a woman has long hair, it is a glory to her*. And glory for ourselves was the last thing we wanted as religious.

Aidan leaned over, so close I could smell a lotion of some kind. He spoke in soft tones. "This is Colleen Shane. She's finishing her master's in our department."

"I've seen you around campus," Colleen said. "I'm so sorry to meet you this way."

I nodded and gave her and Aidan a weak smile. "It's good of you to come all this way." I had a hard time picturing Colleen's beautiful tresses draped over a Latin text on the Uncaused Cause. I wished Aidan had been more specific. His girlfriend? A cousin? Surely he wouldn't take a casual acquaintance on a four-hour drive to O'Farrell's Funeral Home.

"Hey, Aidan, thanks for coming." Timothy had left his seat at the end of the row to greet his new friend and future roommate. It was the first sign of life he'd shown since the start of the wake. He'd avoided talking to me at all and I wondered what I'd done to deserve his disapproval, other than live my life in a way he didn't understand.

Timothy had managed to turn Aidan and Colleen away from me, so I only heard the end of their conversation.

"No, we can't stay for the funeral," Aidan said. "Colleen and I both have a class in New Testament. That way I'll be able to take notes for your sister." He turned and gave me a smile that caused another wave of red to cross my face. I counted on O'Farrell's dim lighting to conceal my reaction.

"Thanks," I said, "but I'm not in that class. My first class of the week is with Father Glanz, on Tuesday."

Aidan snapped his fingers. "Right," he said, turning to Colleen. "Sister Francesca is taking research methods instead. Much tougher."

How did he know my schedule? I wondered. He knew entirely too much about me. I was glad Sister Magdalene, several rows back on the other side of the parlor, had her head in her prayer book. Colleen is useful after all, I thought. If Aidan is seen as safely attached to another woman, Sister Magdalene would have a better interpretation of our connection.

I'd been prepared to introduce Aidan as a friend of Timothy's. That would require admitting that Timothy had visited me in the Bronx, but it wouldn't be quite so bad as owning up to a male friend who'd come a great distance to offer me condolences.

I couldn't remember another time in my life when I'd had to skirt the truth so often. In retrospect, I established a new bond with my Uncle Eddie, who did undercover work for the NYPD before retiring to Potterstown.

I convinced myself my little distortions of reality were for a good cause. I'd managed to turn slippers and bedspread flaws into a reasonable murder scenario. I was more sure than ever Mother Ignatius did not slip away unaided and felt I needed to go back to the Bronx to help bring her killer to justice. Even if I were pulled out afterward, I'd consider my time there was worth it.

I wished I could telephone Sister Ann William. In a short time, I'd gotten used to having someone to talk things over with. A fellow traveler. A friend. I glanced at Aidan, then at Sister Magdalene, who was looking my way. I quickly lowered my eyes, lest she read in them a violation of our Holy Rule.

Just before Sister Magdalene and I were due to leave, a large man stepped to the kneeler, his mane of white hair a match for the mums and lilies surrounding my father's casket.

Jake Driscoll.

I hadn't seen him since he'd caught me and Sister Ann William in his trailer. I wondered if he'd done anything about the incident. I pictured a summons from the Bronx police waiting in my mail slot at St. Lucy's. How did my life get so complicated?

I could feel another white lie coming on if I were questioned about the presence of yet another resident of the Bronx. I wouldn't blame Sister Magdalene if she told Mother Julia there was evidence I'd been acting like a coed with a robust social life.

"My condolences, Sister Francesca," he said simply. I read nothing in his eyes. If he had turned me in, he wasn't gloating. To my relief, he moved on quickly to Timothy who introduced him to the family.

As he spread his charm among my sisters, I held fast to my belief that Driscoll was the best candidate for murderer. He fit all the clues. He'd shown an irresponsible, cavalier attitude towards business fraud while Sister Ann William and I were captive in his trailer. The cufflink I'd confiscated from Mother Ignatius' desk matched his tie clip. And he might well be the person I'd heard Sisters Teresa and Veronique talk about—Driscoll obviously had a career and family ties that would be hard to leave, and involvement with a nun could ruin his career.

On the other hand, here he'd driven four hours to attend a wake for the father of a nun he'd just met and a young man with only tentative employment as a casual laborer. I was in my usual quandary regarding Jake Driscoll. A Good Samaritan? A killer? Or both?

I looked again at the three men chatting in the corner of O'Farrell's parlor—my brother Timothy, Aidan Connors, and Jake Driscoll—symbols of my new life in the Bronx.

I imagined the ride home with Sister Magdalene and said a prayer of thanks for our rule of silence.

Father O'Shaughnesy ushered the earthly remains of Brendan Patrick Wickes into the ground on a sunny Monday morning. I hugged my sisters good-bye and left my Motherhouse.

Between stress over my family's latest burden and the murder that was always in the back of my mind, I felt as wound up as the new alarm clock Mother Julia had put into my going-away packet. She'd been correct to assume there'd be no tower bells to wake us at five o'clock at St. Lucy's Hall.

Not until I was on the bus headed for the Bronx did I take a normal breath.

Until then, I expected any minute Mother Julia would interrogate me about my friends. But either Sister Magdalene had chosen not to report on me, or my superior was giving me the benefit of the doubt.

I also expected criticism from Timothy since I wasn't allowed to go to the Wickes family home after the funeral service, but he was in a surprisingly good mood and gave me no grief.

As I left Potterstown, the final words I'd heard were, "God bless you, Sister," from Mother Julia, and "See ya in the Bronx, Sis," from Timothy, out of earshot of my Superior.

I could hardly believe my good fortune.

It was nearly six o'clock when the bus stopped on the Grand Concourse. Sister Ann William's garment bag was heavier on the return trip, its many zippered compartments crammed with containers of food. Patty had obtained Mother Julia's permission to pack up selections from the elaborate buffet I'd be missing.

I trudged toward St. Lucy's Hall, the smell of corned beef sandwiches, potato salad, and brownies trailing behind me. How far I was from the ideal of my patron Saint Francis of Assisi who admonished his followers to *take nothing for your journey, not shoes nor clothing.*

It was a toss-up as to which weighed me down more—my luggage or my duplicitous life.

I was happy to find the Sisters of St. Lucy's were still at dinner when I arrived at the house. I wanted nothing more than to go straight to my room and remain anonymous for as long as possible. Better still if I could set the calendar back a week and start again. I climbed the stairs to the third floor thinking what I would change. To begin with, no conspiratorial chats with Mother Ignatius. No prying into legal matters and real estate deals. No smiles that could be interpreted as welcoming friendship. Certainly, no favors from lay men, young or old.

By the time I reached my room, I'd come up with at least six more decisions and behaviors I'd regretted. Strangely, since St. Lucy's was kept very neat and clean, I had to climb over several carton boxes to get my door. I dumped my luggage on the floor near my bed and went back through my doorway to see what had been left in the corridor.

Only then did I notice the room next to mine—Room 26, Sister Teresa's—was empty. The bed had been stripped, the desk cleared. The boxes were spread in the hallway outside her room, neatly labeled with her name and an address in Michigan. There was no sign of Sister Teresa.

I rushed down the hall to find Sister Ann William.

My new start would have to wait.

CHAPTER 27

I caught up with Sister Ann William just before she reached our floor. She climbed the stairs slowly since, true to form, she was carrying a tray of food for me.

"I thought you might be hungry after your long journey," she said, as if I'd crossed the ocean like the first SMIs to settle in the United States a century ago.

"This time I have food for you," I told her, leading the way back to my room. I pulled packages of all sizes from the compartments of her garment bag. The aromas of spiced meat and chocolate leaked from wax paper wrappings and filled the small space. "But first, what happened to Sister Teresa?"

She shrugged her shoulders. "I guess she slipped away over the weekend. I came down here to put some mail under your door and noticed those boxes. Her door was wide open, the floor had just been waxed, and the place was stripped of personal belongings."

"Has Sister Felix said anything?"

She twisted her hand back and forth in a way that said *sort of*. "At the noon meal yesterday, she announced simply that Sister Teresa Barnes was taking a leave from her studies and had returned to Michigan. That's all she said."

No great loss, I thought. Sister Felix had lied more than once already. She'd lied to me about Mother Ignatius having a meeting on the evening of her death, and she'd made up a story about my behavior to Sister Magdalene. Why would we trust her information concerning Sister Teresa's whereabouts?

"What about Sister Veronique?"

"I haven't talked to her, but Sisters have been coming and going in her room all weekend."

Sister Ann William had set down the tray of food—its congealed potatoes and gravy notably less appetizing than the treats I'd brought from the kitchens of Potterstown. "Now that you're back …" She trailed off.

"Yes?"

"Well, I didn't feel free to barge in on Sister Veronique with questions by myself, but …"

I took the cue. "Maybe we could both go—after all, the four of us did walk home together once. Doesn't that make us bosom buddies?"

We laughed at that and walked downstairs to visit Sister Veronique, whose room was on the second floor.

I haven't even unpacked, I thought. My father's body is barely settled at Holy Family Cemetery, and all my Motherhouse resolutions have already faded.

I sighed, resigned to my lack of will power, and followed Sister Ann William to Room 19. Two Sisters were leaving as we approached, and Sister Veronique waved us in, as if she'd been expecting us. She sat facing the doorway, her wide body taking up all the available space in the center of the room. I suspected she liked her role as the chief source of information.

"Francesca, you're back. I hope your family is OK. Ann, come on in."

Until now I'd seen only my own room and Sister Ann William's, neither of which had more than the standard St. Lucy's furniture. Sister Veronique had managed to squeeze in several extra pieces—including two bookcases and a filing cabinet, giving her room the look of a crowded office or study instead of a nun's cell. Every level surface was overrun with knickknacks—religious statues of all sizes, ceramic animals, candles, mugs with colorful logos. Her windowsill was lined with cola bottles, most of them empty, and on her bed was the largest bag of potato chips I'd ever seen.

"Snack?" she said, holding out the bag.

I declined, but Sister Ann William reached inside and took one. Part of her politeness program? I planned to ask her sometime for lessons. I hoped I didn't have to go to Texas to learn charm.

"Mmm," said Sister Ann William.

Sister Veronique swept her arm across her bed, indicating we should sit on her non-standard bedspread, a deep rose that matched curtains she'd hung on her window.

"So, you've probably heard about my friend, Teresa."

We shook our heads, leaning forward together.

Sister Veronique sat up straight and lowered the pitch of her voice, giving it a solemn tone. "Teresa is with child."

The room seemed suddenly quiet, not even traffic noise from Marion Avenue disturbed the moment. I thought the Angel Gabriel could not have done a better job of staging the announcement.

Sister Ann William stopped chewing her potato chip. My mind flew quickly to D, E, and F, wondering which one was the father.

"If you're wondering who the father is ..." Sister Veronique said. I lowered my eyes, in case she'd read the question in my expression. "It's a big surprise." She rolled her eyes, to indicate just the opposite was true.

We said nothing. I sensed Sister Veronique wasn't finished, and my patience was rewarded. She continued almost immediately, leaning forward.

"I'll just give you a hint that he's a member of the clergy, chaplain of a community of nuns, recently appointed dean ... are you getting the picture?"

Sister Ann William and I blew out long breaths simultaneously.

Father Malbert.

Sister Veronique sat back and folded her arms across her chest—no small task, given her girth—seemingly satisfied at our reaction.

"Is she sure about the father?" I asked and regretted my question at once.

Sister Veronique frowned at me. "Sis ... Teresa wasn't promiscuous." As if intimacy with only one man were a virtue for a nun to aspire to. I held my tongue. "Sorry to jump at you. But I'm very upset about my friend. She seems to be the only one paying the price."

"Where is she?" Sister Ann William asked.

"She went to stay with her brother and his family in Lansing, Michigan. Meanwhile the jerk in the Roman collar—not that he ever wears it—is happily continuing his life. I tried to tell her, but she wouldn't listen."

I remembered overhearing at least one argument between them that verified Sister Veronique's assertion.

Sister Veronique adjusted her glasses on her nose. "Sometimes I wish we'd never changed the rules."

Indeed.

We left Room 19, each with a napkin full of potato chips, and sat across from each other at a card table in a newly created lounge.

Sister Felix had converted a large storage area on the third floor into common space, as requested by the Sisters who wanted a room to congregate in. Apparently, visiting, fully dressed, using the two parlors on the main floor was inconvenient. A note on the wall of the lounge contained Sister Felix's promise to replace the rickety furniture with more comfortable pieces, plus a small refrigerator and hot plate, soon.

"Oh dear," Sister Ann William said. "Father Malbert. It's as if all the warnings are coming true. First you're being polite and friendly, talking about classes ..."

I nodded. "Then you start meeting outside of the convent."

"Just to have lunch, since you have to eat, anyway."

"Then you go to a movie on campus."

"And you sit around discussing its spiritual implications."

"And it's late at night."

We took turns developing our slippery slope as naturally as if we were reciting alternate antiphons of the Holy Office, except our phrases were punctuated by nibbles of salty chips. And the images in my mind were not of the Holy Trinity, but of Aidan Connors in his blue sweater, chatting with me about vocations and Kadota figs.

"The next thing you know, you're going to have a baby," Sister Ann William said.

I shuddered and cleared away the inadvertent connection. "But what could this have to do with Mother Ignatius' death? So what if Mother Ignatius threatened to expose them? It's not as if it could be kept secret very long."

"But no one ever knows for sure who the father is."

"You're right. Father Malbert could certainly deny it."

"Maybe Mother Ignatius saw them … together?" Sister Ann had as hard a time as I did with the language of unchaste behavior.

The picture was fuzzy in my mind. I'd heard Mother Ignatius hardly ever left St. Lucy's. It's what made her "naïve about the world" according to Sister Veronique and Jake Driscoll. So where could she have seen Sister Teresa and Father Malbert carrying on? In the main parlor? In the basement by the ping pong table?

"I think we need a break from this," I said.

Sister Ann William gasped, as if startled into a new insight. She broke a large potato chip on the way to her mouth, the crumbs scattering over her blue habit.

"You don't think you and I … talking … and … being companions … You don't think we're doing anything wrong, do you, Sister?"

I swallowed. "No, Sister. I don't," I said. I emphasized her title, thinking how little we had left of the formality required of us.

We left our places at the wobbly card table and went silently to our rooms.

Unlike the practice at our Motherhouse when a Sister left the order, there was no constraint on chatter about the defector from St. Lucy's. Breakfast on Tuesday morning was a great source of information on Teresa Barnes and her affair. I learned Father Malbert would keep his new position as Dean of Academic Affairs, announced the Friday before. The administration had issued a second statement immediately, on Monday morning, asking faculty and students to disregard the "unfortunate rumors" and help the new Dean do the Lord's work at St. Alban's.

"I suppose it had to happen sooner or later," said Sister Miriam, draining her glass of orange juice. "They spent a lot of time together." Her pale blue eyes danced, as if she were enjoying a private vision of the couple on a date.

"Poor Teresa," said another Sister. "I wonder how she'll manage. It's not like she'd have any savings or anything."

"God works in strange ways," said Sister Miriam. "In the end, everyone will be fine."

Except Mother Ignatius.

I reviewed the order of events—Mother Ignatius dies, Jake Driscoll gets his new contract, Father Malbert is named Dean, Sister Felix is named superior, Sister Teresa leaves.

The sequence cried out for more than just flimsy connections, but I was unable to fill the gaps.

Sister Ann William and I exchanged awkward glances whenever we caught each other's eye during the morning exercises—answering the bell for mass, lining up for the refectory, taking a place at table.

After breakfast, she slipped me a note. On the way to my room to collect my school bag and umbrella for a rainy walk to class, I read her neat writing.

+ *Sister Francesca, I've thought about it, and I don't believe our walking to campus together amounts to a breach of Rule or constitutes a particular attachment. Meet me in the foyer at 9:30 if you agree. + SAW*

"I agree," I said when I joined her for the trip to St. Alban's.

"I guess what happened to Teresa has thrown me off balance. It's not as if you and I are going to …"

"Not at all. I think we need to use common sense."

Sister Ann William smiled. "Exactly. And it's much safer to have a companion on Southern Boulevard."

I thought about the one time I'd walked home alone—the bruises from that day were nearly gone, but not the memory.

"I can't argue with that."

I wondered whether Mother Julia in Potterstown or Mother Clarisse in Texas would have been so quick to concur.

CHAPTER 28

The steady rain mixing with street debris produced a muddy Southern Boulevard, not the best-swept avenue in the city in any weather.

I finally told Sister Ann William my new evidence, loosely defined, that Mother Ignatius' death was not natural. Spoken out loud, a corpse in bed with slippers and a few pulls on a bedspread seemed less conclusive than I'd first thought.

She gave me a characteristic "Hmmm …" and was silent for a few minutes.

I checked the status of an abandoned car, a cream-colored sedan that had been at the same curbside spot the whole week. Clearly a magnet for vandals. Each day a new piece was missing—first the hubcaps, then the seats, then parts under the hood—until finally only the rusty shell remained.

A metaphor for the most intense week of my life?

At the next bend, Sister Ann William shared her thoughts. "Maybe we should make one last stab at tying Mother Ignatius' death to poison." Obviously, she hadn't been meditating on the deterioration of an automobile.

"But the autopsy report … "

She shook her head before I could finish. "There are so many substances—too many to screen for unless you know exactly what you're looking for. Last night I was reading about succinyl choline."

I winced, thinking of my high school chemistry class. If I'd ever passed a test with those words on it, it was pure luck, or my novena prayers.

Sister Ann William had no such trouble, as the science rolled off her tongue. "Both succinyl and choline occur naturally in the body, but they're also poisonous in certain doses, and it's almost impossible to tell if the compound has been administered or was there all along. It takes a special machine and there are only a few in existence."

"Interesting. But now it sounds even more hopeless. Not detectable. No machines. What can we do?"

"Approach it from a different angle. I'm going to try to get ahold of the log for the pharmacy, where all the drugs are kept. Maybe I'll see the name of someone who's not supposed to be in there."

"Is a murderer going to sign in?"

She sighed. "I suppose not. But there's always a clerk at the window, and theoretically you can't get past her to the drug supply without checking in."

"Then the killer would have to be someone at least familiar to the clerk, or with an ID that lets him or her in."

"Right. And I'm going to find out exactly who else can get access to my poisons." A frown accompanied her proprietary declaration.

As she turned down the path toward her building, I wished I'd persuaded her to drop the undertaking. I had the strange feeling we should quit before something disastrous happened, for no apparent reason other than the word *poisons* sent a chill up my spine.

"Be careful, Sister," I said, but she was too far away to hear me.

———————

I stepped into St. Thomas Aquinas' main lecture hall for my second class in Church Liturgy with Father Glanz.

"Wait till you see what he has in store this time," Aidan said, catching up with me near the top row. "I have the inside scoop from Colleen. She's his TA. Remember her?"

How could I forget? Colleen, the beautiful young woman who attended my father's wake, who might be Aidan's girlfriend.

I nodded. "I suppose Colleen is going to say mass for us today?" I hoped my smile took the edge off my remark.

He laughed. "You're close."

I stared at Aidan, wide-eyed, but Father Glanz appeared before I could get more details. I didn't have long to wait, however.

"We're going to do a little field work this morning," Father Glanz said.

Oh-oh. I turned my head to catch Aidan's eye. He was smiling. "Told you," he whispered.

Father Glanz looked at his watch. "In fifteen minutes, we'll all reconvene across campus at Xavier Hall. There's a room on the first floor—Room 131—we've been using as a chapel. We're going to celebrate what some are calling experimental liturgy. It's an example of what Vatican II is doing for us."

Or to us. My muscles tensed. A lump formed in my throat. Could he do this—force us to attend an unorthodox mass?

The dozen or so students around me seemed excited, uttering phrases like *it's about time*, and *just what I've been waiting for*. I joined the exodus on a rainy walk toward Xavier Hall, Aidan by my side. He refrained from cheering with the others, possibly out of respect for my feelings.

Was this a test of my faith? Was this where I was supposed to suffer punishment for refusing to stray from authorized liturgy? I remembered the true martyrs who had died for their faith, defending matters of dogma against heresies. I had to admit, changing the liturgy was not the same as heresy. It didn't begin to approach the seriousness of doubting the divinity of Christ, for example, or the virginity of Mary. Those were matters of doctrine.

"Are you all right with this, Sister?" Aidan asked me.

"I guess so. I don't have to take Communion, do I?" I asked, as if he would know the answer.

"I don't think it will affect your grade if you don't. Colleen says he's a good guy."

Colleen again. "I don't remember a requirement that priests be good guys."

Aidan laughed. "So you believe all priests, even if they're nasty men, even if they voted for Barry Goldwater for president, are God's messengers on earth, and that's all that matters."

"Yes." That's why I can go to confession to Father Malbert, I thought, wondering if Aidan knew of the new dean's most recent transgression.

"Colleen says this mass will be in English for sure. You can't object to that?"

I sighed, ready with my usual defense of the Vulgate. "The idea behind using Latin in the first place is so we can go to mass anywhere in the world and it will be the same."

Aidan was ready for me. "Right. Wherever you are, no one will be able to understand it."

I laughed. Not a bad point.

The so-called chapel in the office building known as Xavier Hall was a small, unadorned room with a simple wooden table at the front, not even raised from the level of the carpet we stood on. No pews or stained-glass windows. No crucifix. No candle to indicate the presence of the Blessed Sacrament.

I'd heard the floor below us housed the University's new computer center. I pictured long, narrow cards with holes punched in them being mistaken for Holy Cards.

I was surprised to see Sister Miriam from St. Lucy's organizing the singing group. She handed out copies of a brightly colored paperback book, "Songs of Praise for the Liturgy," to a varied collection of seminarians, lay students, and Sisters, some of whom held guitars.

Sister Miriam's blond hair seemed to have been styled since the last time I'd seen her bareheaded. Still short, it fell in soft waves around her ears. I wondered how she decided when to cover her head and when to tuck her veil in the pocket of her jacket, as it was now. She caught my eye and motioned to me.

"Francesca, how nice to see you here. Do you want to come up front and join us? We're just here to get each song started. Everyone sings." Sister Miriam swung her arms in an arc to include the entire congregation.

I shook my head. "No, thank you." I whispered, although I realized technically I wasn't in church.

On the table were facsimiles of the elements of mass—a basket of bread that looked like chunks of a fresh-baked wheat loaf, not the lily-white unleavened wafers that had served the church for … for how long? I was amazed to realize I didn't know. I was sure Father Glanz would be happy to enlighten me.

The bottle of wine next to the bread could have come from the liquor store down the street—quite a different container from the sacramental wine I'd helped set out for our chaplain at the Motherhouse.

About thirty people had gathered, each holding a mimeographed sheet with the "program" for mass. They'd been distributed at the door by a seminarian with a wide grin, as if he'd just been rescued from the Dark Ages.

Guitar chords were struck, and Father Glanz entered the room wearing the strangest vestments I'd ever seen. His chasuble was clearly hand-made, with patches of brightly colored felt in different shapes. I recognized the forms of a chalice, a Host, several candles. Slogans seemed to have been stitched into the fabric of his stole, the words running at odd angles down its length. *Peace. Love not War. We are One.*

"I come to the altar of God," Father Glanz said.

We answered, following the script printed in purple on our programs. "To God who gives joy to my youth."

A reasonable translation of the official opening of mass. Not bad so far, except for the irregular ambience. I had an easier time than I thought following the essential parts of the Holy Sacrifice, in spite of the colloquial English.

Father Glanz used his homily to explain changes to the liturgy, which he termed "a living ritual, subject to reconstruction throughout history." He leaned forward and lowered his voice as if to share a secret with us. "A wise man once wrote: It is the customary fate of new truths to begin as heresies and end as superstitions. Let's be careful we don't turn our liturgical practices into superstitions."

Something to think about, I had to admit.

The hardest part for me was the idea of taking the bread in my own hands. From the time we were children, Catholics were warned—never touch the Holy Eucharist. The Host was placed on our tongues by the sanctified fingers of the priest—it should not come in contact with our hands, our teeth, any part of our bodies. Every seven-year-old First Communicant lived in fear that the thin wafer would stick to the roof of her mouth—a mouth dry from strict fasting, even from water, from the night before.

I watched as Aidan joined the long line of people holding out their hands for what looked like a hunk of bread from a deli. He moved aside to let me get in front of him.

I'd heard Father Glanz's words at the Consecration. I presented myself with the logic: If I believed a priest could transform unleavened bread into the Body of Christ, I had to assume he could transform anything, including this loaf of whole wheat.

I looked at Aidan, his eyebrows raised in a question, waiting for my decision.

I shook my head slightly. Not this time.

At the kiss of peace, which I'd gotten used to from St. Lucy's, a lay woman on my right had given me a bear hug. I was grateful Aidan's greeting was more like a handshake.

But the challenges of dealing with Aidan Connors were far from over.

"Let me drive you home," he said as we left Xavier Hall. "It's pouring."

"Thank you, but I have an umbrella."

As I said this, at least two enormous umbrellas held by passersby turned inside out from the strong wind. Aidan stood in the doorway with me, arms folded across his chest. Waiting me out. I wondered if he'd learned the maneuver from his brief contact with my brother.

I thought about my trip home. Sister Ann William planned to pick up the medal she'd ordered for her brother. She was to meet Sister Veronique later and walk home with her. I wasn't eager to trek along

Southern Boulevard by myself. Getting knocked down in the rain would be even more unpleasant than the first time.

"If it would make you feel better, I could get Colleen to ride with us."

Who is this girl who seems to be at Aidan's beck and call? A date at a wake. Chaperone duty at a moment's notice.

"I don't want to inconvenience anyone."

Aidan's face brightened. "Not a problem." He looked at his watch. "Colleen's a good friend, I know she'd be glad to come."

"Never mind," I said, my voice wavering.

He frowned. "You won't take a ride?"

"I'll take the ride. Never mind getting Colleen."

"Terrific."

"Thanks, I appreciate your offer," I said, my voice weaker with each syllable. I swung around and scanned the hallway, still echoing post-liturgy conversation.

I sighed. No sign of Mother Julia.

CHAPTER 29

I stood at the glass front doors of Xavier Hall, waiting for Aidan. Through sheets of rain, I had a view of the two Student Union Buildings, one old, one under construction. The small contractor sign had been replaced by a billboard of grand proportions. EDSON & SONS had obviously grown in importance since I'd last looked. At least it wasn't another conquest by DRISCOLL & SONS, who'd eaten up St. Lucy's grounds.

To avoid reexamining my decision to ride home with Aidan, I distracted myself with the signage. The new billboard boasted of other campus structures by the same firm. Coming soon were new bleachers for the stadium, renovation of the old performing arts theatre, an extension to one of the dorms. Busy Edsons.

My thoughts drifted to Sister Ann William, perhaps because I thought I should be walking with her, not waiting to get into an automobile with a layman. I was happy she'd been able to order the medal for her seminarian brother but felt a twinge of envy. The most I could hope for my own brother was a return to the faith as a law-abiding citizen. I wondered what I could have done differently when he was ten years old.

I bargained with myself—I'd give Aidan two more minutes, then head home on foot. Not because he was taking too long, but because I questioned the wisdom of my choice. Maybe his delay would be a sign I should reverse my decision.

Lacking a watch, I resorted to an old trick. *One-one thousand. Two-one thousand. Three-one thousand.*

Too late. Aidan pulled up in a blue Volkswagen, coincidentally the color of his eyes and most frequently worn sweater. No turning back. Why had I rejected the idea of including Colleen? I hoped it had nothing to do with wanting Aidan to myself.

He came around to the curb and opened the door for me. I was clumsier than usual gathering my skirts, umbrella, and schoolbag into the small car.

"So, dare I ask? What did you think of the liturgy?" he asked.

"I missed the little bells at the Consecration." Aidan looked at me, probably to see whether I was serious. I kept my head straight, the sides of my bonnet blocking his view of my face. I sensed him leaning forward to check on my expression, and in the interest of safe driving, I turned to show him a smile. "Really, it wasn't as bad as I expected."

He laughed, and we fell easily into a dialogue about the role of priests and nuns in the church.

"To set themselves apart from the laity as examples and ideals to strive for, the keepers of a life of prayer," I said, echoing the training I'd received from Mother Julia and the elder Sisters at the Motherhouse.

"Or to be part of the world, carrying out a special mission while living among the laity, distinguishable only by their spirituality," Aidan said. I'd known for some time I'd been misled by his blue rosary the first day I met him. Not a traditionalist at all, but someone who was trying to balance the old and the new.

"This reminds me of an earlier conversation we had," Aidan told me. I knew his easy manner was purposeful, to lure me into another discussion of the pros and cons of the modern Church. "Are you still holding on to *your love it or leave it* position?"

"I haven't given it any more thought."

He scratched his head. "I guess that's one of the reasons I left the seminary. At the time it was a closed society. No awareness of what was going on in the world. As if war didn't affect us because we'd taken vows."

It was a debate we'd all been drawn into since the start of Vatican II. I was distressed at how my confidence in my position had eroded after one short week in the Bronx.

"Why now?" I asked him. I was sure Mother Julia and Sister Magdalene hadn't had to wrestle with these issues when they were young nuns.

"I don't know," Aidan said. "We're all more aware now. Maybe TV did it." And maybe our rule about no TV was wiser than I thought. "The point is now that we're aware we can't close our eyes." He paused. "But you know what, I think this conversation is ruining our day."

"I think you're right."

Aidan drove carefully through the rainy streets, laughing about his noisy windshield wipers. I enjoyed his amusing anecdotes about his part time job at Lloyd's Used Cars.

"Believe it or not, there are cars in even worse shape than my bug," he said.

By the time we reached St. Lucy's, I'd had such a pleasant time, I knew I'd done something wrong.

I'd just reached my room and toweled raindrops off my bib when I heard my call signal. I picked up the hallway phone and heard a breathless Sister Ann William.

"Sister Francesca, I'm so excited. I couldn't wait to tell you. I may have what we need."

I drew in my breath. "The sign-in sheet for the drug room?"

She laughed. "We call it the pharmaceuticals lab log. But yes."

"How did you manage to get it? Have you had a chance to look at it?"

A tingle of excitement coursed through my body. Perhaps there was one good thing I could do before Mother Julia pulled me from my studies for my transgressions—so many I was beginning to lose count. I pictured myself bringing to justice the murderer of sweet old Mother Ignatius.

"I don't quite have it, but I will almost certainly by tomorrow." Sister Ann William lowered her voice, making it even harder to hear her above the background noises. I assumed she was calling from a campus phone booth. "I'm not exactly proud of my tactics."

"Oh?"

"Well, I sort of used my habit to persuade the pharmacy clerk that I should have a copy of the log. I could tell she was one of those Catholic school girls who'd think a nun can do no wrong."

"What did you tell her?"

Did I want to know? I already felt guilty about Sister Ann William's questionable behavior.

"I … I told her I needed the information for a survey. We sort of do, don't we?"

"Hmm. We need to survey the list, for sure."

"That's what I was thinking. Grace—that's the clerk—said she'd have to check with her supervisor, but she doesn't think it will be a problem as long as it's a Sister who made the request. That's where I felt a little guilty." I could see why but chose not to express it. "Grace said to come back tomorrow, and she'll have it for me."

"Good work."

"Thank you, Sister. Won't it be wonderful if we can solve this crime?"

"It certainly will."

"Well, I have to get ready for my one o'clock class. Then I'm meeting Sister Veronique at two-thirty. So I'll be back to St. Lucy's by three."

"Did you already pick up your medal?"

"I did. It's lovely—a large silver oval, with a matching chain. And a handsome etching of Saint William, meditating in his cave."

"It sounds perfect. I look forward to seeing it."

"I'll check in with you as soon as I get home."

I hung up with Sister Ann William, remembering conversations as a teenager in Potterstown, chatting on and on with my friends, though we'd hardly been apart a few hours.

Apparently, I'd reverted not just to a laywoman, but to a high school girl.

At a little past three I knocked on Sister Ann William's door. No answer.

And no excuse to avoid my homework assignment from Father Glanz. He'd asked us to write a two-thousand-word critique on the liturgy we'd attended in Xavier Hall that morning.

"Don't tell me whether you liked it or didn't like it," he'd warned. "I don't want to know if it moved you to tears for whatever reason, good or bad." He'd paced behind the large counter in the lecture hall, using his long fingers to count off his requirements. "I want analysis, documentation, evaluation. Use Scripture, exegesis, encyclicals, the documents of Vatican II. I want historical arguments, pastoral arguments, theological arguments."

I sighed and opened my copy of The Constitution on the Sacred Liturgy, barely two years old.

"It is the wish of the church to undertake a careful general reform of the liturgy … "

I outlined my paper, reluctantly acknowledging Father Glanz had not tampered with what Vatican documents called immutable elements, such as the Consecration of bread and wine. I had to admit, he'd stayed within the norms for reform of the variable elements—the music, the language, the vestments. I tried to open my mind to the church's deep interest in adapting to the changing needs of the faithful.

The modern world seemed to be drawing me in. I prayed fervently I'd be able to embrace sensibly it and still keep my spiritual commitment.

When my call signal rang for the second time that afternoon, I envisioned an annoyed Sister Felix reporting my decadent social habits to Mother Julia.

As I passed Sister Ann William's room I checked it again. Still no sign of her. I picked up the phone, thinking she might be calling to tell me why she'd been delayed.

Instead, Timothy was on the other end of the line.

"Hi, just want you to know I'm back in town."

"I'm surprised to hear from you. I thought you'd stay home longer. But … welcome back."

It was always a struggle for me to strike just the right note with Timothy. Not criticizing him for leaving Potterstown early. Not too happy he's back, so he won't rebel against my enthusiasm.

"Yeah, well, I need to get to work. I'm going to start at Mr. Driscoll's site in Westchester tomorrow."

"What's in Westchester?"

"A new shopping plaza. He has things going on in about five parts of the city right now. I had my choice, so I thought I'd start in a high-rent district."

"I thought he was anxious to start the development in St. Lucy's back yard. The new housing and recreation center."

"Not really. In fact, he doesn't think he can get that going for a year or so. Too busy."

So why would he want Mother Ignatius out of the picture now, if his business is booming?

"Then I wonder why he was so anxious to renegotiate the contract with St. Lucy's?" I hadn't meant to ask Timothy, but he was ready with an answer.

"He mentioned how he wanted to make sure no one else got the property." Timothy paused and continued on an upbeat note. "I'm already learning a lot about this business."

What Jake Driscoll wants you to learn, I mused. I wasn't ready to cross him off my suspect list, but I certainly had to alter the motive I'd assigned him. I needed Sister Ann William's opinion, and wished she'd hurry back. I stood facing her end of the hallway to monitor her doorway.

"He likes you, you know," Timothy said.

"What?"

"Mr. Driscoll. He likes you. Says you're feisty."

One of my least favorite words. In my mind, *feisty* called up an image of a bent old lady beating a dog with her cane.

I changed the subject. "How's everyone doing?"

"You mean all the Wickes? OK, I guess. Patty's stepped up her Church visits, Kathleen and Neal went back home to their little love nest, and Gabriella's back in her shopping mode."

I smiled at Timothy's pithy summary of our family. "And you?"

"I'm fine. I'm calling from Aidan's. He likes you, too. Want to come over?"

I took a deep breath to prepare my response, but Timothy cut in.

"Never mind. I'm just kidding and I'm going to lay off that for a while. Your life is your life. I don't want you to tell me how to live mine … and so on and so on, Rory Mory."

We laughed at one of my father's favorite expressions. We never knew who Rory Mory was, but we knew the song by heart. Timothy and I sang together, from one end of the Bronx to the other.

Oh Rory Mory, get out the dory
There's a herring in the bay.
We'll work all night
With all our might
Let not one get away.

By the end of the ditty, we were both on the verge of tears. I didn't know about Timothy, but my sadness encompassed more losses than that of Brendan Patrick Wickes.

CHAPTER 30

I looked around the refectory, up and down the length of the two long tables, in case I'd missed Sister Ann William's arrival on the top floor. She was nowhere to be found.

Halfway down my row, I saw Sister Veronique, Sister Ann William's scheduled walking partner. I tried to catch her eye, but her attention was on her neighbors as she chatted in her usual animated style. I'd have to wait until after dinner.

I thought about where Sister Ann William might be. Knocked down on Southern Boulevard? I prayed not. I couldn't remember her saying anything about a study group or another meeting. In fact, every time I replayed our last conversation in my mind, I distinctly heard, "I'll be back to St. Lucy's at three."

I felt strangely nervous, as if a dark cloud were hovering over me. My last hope was she'd been feeling ill and had gone straight to her room while we were at dinner. Or even earlier—she may not have heard my knock. I considered bringing a tray of food to her for a change, but when I looked at the heavy meatloaf and gravy I had no interest in either eating the meal or packing it up for transport.

I kept my eye on Sister Veronique and caught up with her as soon as she left the refectory. She was carrying several cookies from the dessert tray, partly wrapped in a handkerchief. When I approached, she offered me one.

"My favorite kind," she said.

"No, thank you. I was just wondering—did Sister Ann William come home with you?"

She shook her head and swallowed the last of a cookie. "I'd planned to meet her, but I got a message to report to my department chairman at the same time. Can't ignore it when Father O'Neill summons his minions." She laughed in a way that said she was actually flattered by the order to appear. "So I called the pharmacy office and left a message for Sister Ann William to go on without me."

"Do you know if she got the message? Maybe she's still waiting for you."

Sister Veronique pointed to the clock on the wall over the refectory doorway. Six-thirty.

She laughed and rolled her eyes. "For four hours? She's not that dumb."

I bristled. When Sister Veronique turned to go upstairs, I tugged at her sleeve.

"Sister Ann William's not dumb at all. She was counting on you to walk home with her."

My head was pounding, my voice raised well above the level for normal conversation. As the rest of St. Lucy's filed past us, some Sisters gave us curious looks, apparently wondering what the excitement was about. I wanted to pull each Sister aside and interrogate her as to Sister Ann William's whereabouts, as though one of them might have kidnapped her and held her hostage under flowing skirts.

Sister Veronique gave me a surprised look as she steadied the cross that hung around her neck— my jerky motion had set it swinging from side to side.

"I'm sorry, Sister," I said.

"It's OK," she said, pocketing her cookies and taking a step back.

"But I'm worried about Sister Ann William. She was supposed to be home by three …"

"Well, she could be anywhere. Maybe someone invited her for coffee or something."

I started to explain how unlikely that was for Sister Ann William, but stopped when I realized Sister Veronique and the former Sister Teresa had probably engaged in impromptu social intercourse routinely. Certainly, one of them had. I suspected it was not unusual for Sister Teresa to simply not show up in her room of an evening. No wonder Sister Veronique didn't understand my concern.

Sister Felix gave me no more satisfaction. I'd stopped at her doorway, still wound up from my interaction with Sister Veronique.

"Sister, it's barely dark out." Sister Felix spoke from behind the small mahogany desk that had once been Mother Ignatius'. The desk that had held a cuff link with the letter D, and a package of letters from Mother Consiliatrix. What would Sister Felix think if she knew I'd …

Back to the present.

"Did she call and say she'd be missing dinner?" I asked.

"No, she didn't. Many don't."

"I suppose you mean Teresa Barnes. And we know what happened to her. Sister Ann William is not like that."

Sister Felix stood up, her palms flat on the desktop, and leaned over to me. "You don't know that, do you, Sister? Perhaps if the two of you were not such busybodies, Sister Ann William would be in her room right now."

I gasped, partly from repugnance at my own outburst, and partly at what Sister Felix was implying. What did she know of our activities? And what did they have to do with the missing Sister Ann William? Before I could think better of it, I asked her outright.

"What are you saying, Sister Felix? That Sister Ann William is in trouble?"

Sister Felix came from behind the desk and glared at me. Although I was younger and probably stronger than she, the look in her eyes frightened me.

At that moment, a woman I vaguely recognized stepped into the doorway and knocked on the frame. Sister Felix's expression changed to a warm smile.

"Pamela," she said. "How nice to see you."

When she said her name, I remembered—Father Malbert's sister, who'd had dinner with us a couple of times. Evidently she rated a more cordial welcome than I ever did.

Pamela looked at me, her perfect hair unaffected by the wind I'd noticed whipping up the leaves in the back yard. "I'm sorry to disturb you, Sister. I thought Sister Felix and I were going to meet at eight."

Sister Felix gave me a cold stare and addressed her visitor. "We are. Sister Francesca was about to leave."

And I did.

A walk in what was left of St. Lucy's garden would calm me down, I decided, before I alienated everyone who lived there. It was a cold, windy evening, and following the rule—no woolen shawls before the first of October—seemed meaningless in the light of all the customs I'd already abandoned. I went upstairs and got my shawl out of the armoire, checking Sister Ann William's room before and after the errand.

I paced the short walkway in front of the shrine of Our Lady, hugging the black wool square to my chest. My teeth chattered, certainly not from the temperature. I'd been inclined to think Sister Ann William's disappearance—four hours was enough for me to label it that—was related to our murder investigation, and Sister Felix's comment convinced me further.

I created the most likely scenario—it must have to do with her making inquiries about the sign-in sheet for the pharmacy department's supply of drugs. I was afraid the murderer had attacked Sister Ann William while she was walking home alone. If she'd been detained for any other reason, she would have called me. She'd made a spontaneous phone call to update me on her progress with the clerk, surely she'd make another if she'd changed her mind about coming home right after class.

How lucky for the murderer that Sister Veronique was called away.

I stopped short.

My hands went to my face, leaving my shawl to fall to the ground at Our Lady's feet. The soot-streaked yellow brick tenements of the Bronx, darkening with the evening shadows, seemed to close in on me.

What if it wasn't a coincidence? What if the murderer lured Sister Veronique away to create the opportunity? The assault I'd invented against Sister Ann William was as real to me as my own on Southern Boulevard.

I gathered up my shawl and hurried back to the house and straight to Room 19. Sister Veronique was at her desk, her door open. The pile of cookies I'd seen in the handkerchief was next to her notebook, down by half.

Looking at her large body, it occurred to me that Sister Veronique herself might have been an accomplice in the crimes—both Mother Ignatius murder and Sister Ann William's present predicament, whatever that was. I thought it unlikely, but chose to remain on her threshold, one foot in the hallway, just in case.

"Sister, first let me apologize for my behavior."

Sister Veronique waved her chubby hand. "Don't worry about it, Francesca. I know you're worried. I'm starting to wonder myself."

"May I ask—what was your meeting about?"

She gave me a questioning look.

"The meeting with Father O'Neill—the one you were called to suddenly."

"Oh that. Funny thing. When I got there, all out of breath I might add, since I didn't have much notice, Father O'Neill was gone. And his secretary said she didn't know anything about a meeting with me." Sister Veronique shrugged and took a cookie from the dwindling pile. "There must have been some mix-up."

I shivered. Anyone could have pretended to be calling from the chairman's office. Or did I now have to add Father O'Neill to my list of suspects?

I wrapped my shawl around my shoulders, but no amount of wool serge could keep the chill from my body and soul.

CHAPTER 31

I'd waited around long enough. If no one would help, I'd have to take care of things myself. I climbed the stairs to the third floor, peeked once more into Sister Ann William's room, then went to the phone.

"NYPD, Bronx," a gruff male voice answered.

Having had a little practice interviewing Mother Consiliatrix in New Mexico, I was prepared for this call. I introduced myself and, with relative calm, told the officer of my concern.

"How long did you say she was missing?" he asked. I was disappointed he didn't address me by my title, as a Catholic would have. I'd been hoping for special treatment, of the sort Grace, the pharmacy clerk, had given Sister Ann William. Of course, it was the special treatment that might have gotten her in trouble, I reminded myself.

"She was due home at three. It's now nearly eight and there's no sign of her."

He grunted. "Five hours? It has to be at least forty-eight for an adult before we can do anything."

"Two whole days? She has to be missing two whole days before you'll look for her?"

My calmness had gone the way of my rules and customs. I walked up and down in front of the telephone base, as far as the cord would allow.

"I'm afraid so," he said.

"Don't you even want her description? In case ..." I gulped. "In case she's found at a hospital?"

I heard a heavy sigh, the sound of a man resigned to doing something he thought useless. "Sure, ma'am, why don't you tell us what she was wearing."

Ma'am. Definitely not Catholic. Not even a lapsed one. He was humoring me, but he was all I had.

"Her habit is a bright blue, with white trim. Her veil is blue also. She's about my height—uh, she's about five feet eight and thin."

"Glasses?"

"No."

"Give me your name again, and if we hear anything we'll call you."

My turn for a heavy sigh. I recited the information and hung up the phone.

As I passed Sister Ann William's door, I knocked half-heartedly. I knew she wasn't in, but it gave me a feeling of connectedness to her, as if I were tapping my friend's shoulder, reassuring her I hadn't forgotten her.

Kneeling in the front row of St. Lucy's chapel, I focused on the statue of Our Lady. I breathed in the sweet waxy smell from the candles and asked myself how I'd managed to stray so far, so quickly, from the folds of her mantle. I said one rosary, then another, with a plea that Sister Ann William would be all right. I wasn't sure whether a promise never to speak to her again might work in my favor. I was prepared to offer anything.

The chapel was dark except for the row of votive lights to the side of the altar and the sanctuary candle in its ornate gold casing by the Repository. I heard a noise and glanced toward the side door.

Father Malbert.

Here for a nighttime visit? I didn't think he was the type. It was hard to look at him without thinking of his affair with Teresa Barnes. The red flicker from the stubby votive candles cast shadows on his face, giving our chaplain the look of the devil himself.

"Sister Francesca, I thought you might be here. Sister Felix tells me you're worried about Sister Ann William." I raised my eyebrows in surprise. Sister Felix certainly hadn't given me any indication she'd cared. Father Malbert leaned closer to me, apparently close enough to see tense facial muscles and a deep frown. "Are you upset?"

Tears spilled over onto my cheeks, in spite of my best attempts to keep my emotions in check. Perhaps because someone finally seemed to care. I told him Sister Ann William's plans for coming home, and how positive I was she was in harm's way.

"And the police won't do anything for two days. She could be ..."

Father Malbert put his hand on my shoulder. I shrank back. A reflex I regretted. He was, after all, showing concern for my plight.

"Let's see what we can do about that," he said, removing his hand. "I have a few friends at the precinct."

A surge of hope. "You know a policeman?"

He smiled and nodded. "Come back to my office and we'll make some calls."

I followed Father Malbert past the altar rail, through the sacristy to a small room with a desk and two chairs. I'd never been to this part of the first floor. His counseling area, I guessed, since there were no papers or office supplies in sight.

He motioned me to a soft chair while he took his place behind his desk. I stared up at the crucifix while he dialed.

"Is Charlie Ahern there?"

He seemed to know the number by heart, and I wondered how often he had occasion to call in favors from the police department. I hoped Charlie Ahern wasn't the gruff officer who'd taken my call.

"Charlie, Father Dave here. How's it going?"

I listened as Father Malbert gave Officer Ahern a summary of the day's events.

"She would have been walking from St. Alban's campus to St. Lucy's. So somewhere along Southern Boulevard ..." He cupped his hand over the telephone. "Is that the route you usually take, Sister?"

I nodded.

Father Malbert made some notes on the pages of his desk calendar. He hung up the phone and addressed me.

"OK. He gave me some contacts in the hospitals and emergency rooms in the area. Charlie always gives me the code to identify myself. It changes every week or so."

A wave of relief flooded over me, until I realized I might be close to having my worst fears confirmed. I preferred the other possibility— that I'd feel completely foolish learning Sister Ann William was not in a hospital ward. In fact, she'd just slipped into the chapel for a visit after having caught a movie on campus with some classmates.

Father Malbert made several calls, each time giving the code—42 Pelham. I found it frustrating hearing only one side of the conversations.

"A young woman in a nun's habit." Pause. "Yes, blue and white." Pause. "Any time between about three o'clock and now. " Pause. "Thanks, anyway."

And then finally, on the third call, the moment I'd both hoped for and dreaded.

"You do?" Pause. "Hmm. No clothing?" He tapped his pencil on the desk. I sat up straighter and fingered my rosary, matching his rhythm. "How old? Uh-huh. On the thin side, fair skin." Pause.

Father Malbert's face took on a somber look as he hung up the phone.

"St. Anselmo's Hospital on the Parkway. It might not be Sister Ann William. I'm going over to check. You stay here."

Father Malbert sounded excited and ready to take charge. I started to shake my head, but his confident and kind manner persuaded me to do as he said.

"I'll take Sister Felix with me. Stay by my phone and I'll call you at this number as soon as we know anything, either way."

Father Malbert put his hand on my shoulder. I didn't flinch. "Try to relax," he said, his voice gentle. "Promise?"

I nodded. I wasn't sure I could stand up, anyway. My heart had fallen to my feet, my sturdy black shoes seeming to collapse under the burden.

CHAPTER 32

I waited an eternity in Father Malbert's office. To distract myself, I studied the few items on his bookshelves. Extra copies of the new hymnals I'd seen in the Xavier Hall chapel. A row of Bibles of different sizes. A photo of himself with a group of Sisters from St. Lucy's, taken on the grounds that now belonged to Jake Driscoll. The sight of Mother Ignatius in the front row saddened me further. The ex-Sister Teresa stood next to Father Malbert. I wondered if they'd been dating at the time, and who knew about it.

Another frame held a photo of Father Malbert's sister, Pamela Edson with a man I assumed to be her husband, in front of the partially built student union building. Edson & Sons. The contractor. Father Malbert's brother-in-law was the contractor for all the new campus buildings. After my preoccupation with real estate signs, how could I have missed the connection?

Interesting.

I'd started down new lines of thinking when the phone rang. I jumped, as if I'd been caught snooping again. I hesitated to answer but remembered Father Malbert's instruction and picked up the phone. Sister Felix was on the line, calling from St. Anselmo's Hospital. I heard none of her introductory remarks, only the summary at the end.

"… and the doctors say she's in a coma."

I wasn't sure anyone but me could hear my moan, which seemed to go on forever.

"I am so sorry, Sister Francesca. I don't know what to say, except please try to stay calm. Father Malbert and I will be home shortly. There's nothing anyone can do here right now."

In the background I could hear hospital noises—pages, bells, unintelligible conversation bouncing off bare walls. I thought of Fishkill General, where my father died a few days before, and imagined my family in just such a waiting area.

What of Sister Ann William's family? "Her community in Texas …" I said to Sister Felix.

"I'll take care of it when I get there, Sister. For now, try to rest. When she wakes up, Sister Ann William will need you. You must stay strong for her."

I had a flash of hope. Sister Felix assumed Sister Ann William would be waking up. I started to think rationally, wanting information. What exactly was a coma? Did people recover from them? Did St. Anselmo's have a competent staff? If only I had her Uncle Jeb's number in Texas, so I could ask him all my questions.

I wished I could wind back the clock and relive my entire life in the Bronx.

I went out through the sacristy to the chapel and knelt in the front pew until Father Malbert woke me up some time later.

"Sister Francesca, this can't be good for you."

I shook my head. My neck hurt from the unnatural sleeping position. Since I could barely straighten my knees, I slid back onto the pew without unfolding my legs.

Father Malbert sat down next to me. He described Sister Ann William's condition as best he could—she'd been found naked, badly beaten, in some bushes on the Botanical Gardens side of Southern Boulevard.

I shuddered at the image. But at the same time my brain processed an inconsistency. "That's not the side we usually walked on. We never cross the street until we pass Webster." As if a week of walking to and from class together established an iron-clad habit. In my mind, it did.

"Whoever it was must have lured her over there," Father Malbert said. "Probably because it's easier to hide someone in the shrubbery on that side."

"It's all my fault," I told him.

"Now, how can you blame yourself, Sister?"

"I led Sister Ann William into foolish behavior." I started recounting instances of my bad influence, my breath labored. I realized I might as well seek absolution at the same time.

"Father, I'd like you to hear my confession."

"Certainly, Sister." He went to the sacristy and returned wearing his purple stole. I was glad to see he wore the official narrow mantle, and not some updated multi-colored version.

Once in the booth, my breathing returned to normal. I was comforted knowing my soul would receive the grace of God through the sacrament, even if couldn't think clearly, and even if I had little respect for a Confessor of questionable morals, including fathering an illegitimate child. He had, after all, located Sister Ann William for me.

Father Malbert was so sympathetic, I was afraid I was going to have to assign my own penance once more.

"It's not your fault. It's the mugger's fault," he told me. He laughed—a low, throaty sound to signal irony. "Times have certainly changed when someone would attack and rob a nun. Only a lowlife. I'll bet he was disappointed to get a mere few coins and a Saint William medal."

I nodded, though I knew he couldn't see me clearly. I'd also wondered what attraction a nun would have for a robber. And why Sister Ann William would follow a lowlife across the street.

The Saint William medal.

The light flooded my brain with the intensity of a cathedral full of Christmas candles. Who knew Sister Ann William had been carrying the medal she'd bought for her brother? Only me. And her attacker. She'd just picked it up at the campus store.

Within seconds, all the other clues fell into place.

D for Dave. And Dean. I remember Father O'Neill's comment about the dean's office not being for sale, or something like that. Mother Consiliatrix's words also came back to me—manipulating the administration for personal gain. I was certain Father Malbert got the position under false pretenses, though I didn't know the details.

E for Edson, Father Malbert's brother-in-law. I'd started to put it together when I saw the photo of the Edsons in Father Malbert's office. Mother Ignatius had written that the shady real estate deal was for campus buildings. Driscoll & Sons' buildings were off campus. Father Malbert probably finagled the contract bidding to favor his sister's husband. How could I have missed that possibility?

And F for father, his child with Teresa Barnes.

All the code letters Mother Ignatius used with Mother Consiliatrix were about the same person. Father Malbert was D, E, and F.

Sister Ann William's report on Father Malbert's eulogy at Mother Ignatius' wake came back to my mind, its significance now clear. He'd said she was in white, head to *toe*—he must have seen her in her slippers.

All of this came to me in seconds, together with gasps I tried to stifle.

"Sister Francesca?"

I jumped, hitting my fist on the small counter at the bottom of the grille between us. "I'm fine, thank you, Father. I'd like to make my Act of Contrition now."

My voice trembled and I worried that I'd alerted him to my new awareness—our chaplain was a fraud, a father, and a murderer. I said my Act of Contraction so rapidly, the opening *Oh, My God ...* became one syllable with the ending ... *and amend my life. Amen.*

I pulled the heavy curtain aside without waiting for the blessing.

A mistake.

I heard a low moan from Father Malbert. Apparently that gesture was the last thing Father Malbert needed to assure himself he'd slipped up.

He opened his door in the center of the booth and stood facing me in the aisle. His stylish brown hair seemed messier than when he entered, and I couldn't imagine how it got that way. His dark eyes were different—staring, without the gentleness I thought I'd seen while he was helping me find Sister Ann William. I realized what I'd mistook for sympathy was relief as he thought he'd gotten away with murder.

"Sister Francesca, what are we going to do now?" His voice seemed higher pitched than usual, as if a deranged demon had taken over his body. I wanted to scream out for an exorcist, but I couldn't catch my breath enough to make anything but the tiniest of sounds.

He moved toward me. "You and your little friend couldn't leave well enough alone."

As Father Malbert talked, he stared over my shoulder at the altar, as if into the future. As if I wasn't part of the future he envisioned.

I turned and ran toward the front of the chapel, to the hallway door. But, unencumbered by skirts or a heavy rosary, he was faster than I was.

He caught up with me halfway down the aisle and grabbed me around my waist. He landed on top of me. My bonnet fell off, leaving my carrot-red stubble wrapped only in the narrow white band pinned at the back of my head. I struggled to get from under him, but I couldn't muster the strength. My limbs were weak as the palm fronds that greeted Our Lord before his crucifixion.

What time was it? I wondered vaguely if it were close to dawn and Sisters would be pouring into the chapel for mass. I knew I'd been screaming, not because I heard myself, but because my throat was hoarse. Where was everyone? I'd lost track of the day, the time, the place. I felt every nerve in my body at the edge of my skin.

Father Malbert hadn't stopped talking since he left the confessional. I tried to listen, in case what he said was important in my struggle for my life. I was horrified by his words.

"She was old. She'd be dying soon. I figured a few months quicker wouldn't do any harm."

"You're a priest. How could you think that way?"

Not smart, I told myself. For once, don't argue.

"She wouldn't give up. All she had to do was wait until I'd been appointed. A matter of days. Then nothing would have mattered. But once she found out, she was determined … never mind. It's over."

What's over? My life, too? In a burst of energy brought on by fear, I freed one arm and reached into a pew near me. My fingers landed on a missal tucked into a rack near the floor. I picked it up and swung back as far as I could, smashing the hard cover into his eyes. The first time I'd ever picked up a holy book without kissing it. The first time I'd ever deliberately struck someone to hurt him. I made the sign of the cross mentally to take the curse off my action.

He screamed and let go of me, covering his eye. No blood that I could see, so I thought I didn't have much time. I gathered up the skirts of my habit and ran.

He overtook me again.

"You're so light, Francesca. Just like Mother Ignatius. Some mornings it's harder to lift the chalice above my head than it was to get her onto that bed."

He put his body between me and the door, leaning his arm on the altar rail. His laugh sent a chill through me. He pressed against me until I was bent over backwards on the altar rail.

"What shall I do with you, Sister Francesca?" he asked again. His voice was sing-song, like a child reciting his nighttime prayers.

It was my question also. What did he intend to do with me? There were forty other people in the house, one of them, Sister Felix, not too far down the hall from the chapel. Surely he couldn't kill me here. I had a frightening image of Father Malbert hiding my dead body in his office until he could remove it to some remote location. Another roadside attack on a nun, the police would say. His friend Officer Charlie Ahern would never suspect St. Alban's new dean.

Father Malbert had another idea. "Maybe they'll find you in the morning. A despondent nun who couldn't live with the burden of causing her friend to lie in a coma."

"Poison?" I could hardly get the word out.

"It worked before."

Too much talk. Not enough action.

For leverage, I braced my foot on the marble step leading to the altar and thrust myself from his grip. In the next motion, I grabbed lit votive candles from the metal rack by my side and hurled them, one by one, at Father Malbert's face. I thought of snowballs in the winter fields of Potterstown, of pitch-till-you-win at the county fair booth, of volleyball practice in my high school gym.

Anything but throwing burning candles at another human being.

Father Malbert's stole caught fire first. He whipped it off but couldn't contain the blaze that had shot up his neck. The smells mixed together. Singed hair. Burning flesh and plastic from his Roman collar. Vanilla wax from the candles.

As I ran to the safety of the hallway and Sister Felix's bedroom, I had a final glimpse of a fallen priest, flailing about in flames, as if he'd been caught unexpectedly in the fires of Hell.

CHAPTER 33

Just as well I'd been naïve about the real challenges awaiting me in the Bronx. I'd never have thought I'd be able to cope with friendships, reformed convent life, unorthodox professors, barely recognizable liturgy—let alone murder. And my sorrow at the death of my father had only intensified every experience.

A few days after Father Malbert had been taken into custody, Sister Ann William regained consciousness, and I had renewed faith in the God of justice and mercy.

Unwilling to rehash my role in the incidents leading up to Father Malbert's desperate assault, I kept my distance from Sister Ann William's visitors from Texas. I did overhear the Sisters in the parlor with Sister Felix, however.

"We're simply not used to this sort of thing in Houston," Mother Clarisse said.

"Neither are we, believe me, Mother," Sister Felix had answered.

Sister Felix had softened her approach around me. I guessed she felt badly about not responding to my concern when Sister Ann William was first missing. When her order appointed her officially Mother Superior at St. Lucy's, I wrote a note offering my prayers for the new assignment.

"Sister Francesca, thank you," she'd written back. "I look forward to a new start."

I thought I knew what she meant, and I resolved to give her no more trouble. No more extra pillows, and no more impertinence.

———————

I reformed my truant ways somewhat and asked Mother Julia's permission before visiting Sister Ann William in the hospital.

"I consider that a corporal work of mercy, Sister Francesca," she'd told me by telephone from Potterstown.

"Yes, Mother. Thank you, Mother."

I'd spared Mother Julia the details of what brought about Sister Ann William's encounter with violence. I guessed an incident in the Bronx wouldn't reach the four-page Potterstown weekly newspaper. At least not the front page, which was all Mother Julia scanned for us.

Sitting up in the hospital bed, Sister Ann William was in good spirits, in spite of her weak and vulnerable appearance. The first few times I'd seen her, she seemed shaky and easily startled, jumping each time a new person entered her room.

Sister Ann William's Superior and another Sister of her order had come to the Bronx to satisfy themselves she was no longer in danger. They'd brought her a cotton robe, the same shade of blue as her regular dress, and a special cap to cover her head and neck. A strangely modified habit.

"Think of all the effort we went through to learn about poisons, and in the end we didn't need the information at all," I said.

"And I never did get the pharmacy log." She sounded disappointed, as if she'd failed a test, instead of avoiding a transgression. "We can only assume Father Malbert's name was on it. I hope eventually we'll find out exactly what he used to … subdue Mother Ignatius."

"Mr. Driscoll promised to let us know what the police labs turn up."

"I hope they tell us more than lab results," she said.

I nodded. "Like how did Mother Ignatius find out about his evil ways …"

Sister Ann William brightened. "I do know one loose end. Did I tell you how Father Malbert found out I'd asked to see the log?"

Something I'd been wondering about, since very little time elapsed between Sister Ann William's call to me about her success with the pharmacy clerk and the assault on her life. I shook my head.

"Grace—the clerk I talked to?" Sister Ann William's accent had reverted to its original intensity in the days after her hometown Sisters' visit. "Grace came by here to see me? She told me she couldn't locate her supervisor for permission to give me the log, but she ran into Father Malbert right after I left, and since he was Dean ..."

"She thought she could trust him."

She nodded. A sad look came over her, and I guessed she'd already forgiven Father Malbert and was more concerned for his soul than for her body.

I tried a distraction, in case she was reliving an ugly moment in her life. She hadn't talked much about the experience except she thought she fainted early on and was mercifully unaware of what happened to her.

"Your poison tutorials weren't wasted, by the way. I learned a great deal. For example, I never knew the median strip on New York's highways were lined with hemlock."

She chuckled, then grimaced as if the movement of the laughter muscles caused her pain.

I sprang up to help. "Shall I get you an aspirin?" I paused mid-step, remembering one of her explications on the way to campus. "Uh oh, aspirin is toxic, isn't it?"

"Only if you take it in huge amounts."

"Right. I suppose even ice cream can kill you if you eat too much."

We both laughed, and Sister Ann William grimaced again.

———————

It seemed Father Malbert wasn't the only one who had connections in the precinct. Jake Driscoll came through with a full report from the police. He'd volunteered to share what he'd learned with all the Sisters in the house but offered to tell the story to Sister Ann William and me in a private session.

"Since you're among the principals," he'd said, with a grin.

The day after she returned to St. Lucy's, Sister Ann William and I sat in the parlor with him, taking the same seats we had when he'd brought us Mother Ignatius' autopsy report. I thought back to our breaking into the Driscoll & Sons construction trailer and accusing him of murder, for all practical purposes. I also recalled, with some embarrassment, my own rude behavior to him on several occasions.

All in all, Jake Driscoll had been pretty patient with us, I decided.

"The police found your habit in a duffel bag in Father Malbert's office. The one off the sacristy here," he told Sister Ann William. He pointed in the direction of St. Lucy's chapel. "They were all tangled up with his sweaty gym clothes."

"Why do you think he … removed …?" she asked. Her voice was so shaky I was afraid of relapse, if there were such a thing for comas.

Jake Driscoll came to her rescue. "The cops figure he removed your clothes to delay an investigation. He probably intended to burn the whole bag eventually. Everything was pretty torn up and bloody and …" He paused. "Well, it's over now. He knew it would have been too easy to ID you with your habit on, and it's always better for the criminal when the trail is cold."

"But he was the one who located me at St. Anselmo's," Sister Ann William said, expressing my own thoughts. Apparently we had a lot to learn about the criminal mind.

Jake Driscoll nodded in my direction. "Because Sister Francesca was so … persistent." He looked at me and smiled, as if to remind me there were harsher terms he might use. "Evidently, he thought it would remove all suspicion if he showed sympathy and helped her out. He never expected her to put all the pieces together."

He gave me a smile meant to show pride, I sensed, but I wasn't in the mood for praise. Instead, I thought how I'd sat in Father Malbert's office for more than an hour, how close I was to his evidence-laden closet while he'd called the emergency rooms. And all during the time I waited for him and Sister Felix to phone me from St. Anselmo's Hospital, Sister Ann William's bloody habit had been a few feet away.

I'd snooped in two offices—Mother Ignatius' and Jake Driscoll's—and minded my own business in the one that mattered. Nothing to be proud of.

"Chloroform," Sister Ann William said, as if she'd just processed the information Jake Driscoll had given us at the beginning of our meeting. "Such a simple method. As old as she was, Mother Ignatius would have only a few moments before her heart would stop."

"And there was no way to tell from the autopsy?" I asked Sister Ann William, who was a medical expert compared to me.

She shook her head. "There might have been a slight rash on her face, or irritation in her nose and throat. But everyone was focused on poisoning and looking for a disruption of her internal functions."

I was still puzzled. "What possible reason would Father Malbert give for checking chloroform out of the pharmacy?"

"He didn't," Jake Driscoll said. "He slipped it into his pocket on what he called a routine visit as a faculty member in line for an administrative position. Wanted to familiarize himself with all parts of the campus, he told the clerk. He signed in and out but didn't indicate he was removing any controlled substance."

"If anyone noticed and asked, he could always say he had some heavy-duty cleaning agent for a project," Sister Ann William added.

Like no household chores I'd ever done, I thought.

Jake Driscoll gazed over my shoulder as if he were watching a scene play out on the parlor wall, next to the painting of the Sacred Heart. "Poor old nun. In the wrong place at the wrong time, I guess."

"What do you mean?" Sister Ann William asked.

He lowered his eyes to our level. "That's right. You wouldn't know. Father Malbert is cleansing his soul by talking to anyone who'll listen. I guess the Church doesn't provide very good attorneys for murderers."

Sister Ann William and I were perched on the edges of our chairs. Jake Driscoll, on the other hand, looked relaxed, lounging back on the sofa, apparently enjoying his role as our source of news.

What's Father Malbert saying? we wanted to know.

"For one thing he's remorseful. He's sorry he knocked you down, Sister Francesca." So it was connected. I reached for my thigh surreptitiously, as if to apologize to my body for getting into trouble. "He says he's almost glad some young lovers crawled into the bushes where he'd dragged Sister Ann William."

I gasped. "I never thought of that. His real aim was to kill her ..."

Jake Driscoll nodded. "He had to run off before ..." He paused. "I'm sorry, Sisters. Maybe we should stop here."

Sister Ann William swallowed hard enough for me to hear. I reached out and put my hand on hers.

For a moment we were all silent.

I'd seen Sister Veronique's white habit flutter by several times during our conference. Finally, she appeared in the doorway, carrying a plate of cookies.

She cleared her throat. "I thought you might like a snack. I brought a little something from the kitchen."

Or from the supply in your room, I mused. To cover up my uncharitable thought, I gave her what I assumed she wanted.

"Come in, Sister. Mr. Driscoll was about to tell us some of the details Father Malbert has given to the police."

"Thanks, Fran. I don't mind if I do."

I smiled at her but grimaced inwardly. Now we were down to nicknames.

Jake Driscoll stood when she entered and sat again after Sister Veronique—Ronnie?—had taken a seat next to him on the sofa. Ever the Catholic gentleman. He continued with his story.

"Mother Ignatius was in his office one afternoon, about a week before she died—the girl who was supposed to clean in there didn't show up one day and Mother Ignatius decided to substitute so the good Father would have a spick and span place to work." He shook his head as if to indicate the futility of it all. "She overheard a telephone conversation or found some documents ... or both ... the story changes."

"About the Edson contract?"

He nodded. "And the Dean's position. It was all connected—he got inside information from Father O'Neill, for his brother-in-law. That way Edson could bid lower than anyone else. Then, he held that over Father O'Neill's head. *Make me Dean or I'll tell all.*"

"But that would have exposed him and his brother-in-law also," I said, stretching my brain to understand the world of business and high finance.

"The repercussions would be worse for Father O'Neill and St. Alban's administration. Everybody expects contractors to be crooked, anyway. Right, Sisters?"

I tried to look suitably contrite.

Sister Veronique swallowed some part of a cookie and spoke up. "Well, I have a few details of my own, if you're interested."

The affair with Teresa Barnes. None of us had brought it up, but the prurience of the topic didn't keep us all from listening intently.

Sister Veronique was ready with her story. "David's intention was to keep his affair with Teresa a secret until he made Dean, then leave the order. He'd have a contract by then and they wouldn't let him go." She took another bite of cookie. "Whereas they could refuse him the post if he left the order first. So the plan was, he'd be Dean, then he and Teresa would leave their orders and get married." She spread her hands. "Ta da. Happily ever after."

Sister Veronique's frown contradicted her words. "Instead, when he found out about the baby, he pushed her aside. She had no choice but to go home to Michigan."

"Did Mother Ignatius overhear all that, too?"

Sister Veronique shook her head, her mouth falling into a sad expression. "Teresa told Mother Ignatius. She confided in her." I saw a surprised look on Sister Ann William's face, echoing my own feelings. "I know you think we're radicals and hated Mother Ignatius, but that's not true. Teresa ..." Sister Veronique's voice cracked. "Now I can't bear to tell Teresa she may have been to blame for Mother Ignatius' death."

"Don't do it, Sister," Jake Driscoll said, with vehemence. "Father Malbert is the one responsible, and there's no sense thinking what we all might or might not have done differently."

I agreed, except for one other matter. While we were on the topic of blame, I had a question for Jake Driscoll. I'd been sleeping badly since my adventure in the chapel with Father Malbert. Prisoner David, I realized, curiously aware of how titles and relationships were so closely linked.

My attack on David disturbed my dreams. In one, I saw myself hurling flames at his naked body. In another, I ran screaming while my own habit was red with blood and fire.

I'd asked myself over and over if it had been necessary for me to resort to violence.

"How is Father Malbert?" I asked Jake Driscoll.

"David," Sister Veronique said with a twist to her lips. "He won't be hearing anyone else's confession very soon."

"He's badly burned, of course. He'll be all right, but he's probably scarred for life."

In more ways than one, I thought.

"It's not a sin to defend your life, Sister Francesca," Jake Driscoll said. I shrugged my shoulders. "If you're thinking of the martyrs, it's the wrong analogy. It's not as if you'd have been dying for your faith." When I pushed my feelings aside, I knew he was correct. "You did what you had to do."

Sister Ann William nodded vigorously.

"Absolutely," Sister Veronique said. I had the vague feeling she wished she'd thrown the candles herself.

"One more thing," I said to Jake Driscoll as we stood to leave. I reached into my pocket and pulled out a single onyx cuff link with an elaborate silver letter D. The D that was different from the D between Mother Ignatius and Mother Consiliatrix. "I think this is yours."

Jake Driscoll's eyes widened. "Dang. I've been looking for this. Where did you find it?"

"In a compromising place."

A look of comprehension came over his face. "No wonder you thought ... "

I smiled and extended my hand. "Thanks for everything, Mr. Driscoll."

CHAPTER 34

B efore leaving the Bronx for the Christmas season in Potterstown, I'd begun to attend Father Glanz's daily mass in Xavier Hall. I came to appreciate his scholarship, taking us back to the roots of the early Church to find an expression of spirituality for modern times.

"The custom of receiving the Host on your tongue dates to when priests were the only educated sector of society," Father Glanz told us. "Everyone else had dirty hands." He paused and looked at his fingers. "I don't think we have to worry about that now."

Though I never talked to him personally, Father Glanz became my model—someone who'd embraced the changes in the Church while maintaining a deep respect for tradition.

Sister Ann William and Sister Veronique, Aidan Connors, and Colleen Shane, were all part of the new community that was forming around Father Glanz's experimental liturgies.

I tried to tease my brother into attending the new liturgy. He'd begun to turn his life around, rooming with Aidan and doing well at Driscoll & Sons. His new boss had seen an aptitude for mathematics and finance in Timothy and sent him to a class in accounting. My brother, the CFO, I mused. Another big gap in talent between us.

"You might like the new liturgy," I told Timothy. "There's contemporary music, and no Latin mumbo-jumbo, as you call it." I paused before I brought out another compelling reason. "And Aidan comes."

Timothy grinned, signaling he saw through my ploy. "Yeah. Well, I'll think about it."

"Good. I'll wait to hear."

I didn't tell him I'd also pray for him.

The Christmas altar at the Motherhouse was magnificent. White marble overflowing with row upon row of red and green candles, dozens of brilliant poinsettia plants, and a rash of holly berries—whose poisonous quality I pushed to the back of my mind.

All week long, from December 25, we'd enjoyed extra recreation. I realized how much less exciting it was to talk at breakfast on Christmas morning, when I'd been talking nonstop at St. Lucy's Hall.

Holiday programs went on through the days following Christmas. Sister Rosemary, tiny as she was, played Christmas songs on the accordion. Sister Geraldine read poetry she'd written herself in honor of Mother Julia's silver jubilee. The youngest members of the community performed a play based on the life of the late Pope Pius XII.

Since most of the Sisters were of Irish descent, Sister Mary Patrick's step-dancing routines were appropriate at any season, and she treated us to a new round of dances.

Although I was glad to be home, I'd felt less a part of the festivities than other years. I'd been away most of the Advent season when preparations and rehearsals were daily routines. At the last minute, however, Sister Maryanne, the music director, gave me a private practice session so at least I could join the choir for midnight mass on Christmas Eve.

On the day after Christmas, the Feast of Saint Stephen, Mother Julia called a special assembly.

We walked in silence to the main study hall. There'd been no rumors, and I heard no buzzing sounds indicating an exchange of ideas or expectations. Quite different from what I'd come to expect at St. Lucy's Hall.

Mother Julia took her seat at the front of the room and signaled us to be seated. "Sisters, I have news for you from our Archbishop."

A slight shuffle as we shifted on our wooden chairs. For my part, I thought the information might be a new chaplain at the Motherhouse for the coming year. Nothing that would affect me. Or a new appointment in the Chancery office in Albany. Or a large donation to the order's building fund.

I wasn't even close.

"Beginning tomorrow morning, our Liturgy will be in English, Sisters. And we will have the opportunity of receiving the Sacred Host in our hands." Mother Julia cupped her hands and held them in front of her bib.

A wave of tiny gasps rippled through the hall. Mother Julia waited for the sound to subside, without admonishing us, and presented her lesson. Holy Mother Church was moving to a new way of doing things. We'd be seeing many changes, in due time. We were not to worry, however—the reforms were approved by our leaders, a consequence of the Second Vatican Council. *Aggiornamento*, it was called. An updating.

Through most of Mother Julia's discourse, my mind was on the Bronx and the large dose of *aggiornamento* I'd already been through.

"Are there any questions, Sisters?"

"What if a piece of the Host clings to our hands?" Sister Rosemary asked.

Mother Julia made a clucking sound, as if her mind was hard at work. "I'll address that problem in a future lesson, Sister," she finally said.

Wait till you're faced with brownies and milk, I thought.

———————

As I prepared to leave Potterstown at the end of my vacation, Mother Julia called me into her office.

"Sister Francesca, I hope you're not too disturbed by these changes."

I swallowed hard. How much did my Superior know about my life in the Bronx? "No, Mother, I'm not disturbed."

"The bishops are mandated to enforce the new guidelines in every diocese eventually. I'm sure you'll be meeting the same challenges at St. Alban's."

I pressed my lips together, lest I reveal more than Mother Julia was prepared to hear. "Yes, Mother."

"Are you up to these challenges?"

"Yes, Mother."

It was time for me to leave her office. An awkward moment. Traditionally, I'd kneel and ask for Mother Julia's blessing, then kiss the floor. Caught as I was between two worlds, I stood still and looked to my Superior for guidance.

Mother Julia's eyes sparkled, a tiny grin starting at the corners of her mouth. I had the feeling she understood my predicament. In an unprecedented gesture, she reached out and put her hand on my shoulder.

"Take care of yourself, Sister Francesca," she said, smiling.

I took a breath and smiled back. "Thank you, Mother Julia."

It seemed a lifetime since I'd worried about having a mirror in my room.

About the Author

Camille Minichino is a retired physicist turned writer. When her first book, on nuclear waste management, was popular only in academic circles, she turned to cozy mystery novels and has published twenty-eight of them in five different series: the Periodic Table Mysteries, the Miniature Mysteries (**as Margaret Grace**), the Professor Sophie Knowles Mysteries (**as Ada Madison**), the Postmistress Mysteries (**as Jean Flowers**), and the Alaska Diner Mysteries (**as Elizabeth Logan**). She's also written nonfiction, many short stories, and articles on the craft of writing. She teaches science at Golden Gate U. in San Francisco and writing workshops around the SF Bay Area. More information is at **www.minichino.com**.

SELECTED PUBLICATIONS

<u>NOVELS</u>
Writing as CAMILLE MINICHINO
The Hydrogen Murder (Avalon Books)
The Helium Murder (Avalon Books)
The Lithium Murder (William Morrow)
The Beryllium Murder (William Morrow)
The Boric Acid Murder (St. Martin's Minotaur)
The Carbon Murder (St. Martin's Minotaur)
The Nitrogen Murder (St. Martin's Minotaur)
The Oxygen Murder (St. Martin's Minotaur)

Killer in the Cloister (amazon.com/CreateSpace)

Writing as MARGARET GRACE
Murder in Miniature (Berkley Prime Crime/Penguin)
Mayhem in Miniature (Berkley Prime Crime/Penguin)
Malice in Miniature (Berkley Prime Crime/Penguin)
Mourning in Miniature (Berkley Prime Crime/Penguin)

Monster in Miniature (Berkley Prime Crime/Penguin)
Mix-up in Miniature (Perseverance Press)
Madness in Miniature (Perseverance Press)
Manhattan in Miniature (Perseverance Press)
Matrimony in Miniature (Perseverance Press)

Writing as ADA MADISON
The Square Root of Murder (Berkley Prime Crime/Penguin-RH)
The Probability of Murder (Berkley Prime Crime/Penguin-RH)
A Function of Murder (Berkley Prime Crime/Penguin-RH)
The Quotient of Murder (Berkley Prime Crime/Penguin-RH)

Writing as JEAN FLOWERS
Death Takes Priority (Berkley Prime Crime/Penguin-RH)
Cancelled by Murder (Berkley Prime Crime/Penguin-RH)
Addressed to Kill (Berkley Prime Crime/Penguin-RH)

Writing as ELIZABETH LOGAN
Mousse and Murder (Berkley Prime Crime/Penguin-RH)
Fishing for Trouble (Berkley Prime Crime/Penguin-RH)
Murphy's Slaw (Berkley Prime Crime/Penguin-RH)

NONFICTION
How to Live with an Engineer

SELECTED SHORT PIECES
Fiction:
The Fluorine Murder
The Neon Ornaments
The Sodium Arrow
The Magnesium Murder
Majesty in Miniature

Nonfiction:
Essays in *Mystery Readers Journal*

Curious about other Crossroad Press books? Stop by our website:
http://crossroadpress.com
We offer quality writing
in digital, audio, and print formats.

Subscribe to our newsletter on the website homepage and receive a
free eBook.